THE GHOSTS
OF SOUTHWARK

A NICKIE NICK VAMPIRE HUNTER NOVEL

THE GHOSTS
OF SOUTHWARK

A NICKIE NICK VAMPIRE HUNTER NOVEL

by O. M. Grey

BLUE
MOOSE
PRESS

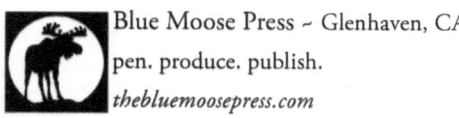

Blue Moose Press ~ Glenhaven, CA
pen. produce. publish.
thebluemoosepress.com

Copyright 2013 by O. M. Grey. All rights reserved.
Cover Illustration by J. R. Fleming
Edited by Sue Soares

ISBN-13: 978-1-936960-80-4
First Edition.

ATTENTION ORGANIZATIONS AND SCHOOLS:
Quantity discounts are available on bulk purchases of this book for educational purposes or fundraising.

For more information, go to
  thebluemoosepress.com
  omgrey.wordpress.com

Library of Congress Control Number: 2013954451
Grey, O. M., 1969 -
  Avalon Revisited / by O. M. Grey
1. Paranormal Romance--Fiction. II. Title.
ISBN-13: 978-1-936960-80-4

Printed in the United States of America

For James Conrad Agin
*Your kindness, support, and friendship
helped return my voice to me.*

For Adrian Hutchens & Bekah June
*Loyal readers who have
become cherished friends*

For Timothy D Morgan
*Your Kickstarter pledge
helped make this book possible*

Also by O. M. Grey

Avalon Revisited

The Zombies of Mesmer

Caught in the Cogs: An Eclectic Collection

Avalon Revamped

The Ghosts of Southwark

...under the name Christine Rose:

Rowan of the Wood

Witch on the Water

Fire of the Fey

Power of the Zephyr

Spirit of the Otherworld

Publishing & Marketing Realities for the Emerging Author

AUTHOR'S NOTE

A few words about historical references and chronological discrepancies...

In St. Saviour's Cathedral, now known as Southwark Cathedral, I describe a beautiful monument to William Shakespeare. Although that wasn't put in the church until 1912, I decided to include it in this 1881 semifictional world because of what Shakespeare means to me and to Nickie Nick. This, among many other things about the cathedral, inspired me to set this book there.

Similarly, the church as it stands now was rebuilt in 1890, but I've described it as it now stands on these pages. Please visit Southwark Cathedral if you visit London and see this awe-inspiring place for yourself. Walk around its walls and picture Nickie doing the same.

Bethlehem Hospital was also called Bethlem Asylum or Bethlem Hospital. It is historically known by its nickname: Bedlam. The building both in this and the first book, *The Zombies of Mesmer*, is described as it stands today. Although it's no longer an asylum for the mentally ill, its current incarnation as the Imperial War Museum is situated on Lambeth Road right between Nickie's house and St. George's Cathedral, south of the Thames.

John Hathorne, the Salem Witch Trial judge is a historical figure. One of his real descendants is Nathaniel Hawthorne, author of *The Scarlet Letter*, among others. Historically, Hawthorne changed the spelling of his name to distance himself from the cruel judge. Nickie Nick's ancestors did the same, changing the spelling to distance themselves both from the cursed judge and the embarrassment of having a writer in the family. Simon's connection with Julian, Nathaniel's son, is pure fiction, as is Nickie Nick's entire immediate family.

All the places in this book are set in London, England, as in all my books. London is the city of my soul. It flows through my veins and is a part of every breath. You can find the above places as well as locations in my other books, like *Avalon Revisited* and *Avalon Revamped*, on my O. M. Grey tour of London map, which can be found on my blog: http://omgrey.wordpress.com

Hope you enjoy the story.

May you find peace.

~Olivia

CHAPTER ONE

IN WHICH NICKIE NICK LAMENTS

February 6, 1881

Stone lips caress my cheek. I laugh, and the sound echoes off the surrounding buildings, darkened by the night. He is my light, my only light. I need no other.

"Ashe," I breathe into his ear then pull his lobe between my lips. A moment later, I'm warming and wetting his lips with my own.

"You're mine, Nicole. Only. Always mine. Forever mine." He whispers each phrase into my open mouth, hungry for more kisses. I'm desperate to taste him again, but he pulls away and looks into me with eyes blacker than the Thames at midnight. Deeper than the tunnels in which he hides from the sun. They search my face. Sincerity flashes quickly into something else. Fear, maybe. Anger. I'm not sure, but it frightens me.

"Don't leave me again," I say. "Please, Ashe. I couldn't survive it. Not again. I belong in the darkness with you." My knuckles whiten, grasping his coat, then arms, then body to mine. I hold on tight, but something is tearing me away.

"You belong in the light." He pushes me away, then claws at me to come closer again.

After his final shove, I'm parted from him, and it's as if he ripped my heart from my bosom. "No! Ashe! Not again. Don't leave me again."

He reaches out to me and I grasp at his outstretched hands, so cold they burn mine, but I don't let go. Not for anything.

Then, just like that, we're in the light. Both of us. He and I are together under the midday sun, and he's all right. Alive, not bursting into flames or turning to dust. Reclining on a blanket by a lake. Daffodils dance, just like the poem, and I smile.

"It's all right, Nicole. I'm here. I'm always right here," he says, tapping the spot between my eyebrows, but something about the movement feels wrong. Condescending or controlling, but I push that offensive thought away. He's here. That's all that matters. He's here. My heart swells beneath my corset as he looms over me and pins me against the blanket with his weight, blocking the sun and blue skies with his dark locks and darker eyes.

His cold lips caress my cheek, then lips, then neck, then lower. Then lower. Then lower.

I grasp his dark curls between my fingers, holding him to me. Cinnamon fills my nostrils, and I laugh again. So full of joy and love.

"Did you bring my favorite for lunch, my love? You know how I love those apple tarts. Second only to you, that is. Come, kiss me again," I say, pulling his head back up to mine, but when my hands reach my face, they are no longer full of his sable curls. Dying grass pokes out between my fingers as storm clouds roll in above me.

The sky turns crimson. Huge red raindrops stain my white skirts. At first, horrified, I think it's blood, but it's cinnamon. "Did you do this?" I call into the wild. "Ashe, my love? Did you make it rain cinnamon just for me? What a gift, my love! What a treasure!" Arms wide, I spin around and around in the cinnamon mist, reveling in the game. "Come out. Come out. Wherever you are. Ashe? Come dance in the rain with me! Come out!"

Then darkness.

Then blinding light.

In bed, snuggled beneath white sheets, I choke on bile as my empty stomach contracts in panic. Again. Just like every morning since that horrible day. Every morning. The torment rushes back and suffocates me.

Cinnamon scented heartbreak.

Fear. Pain. Paralyzed.

I remember now.

He's gone.

The smell of freshly baked apple tarts wafts beneath my sheets. Fanny's tempting me again. My stomach grumbles and I long for the sweet tartness just on the other side of my blanket, but I'm unable to move. I think of pulling the covers down and jumping out of bed, at last. My home for weeks now. I don't even know how many weeks anymore. Is it February yet? March? Next year? Is my life over yet?

Please let it be over. Please let this stop.

I will my arm to move. I will my hand to grasp the top of the white sheet through which the sun brightens the world. A world that is no longer mine, that no longer makes sense.

I will my body to move.

After what feels like hours, it does move, finally, but only to roll over. The soft sheet caresses my palm.

I will my body to move.

I will my arms to throw the duvet aside and lunge toward those apple tarts, but instead, my hands wrap my downy protection tighter around me and tuck it beneath my chin.

He's gone.

Tears roll off the bridge of my nose. They wet the pillow and the sheet and my nightgown sleeve all at once. I don't wail. Not anymore. I don't make a sound. Like the baby with deaf parents, I know my sobs will bring no relief, no peace. They take far too much energy anyway.

Silent tears, my constant companion.

Fanny's voice breaks through my quiet sanctuary, but I don't hear anything but meaningless words and sounds and sighs. They fill the air, yet all I hear is the same mantra repeating in my mind.

He's gone. He's gone. He's gone.

He's gone.

Fanny pulls the blanket off me, exposing me to the world. Morning breaks into my chamber, a thief stealing my protective solitude, ripping it away with force. Violating me. I shade my eyes from the offensive light and back against the wall, looking away from Fanny. She betrayed my trust, exposed me to this dangerous world when she was meant to protect me.

I'll never forgive her for this.

I'll never forgive any of them.

Death to them all, but to me first. Please, let this end.

"Conrad came to see you again last night, my lamb." She leans over the bed and strokes my brow as if I'm sick. As if some kindness and hot soup will cure my ills. Her fingers push the hair from my eyes. "He's worried about you. They all are." The guilt of hurting my friends weighs on me, and I sink into my mattress, trying to disappear. I want it to swallow me, to make me invisible.

Just to fade away, out of Fanny's reach. Out of everyone's reach, but his. Envelop me in darkness with him.

My eyes stare, unfocused on anything, not even the wall before them. I look through the floral wallpaper, past the daub wall into the void.

"I'm worried, too," she continues. "Please, eat something. The cook made some fresh tarts for you again. Your favorite! Please, Nicole. Eat something. You're withering away. You've barely eaten for the past month."

"Leave me alone," I manage through my dry, cracked lips.

Fanny balls her fists up at her side and stomps her boot on the floor. "No. Enough of this!" Her voice is harsh now, scolding.

"Please don't yell at me," I say, crying anew. My eyes seek darkness beneath my arms. That's where I want to be, in the darkness. If I could just find my way back to him, he's waiting for me there. Curled up in a ball against the wall, my nightgown tangled around my thighs, I die again, just like I have every moment since I read his letter. I've read it so many times I know it by heart. It's burned into the crevices of my mind forever.

Don't look for me, for you will not find me.

He's gone. He's gone. He's gone.

I clasp the small key he left me, always next to my heart—the key to his heart, he said—and die again.

The mattress tilts toward the floor when Fanny sits on the edge of the bed. The backs of her fingers press against my head, then cheek, checking for fever. She strokes back my hair, repeating the soothing motion over and over, soothing her and soothing me. My hair must be a frightful mess. The cool touch of her hand on my temple gives me a sense of peace. I always feel lulled into safety when someone strokes my hair, if only for a moment.

"I don't know what to do, Nicole. I can't stand to see you in so much pain. Please, help me. What can I do to help?" Her voice changes quickly from kindness to anger to defeat. Fanny sounds as confused as I feel. She has tried anything and everything to get through to me since he left. Has it been weeks or has it been an eternity? Regardless, I'm no longer here. Nicole Knickerbocker Hawthorn is gone. Only her shell remains, a ghost of her former self. Emptiness.

"Leave me alone." The words come out flat. Numbness takes over again, and I welcome the reprieve from the pain. If I could just find the silence again, the darkness, then I'd be fine. Oh, let it be night! Let me sleep again and feel that sweet relief.

"No." Fanny's voice keeps me tethered to this brash place, forcing me into the harsh light of day. "I shan't leave you alone like this for a moment longer. It's been a month, and I can't cover for you anymore with your parents."

Only a month? Surely not. Please, no. I had held out hope of his return for the first two weeks, getting through New Year and St. Stephen's just fine. Laughing and dancing at the party. I knew in my heart he'd be back, but then after a fortnight, reality set in, and so did the illness that consumes me to this day. He's gone. He's gone. He's gone.

"They've sent word to the doctor, Nicole. They're talking hysteria. Oh, sweet kitten, you don't know the horrors that await you if they're convinced you're suffering from hysteria. You must eat. Please. Just one tart and we'll go for a walk today in the sunshine. Sunlight will do you good."

"No! I don't belong in the sunlight! I belong in the darkness with him!"

"No! You don't, Nicole!" Now Fanny cries with me, which touches me. Her tears melt down my wall of protection, of isolation. I chance a look at her rosy face, and it's wet with tears just like mine. Tear for tear. Sigh for sigh. The release of unspeakable pain manifests as tiny droplets of salt water. That's somehow unjust, too, like this world. It should be waterfalls. It should be thunderstorms and earthquakes, not silent pin drops of water. She cries with me, and I feel loved. No longer alone, if only for a moment.

Two women weeping over the cruelty of men.

"Why are you crying?" I ask her. It wasn't she who was tossed aside like rubbish. She didn't feel his lips, his eyes, his love, then have it ripped away because of some displaced sense of chivalry and honor. Cowardice, more like.

"I know how much this hurts, Nicole. I also know how much worse it can be."

"This is bad enough! If it were any worse I would be dead, Fanny! How can you say that? You don't know what it's like, Fanny. It hurts to breathe—I wish to disappear! Worse?"

"It's not my intention to belittle your pain, Nicole. I do know how devastating this is. No one deserves to be treated thus. When I say it could be worse, I mean on top of the heartbreak. Your entire life. Well..." She pauses then and bites her lip. I've never seen her look so sad, so lost. It's as if she's taking on all my pain and more. Beneath her rosy cheeks, I see a broken woman. Cracked, like me. Before I can think of what to say, she continues, "Please, child, listen to me. Have you ever wondered why I chose to be a spinster? Hmmmm? Why I keep my distance even from Wilfred, all these years later?"

I use the sleeve of my nightgown to wipe my nose. Fanny grimaces and flicks a handkerchief my way. For the briefest moment I glimpse my jolly governess in that scoff, but the shattered woman is back a heartbeat later. I take the proffered handkerchief embroidered with a blue rose and say nothing, no apology for my faux pas. I'm so far past caring about propriety, but she did spark my curiosity, and my compassion. All my attention is on her, eagerly awaiting her story.

Chapter Two

In Which Fanny Tells a Sad Tale

"I wasn't much older than you, my sweet. Eighteen, I was. So many years ago now. Twenty and more, yet I can still see his eyes when I close my own. I can still hear his promises and feel his cheek against mine. There is little in this world more devastating than heartbreak, my dove. Loss by death is crippling enough, no doubt. Add to that the dagger of betrayal and the rejection by someone you trusted, someone you loved. It's a loss of a loved one either way, you see. However, one is natural, part of the cycle of life and death, and the other, deliberate. Beyond cruel. The loss of a love is distressing either way, sure, but even more damaging is the betrayal by the one you love. He who claimed to love you as well. Who convinced you he adored you.

"That shatters, irreparably at times."

Fanny's lip trembles, and she gets a distant look in her eyes. Faraway and empty, except for a hint of pain behind the vast nothingness. "Tell me," I say.

To my surprise, an apple tart warms my hand, which brings the tasty pastry closer to my mouth. In another moment, my teeth sink into the soft, gooey goodness. Mmmmm. It's the first morsel of food I've had in as long as I can remember, save the few crusts of bread Fanny made me choke down now and again, and the cold tea she made me drink. Although she had brought it to me hot, by the time she got it to my lips, it had gone cold in the winter air.

The first glorious tarty taste of cinnamon and sugar melts on my tongue. Crumbs of crust stick to my lips, then one or two fall upon my bedclothes. Until now, I've been far too nauseous to eat, but this morning my body acts on its own while my mind is distracted by Fanny's story.

Fanny's lips turn up in a genuine smile, but her eyes remain vacant. "I was eighteen, and I was so deeply in love. His name was Peter. Oh my," she says, bringing her hand to her mouth in surprise. "Even after all these years it's hard for me to speak that name. I still feel sick when hearing it." She shakes her head, hands pressing into her cheeks. Tears glisten in her eyes. "I can't believe I'm telling you this, dear. I've never told anyone, save me mum and dad. Never anyone, in all these years." Shame dims Fanny's features as her hands cover her eyes, hiding her entire face from the world. Hiding herself away.

I understand the desire, and my heart goes out to her. In this moment, I want nothing more than to comfort her, to relieve her pain. I want to tell her she has nothing to be ashamed of. I love her and will protect her from ever being hurt again. Ever, ever again. It's not something within my power, of course, save protection from vampires. I suppose it's impossible to protect someone from the unseen treachery of another, especially when they're in love. I feel so helpless and sad for her, and then it dawned on me. This must be how she's felt for weeks while I've been in this state. I truly wish to say the right words, to make it all better for her and for me, to make it all go away. Words form in my mind yet I quickly dismiss them as trite or meaningless platitudes, so I just speak from my heart. "You can trust me, Fanny. I shan't betray you, never shall I betray any whom I love, especially not now that I know how damaging such a thing is." Images of Dante's Inferno come to mind. The devil flaps his wings to escape, but the cold wind created by his vigorous attempts keeps the ice frozen—keeps hell devoid of warmth—while he devours the treacherous like Judas Iscariot over and over for all eternity. I continue through gritted teeth, "No wonder the lowest place in hell is reserved for traitors. Rightfully so."

"Yes, I can trust you, my lamb. I can trust you with my life, as you've proven. And you, me." She wipes her eyes dry and composes herself. She sits up tall and lays her hands in her lap, like a proper Victorian lady, taught to hide everything unpleasant and wear a mask of contented beauty. "I'm telling you this, not for your pity but to show you what you've already learned. You just don't know you've learned it yet. It took me years to work it out; such is the way of betrayal by those we had the misfortune of trusting, and loving. Confusing at best."

No truer words. Confusing, indeed. One vacillates between making excuses for them, swearing it's just all a misunderstanding—all because he's scared or inept at what to do or some other of the thousands of reasons that would make it not what it is—and coming to terms with the reality of the situation: betrayal by a lover.

I wait for her to continue her tale, my eyes wide and eager. My lips wrap around each sticky finger in turn, sucking every succulent crumb and morsel of sour sweetness from the tart. I help myself to another, but Fanny still doesn't speak. She opens her mouth, and then closes it again. Her face twists into anger, then sadness, then distress. Imploring eyes flick to mine, then away in apparent shame. Then, remembering herself again, she recomposes her proper mask of serenity. I recognize it so well for the number of times I've done the same thing. The constant struggle between what's screaming inside desperate to be heard and seen and what society demands. What propriety demands. Then, to want nothing more than to crawl into a deep hole so no one can ever see me or hurt me again. I know the maddening process too well, indeed. The only thing I can do is reassure her that she doesn't have to keep up such pretense with me. That I will love her no matter what she says, unconditionally. Still, perhaps in her love for me, she feels obligated to relate on this very painful subject.

I must relieve that expectation. "It's all right, Fanny. You don't have to tell me if it's still too painful." Yet, I hope she does. It's the first thing that has gotten my mind off Ashe.

Oh, Ashe.

Just like that, the abyss beckons me once again. The numbing trance envelops me. One single word, a specific assembly of letters. A series of sounds that had brought such joy to my heart a short while ago now brings pain, suffocation, nausea, despair. The tart turns to sand in my mouth. My tongue swells up, and I cannot swallow without gagging. It scratches my throat as if I had swallowed a rock from the murky bank of The Thames.

Then, the mantra.

He's gone. He's gone. He's gone.

I sink back onto my pillow. The half-eaten tart falls upon my breast, and my hand collapses limp onto the mattress, bereft of all strength, the will to move—the will to even live. Warm tears make fresh trails down my temples.

I see nothing but the absence of him.

"Finish your tart, my lamb," Fanny urges, nudging me, but I don't move. Catatonic. My mind goes around and around and around. Thoughts urge me to look at her, but my body doesn't respond. Fanny grasps my shoulders and pulls me toward her. Like a rag doll, I fall against her, and she pats my back. She says something, but the words flow through my head unintelligible. In one side and out the other, chased away by 'He's gone. He's gone. He's gone.'

"There are so many more tarts here," Fanny pleads, "and they're all for you. Please! Eat up!"

"He's gone," I whisper. No. Not whisper. My lips shape the words but no sound emerges. I mouth the maddening mantra over and over.

"Get up!" she shouts, shaking me to and fro before pushing me away from her back onto the bed. This shocks me out of my stupor and I stare into chilly winter air filling my chamber. She throws her hands up in defeat and says, "All right! All right! Anything to bring you out of this. You are more important than my shame." Fanny's voice sounds angry, but she's not angry with me, despite her rough treatment. "Damnation," she scolds herself. "The shame is not yours. It's his. It's all his." Then, to me, "Please, my lamb. I'm sorry for treating you thus," she says, then pleads with me, "Sit back up and have another tart. Eat. I'll tell you my pitiful tale if you will keep eating, all right? Please don't judge me too harshly, for I was in love." She becomes quiet for a moment and smiles to herself, and then shakes her head side to side as if dismissing a disturbing thought. "I nearly said young and in love, but it was not my age that made me a fool. No. Please, my dear. Have another tart." She holds a tart in front of my face until my eyes focus on it. Then, like coaxing a spaniel with a tasty treat, she pulls it away from me, then pushes it close to my lips, then pulls it away again.

I laugh. It sounds strange, my laughter. Foreign. I never thought I'd laugh again, but this kind woman who raised me and loved me like her own gives me a moment of joy. I've missed Fanny's antics. Then, I realize, I've missed me, too. Much to my surprise, my body responds to the sugary temptation once again.

"Very well," I say, sitting back up to accept the proffered tart. "Tell me, please." I take a bite of the yummy tart and continue, forming the words around the heavenly cinnamon. "I love you, Fanny. You have no need to feel ashamed."

"Wait until you hear my pitiful tale before you say such things. It will be all the worse to see the disappointment on your face." After another heavy sigh and shake of her head—one, two, three times, she starts her story. "I was so in love with Peter. I suppose the story is age-old, isn't it? Such a cliché, really. I was a country girl, not terribly well-born. He was the son of a lord, but he took an interest in me. Said I was so full of life. Said he loved my long red hair." She stroked her phantom locks, once vibrant red but now tinged in grey and pulled back in a tight bun at the nape of her neck. Her eyes sparkles for the briefest moment as she relived that moment in her memory. "I would wander in the woods and the fields, gathering wild herbs for spells back home, for the coven's rituals and for medicines as well. On the few sunny days, I would run amongst the wild flowers and dance to a song only I heard, turning around and around, my long hair fanning out around me. I basked in the joy of life, and I felt so beautiful, Nicole, like a princess. I didn't know anyone was watching. Turns out he was. Looking back I suppose, he thought he must own me, capture such beauty and freedom and joy for his own. Feed on it, for he had none of his own, empty and cruel as he was. I see that now, but then..."

She stops for a moment and finds my eyes intently focused on her, perhaps looking for a hint of either judgment or compassion, but all I feel is curiosity. "What happened, Fanny?"

"He came to me and professed his love one day. Oh, Nicole, he was so handsome and kind, at first. He said he wanted to marry me and take me away from my simple life. He said I would become the lady of his manor. Something inside me knew it wasn't possible. Such was the way of the world then, but my heart wanted to believe. No longer would I dance in the fields alone, but I would dance in fine balls wearing beautiful gowns with my handsome lord in love and joy. It was such a dream, and I gave into it."

Fanny gets very quiet and looks down at her hands resting in her lap. Tears drip from her eyes and her breath comes quick. "He had me, my lamb, after just a few months of courting me, secret meetings and stolen kisses. He had me in the forest. I protested, but he didn't listen. Perhaps I didn't protest strongly enough…but, no, I did. For even a whisper of a protest is strong enough, even an indication—pushing him away or turning away or anything, but he didn't listen. He ignored all my NOs and STOPs and PLEASE DON'Ts, and he had me in that forest on that day. He did what he wanted with no consideration to me. Such is the way of the world, especially between classes, but his betrayal changed me nonetheless. I was no more than a tool for his pleasure, an object for further taking, another thing to possess, to use, to discard. My life has never been the same."

"Oh, Fanny! How horrible! I'm so sorry!"

"It's not the worst of it, I'm afraid. I became pregnant, so I had to tell me mum. There was no hiding that, after all. She believed me and, being a witch herself, knew the wicked ways of mankind, but my father would have none of it. He chided me for being alone in the forest with a man, for being a foolish girl in love. Said I deserved it, he did. I was ruined, of course. Even in all her power, my mother relented to his will. Fear of violation and loss herself, perhaps. Fear is a powerful force on its own, sometimes not even a match for magic. Both of them turned on me in the end. I was truly alone. My parents hid me away for nine months, making excuses to the village about an illness. When the child came, it was stillborn. Just as well, I've always said. Yes, I've never been quite the same."

Familiar tears wet my cheeks, but they represent Fanny's predicament now, not the absence of Ashe. She was right. It could be so much worse.

"Did Ashe"—I cringe at the sound of his name—"So sorry, my dear. Did he ever…"

"No, Fanny! Never! Nothing but a kiss or two only. Nothing more! He was a perfect gentleman, until the end. He gave me his heart, Fanny. He loves me! He said he loves me, so why did he leave? For my own good? It's balderdash, isn't it?"

"I'm afraid so, my lamb."

"Peter said he loved you, too. Didn't he?"

"Yes. Over and over. When we were together, he had to be touching me, always holding my hand or touching my arm–always in contact. I felt so loved. Cherished. Adored, even worshipped. Nothing ever like it before or since. He had the most intense sky-blue eyes, and he would hold me in his gaze for never-ending moments in time. I know now it was him taking possession of my essence, owning me, claiming me—body, mind, and soul—as his, to do what he will. And he did just that."

Fanny pauses, but I can tell she's not finished. I cross my legs and help myself to another tart. Somehow hearing her pitiful tale helps me feel less alone. Not that I'm glad she went through such a horrible ordeal. Not at all! But knowing she understands, that she doesn't see me as foolish or frivolous for being so broken over the loss of a love, really helps. She breathes deeply, then looks at me with a sad smile and continues, "After that day in the forest, I never saw him again. I heard that he married a fine lady and moved to London. For so long, even after the…"—She can't bring herself to say the word, and I can't blame her. Horrific thing to admit happened to you. No—to admit someone you loved chose to force on you.—"I envied her, his new fancy wife. Oh! Our love was like an opiate, my lamb. Do you see? So wonderful but a fantasy. All a fantasy to cover up something so horrible."

"Oh, Fanny! No wonder you never married! How could you trust again after something like that?"

"You do understand, don't you, Nicole?" She grasped my hands in a desperate motion, her eyes wild. "It wasn't worth it, my lamb. The price was too high, you see. I paid for those few moments of heaven with a lifetime of agony and regret. It was too high a price to pay, so

I never chanced it again. I couldn't trust men, and I couldn't trust myself to know a saint from a scoundrel."

I hold her soft hands tightly in solidarity. "Oh, yes! I do understand, Fanny! But my love is not a scoundrel. He is not forceful. He doesn't wish to own me."

"Perhaps not, love, but he did presume to choose what was best for you without consulting you. He loved you and you loved him, yet he turned away from that love out of cowardice. That is what's behind every bully, a coward. Do you know where the word bully word comes from?"

She releases me from her frantic hold, and I take the opportunity to help myself to another tart, my fourth, and shake off the doubts before biting into it.

"It originally meant sweetheart, a term of endearment for a lover, believe it or not. This type of treatment is so commonplace, my lamb that our own language has changed to reflect it. Every maid for hundreds of years thinks that her lover is different. Her lover speaks the truth. Her lover shan't betray her. Alas, most of them are tragically mistaken."

"Surely I can't mistrust every man, Fanny! Some must be honorable."

"Some are indeed. Few and far between, and perhaps your lad is one. Perhaps he is an honorable coward who did have your best interest at heart. It doesn't change that he's left you in such a state for weeks now. He abandoned you, my lamb. Even if he returns, which I have no doubt he will, what's to say he won't do it again? He's already proven that in times of stress or trouble, he turns away from love, not towards it."

"How can I be sure? I can't turn my back on love, Fanny! I love him so much!"

"I know you do. Love is wonderful and horrible all at once. Love alone is not enough to make a relationship work. It takes courage and investment and honesty and being there. True love is not cowardly. I do know that much. Your entire life can be defined by one decision, one foolish decision. That decision almost always comes from cowardice. Not fear. Fear is natural. It protects us, warns us, keeps us alive. Cowardice is something vile, deformed—shrinking away in the face of fear. Making the easy choice even though you know it's wrong or unwise or will greatly hurt another. Courage is acting honorably, with integrity, in the face of fear. It's making the hard decision because you know it's right, not only for you, but for everyone involved. You will learn this, especially in your position as The Protector, Nicole. You must think about others as well during this time, those who are victims of vampires and other such horrors. You don't have the luxury of wallowing in heartbreak. The people need you. Your friends need you."

Her words offend me, and I start, shocked. "Luxury? Do you think this has been fun for me, Fanny?"

"Of course not. You heard my story. You know the damage done to me under the guise of love. It ruined me. I was much as you are for months upon months, struggling between love and anger. The baby came, dead, and still I couldn't face the world, frightened of every sound, every passerby. I acted out of cowardice when I loved him, knowing it wasn't possible but wanting so desperately to believe that it was. I did what was easy, what felt good. I didn't listen to myself when I knew what was true, deep in my soul. I chose to believe the fantasy. Still, his treachery and violation are on his soul and his alone. That is not my doing, nor what I deserve for taking a chance on impossible love, not at all. My father was wrong; it wasn't my fault. Yet, I can't help but think none of it would've happened if I hadn't been so foolish."

"Ashe did it for me! He left for my well-being, so that I could be in the sunlight. So that I could have a normal life! It was a selfless act, Fanny. He loves me!"

"Admirable, indeed. But was it really for you? Or was it for him? Did it make things easier for him? Perhaps he felt too much for you and it scared him, but instead of turning to you, he just left. That's cowardice."

"I can't bear to think of him as a coward. Not after he fought so bravely against Pilkington. We're alive, in part, because of him." There is no convincing her of what I know in my heart, and I don't want to talk about it anymore anyway. I reach for another tart to discover they are all gone. "Aw," I say. "No more? I feel better than I have in weeks, and the tarts definitely helped. More, please?" I smile my best little girl smile and bat my eyes.

"There's more in the kitchen, love. Perhaps a bowl of soup as well and some tea?"

"That would be lovely, Fanny!" I jump out of bed and land on my tip toes. The wood floor is hard and cold beneath them, such a strange sensation after the softness of the bed for so long. I stretch the kinks out of my arms and back, twirling around. "Tea, indeed. Then a walk perhaps?"

"A walk sounds lovely, and training! You must get back out there. It's your—"

"—duty. Yes, I know, Fanny. My sacred duty. First, more tarts!"

CHAPTER THREE

IN WHICH NICKIE NICK WEARS A CROWN

The journey to Barge House Street is surprisingly pleasant. Cheerful, even. My mind is free and focused, like my old self. I turn my collar up to the rain and chase my frozen breath. Tall brick buildings flank me, and I feel an odd comfort between them, like they protect me. Even the chill of a London winter warms me. All this around me—here before *him*, before us. All here still.

Once through the street level door, I shake off the wet and cold, looking up the stairs to where my friends await my arrival. An even deeper sense of safety fills me. I'm so glad I came. Turns out after all, Fanny had promised Conrad I'd pop 'round today, so I didn't have much of a choice, really. Still, it feels so good to be here again.

"Alright, Nick?" Conrad smiles and shows me into the parlor. A fire burns in the hearth, but it's not half as warm as the light in Conrad's smile. Flushed, I turn from him and see his mother knitting in the comfy chair. Her stocking feet are propped up on a small round stool. The flickering light of the flames dances against the hand-knitted pattern, toasting her toes. After that horrible place had been washed away, the stench of Bedlam, not only in scent but in energy, she shone through. It was good to see her looking well, beautiful and rather radiant. Conrad takes after her, indeed.

"Hello, Mrs. Hannon? Nice to see you."

"And you, Nicole. Cup of tea?" she asks, setting down her needles and yarn, eager to serve like a good mum. Mrs. Hannon beams, and it reminds me of something Fanny always says, 'to serve others is the nourishment that feeds one's heart and soul.'

"Yes. Thank you. Cold out there. Tea would do me well."

"That's if I can find my way about the workshop—um—kitchen. We must find another place for Franklin to work!" Her voice holds a mock edge of frustration, but her eyes are all smiles. She's settled in nicely as matron to these boys, and she quite obviously loves every moment.

"Alright, Nick?" Conrad repeats and moves closer. Concern fills his eyes and he's as serious as I've ever seen him.

"Yes. Fine, Conrad."

"Back among the living?" He nudges me with his elbow, trying to be playful, but it has the opposite effect.

"Don't, please." I feel the tears burning behind my eyes. "I can't take your teasing. Not now." I blink hard, willing myself not to cry.

"Oh, Nick," he says and touches my cheek with such tenderness. "I'd never. Not now."

There's something lingering in the features of his face, similar to what I'd seen in Ashe's (to what I'd felt, too), but different at the same time.

Love. Indeed, a special kind of love.

Before I can react, I'm embraced by three sets of arms. Cassie, Edwin, and Rufus all rush me in a simultaneous hug. Honestly, if I didn't have the strength of The Protector, I most certainly would've been bowled over!

Conrad looks at his feet and retreats into his own chair by the fire.

"Are you really well, Nickie?" Edwin says. His big blue eyes look up at me, searching—full of concern as well. Guilt washes over me. My nonsense has hurt all those I love. No more, I vow. No more.

"Yeah, Nick. Alright?" Rufus echoes. He backs away first, controlling his excitement and folding his hands properly in front of him, like a gentleman. He's at that awkward age between child and adult at twelve, just learning to contain himself.

"I'm fine, everyone, truly. So lovely to see you all."

"We missed you, Nickie! Dolly missed you, too!" Cassie's small voice fills my broken heart. Here, all here. These are the reasons to go on. These are the reasons to get out of bed. To eat apple tarts. To walk in the sunshine. Right here.

"Let the poor girl breathe," Mrs. Hannon says as she emerges from the kitchen with a tray of chocolate biscuits. "Come, Nicole. Sit. The kettle's on."

"Hey, Nickie. Missed ya." Franklin pokes his head out of his kitchen workshop and gives me an awkward wave. Not much for socializing, my Franklin.

"Well, hello Franklin. Working hard?"

"Always. Come in after yer tea, and I'll show ya my latest."

"Will do."

Somewhere in the back of my mind I remember that Ashe procured this flat for them. He's here, in every nook. I can feel him here. Here, but gone.

He's gone. He's gone. He's gone.

My stomach clenches and I fear I'll vomit. The loss. The pain. Suffocating, returns.

A single thought brings it all rushing back.

Not here. Not here. Not here. I will myself to keep calm. I can't let my boys see me like that. My hand catches my balance, pressed into the hardness of the wall. I focus all my energy on the way the wall feels beneath my hand. Hard. Smooth. My eyes close, and I focus everything I am on this moment where I am safe and loved.

"Nick?"

Conrad's voice.

The wall and Conrad's voice. I'm all right. I'm safe.

"Nick?" His hand touches my shoulder just as the tea kettle whistles in the kitchen. Together they bring me back.

"I'm fine, Conrad. Thank you. Just need to sit is all." I take off my drenched coat and hang it near the door before taking a seat near in the parlor. Mrs. Hannon takes my faltering as a desperate need for tea, no doubt, for she disappears, but emerges again with the brewing pot in no time. "Thank you, Mrs. Hannon," I say and take a biscuit and the proffered tea. "The tea smells lovely. Is it peppermint?"

"Yes, my dear. My own special blend. Earl Grey with a hint of peppermint. Conrad's father used to—" Her voice faltered. Mine isn't the only broken heart in the room. "Conrad loves it," she says instead, recovering nicely. I could learn from her example.

Must remain distracted. Must stay focused.

I've killed vampires, foiled the plans of a mad-psychiatrist, and saved the Queen of England, so carrying on a simple conversation shouldn't be a challenge. I can do this. I can do this. Distraction. Stories, like Fanny told me. Turn my focus outside of me. To those I love.

"What's been happening? Any news since—" I stumble over my words. Since what? I can't speak his name, not in these walls. Please, let them know not to, as well.

"—since Pilkington was stopped." Conrad saves me.

"Yes. Since Pilkington."

"Nope. All's been rather quiet, really. We haven't wandered out much, knowing what's out and about. Especially with you away. We win what we can each day. Mom helps now, too," he says, full of pride. "We got it pretty well sorted."

Mrs. Hannon blushes, embarrassed of having to steal, which is what Conrad calls "winning." Her hands work faster over the yarn. "It's temporary, of course. I'm feeling so much better. I'll be able to work soon. Make an honest living for these boys."

"A-hem!" Cassie says, crossing her little arms over her chest. Her dolly's limbs flop from the gesture. Its broken face mirrors Cassie's cross look, little brows furrowed in frustration.

"My mistake, of course, Cassie. So sorry. These boys and girl."

"That's better," Cassie says. She plays with her dolly alone in the corner again, keeping herself occupied, but I hear her whisper, "They always forget about us, don't they dolly? We matter, too. We're small and we're girls, but we matter, too. Don't we?"

"We most certainly do, little Cassie. We most certainly do," I say. We do indeed matter. This sweet little girl reminds me of my inherent worth. I do feel safe here, surrounded by my family. They are my family, after all, aren't they?

"Psssst." Edwin is poking his head out of the kitchen, and he says "Psssst" again.

"Yes, Edwin," I whisper, playing his game.

His cheeks and nose turn rosy red with those blue eyes cast down to his toes. "No. Not you, Nickie," he says in normal tones, then "Pssssst!! Cassie!!!" in a harsh whisper, as if no one else can hear him. Cassie holds her dolly close and looks over at Edwin who now frantically flaps his hand in a 'come here' motion. "It's time!!" he hisses.

"Oh!" Cassie's entire tiny frame starts, and she jumps up. Dolly's arms flap about.

Edwin disappears back into the kitchen with Franklin and, I assume, Rufus, since he isn't out here with us. Cassie curtsies and starts to inch her way toward the kitchen. Conrad and his mother look with great intent into their laps, smiling mischievously.

"What's this all about, Cassie?"

"Nothing," she says. "Nothing at all." She smooths out her skirts in a very proper way and looks this way and that, eyes wide, as if she's been caught in a secret and doesn't know what to do next.

Edwin's arm shoots out of the door, grabs Cassie, and yanks her inside.

Conrad bursts out laughing and slaps his thigh. Even his mum must stifle a snicker.

"Conrad? What's happening?"

"You'll see, Nick. Just sit tight." Conrad crosses his arms over his chest and sinks down in his chair, giggling. I don't think I've ever seen Conrad giggle in all the years I've known him. Since we were Cassie's age ourselves.

"Stop it!" I hear from the other side of the kitchen door. "Not like that. Wait! No. Here, hold this end. Ready? One, two, three." The door opens, held by Franklin who stands off to the side to let the other three through. Edwin and Cassie hold either side of a very lopsided cake on a large plate. The icing is melting off one side, slipping into sugary ribbons along the base.

"Oh, my goodness!" I exclaim, genuinely surprised. "For me? You did this all for me?"

The two little ones walk towards me. Each ginger step takes all their concentration to keep the cake properly balanced between them. Edwin, focused, presses his tongue between his teeth. His eyes never leave the cake. Rufus walks in procession behind them, smiling from ear to ear. He keeps his hands behind his back as if he's hiding something. Then Franklin comes, more distracted than anything. His mind is, no doubt, still back in his workshop figuring out a puzzle he's been contemplating for hours, if not days, but his body is out here for the celebration.

Conrad answers, "Edwin has been planning this for quite some time. It was all his idea."

"I helped!" little Cassie says. She stumbles a bit, but they're close enough to me that I'm able to put my hands beneath the platter and save the cake from the floor.

"You almost ruined it!" Edwin chides Cassie.

"Well I did help," she says, tiny balled fists on her tiny hips.

"It's perfect! Thank you, Cassie." After patting her on the head, I look directly at Edwin and wait until I have his full attention. "Thank you, Edwin. This is the nicest thing anyone has ever done for me. Ever." Tears burn my eyes, but they are indeed tears inspired by love and joy, for a change.

"We missed you, Nickie," he says quietly, looking down at his feet.

"I missed you, too. All of you! Did you make this cake yourself, Edwin?"

Edwin nods.

"I helped!" Cassie says.

"You got flour all over your dress is what you did," Edwin says, but he says it with a smile and a teasing edge in his voice.

Cassie's ready to retort, but when she sees his warm smile she giggles. "I did. It was so much fun! Wasn't it, dolly?" She trots back to the kitchen to fetch her constant companion.

"I hadn't made a cake in quite some time," Mrs. Hannon says, blushing.

"I put the icing on myself," Edwin says and thrusts his little chest out in pride, "and I didn't even have one lick for myself. Not one!" His eyes are back on the cake. He's been waiting so long to have some. A treat like this is few and far between for orphans like them. Now with Mrs. Hannon about, perhaps they'll be more times like this. With me, too. They're my family, and I must take care of them, too. Remember to bring them tarts and such from our kitchen. We have so much. It's just not fair.

"Then let's have some now! Everyone!"

Edwin reaches out, finger poised to smear the wavy icing along the bottom, but Mrs. Hannon mothers him. "Uh-uh-uh! Not with your fingers! Go get some plates and forks, Edwin. Enough for all of us. Let's see. One. Two. Three." She counts the rest of us in silence, mouthing four. five. six. seven. "Seven plates and seven forks."

Edwin takes a quick scoop into the icing, leaving a small dent in the sugary goodness and runs into the kitchen laughing. Cassie's hugs her dolly, and they both sit near my feet, waiting for their slice.

"There's more, Nickie," Rufus says. I wonder how Rufus has been since his ordeal with Pilkington. I must remember that I'm not the only one who has been hurt by the events of the last month. I've been so selfish, I decide and chide myself for my foolishness. How trite, a broken heart. Rufus was turned into a mesmerized zombie, not even able to control his thoughts and his movements, and I'm mooning over a boy.

Perspective, Nick. Perspective.

If only it were that easy.

"More? Oh, my!"

"Here," he says. "We found a cracker after Christmas, and we saved the crown for you." He puts a paper crown on my head and gives me a piece of paper. It's a notice from the street. This one says: Medicine Show! Snake Oil to cure ALL ILLS. Feeling depressed? Low? Lonely? Aches and Pains? Peterson's Snake Oil will cure all your ills. Join us!

"No!" Rufus interrupts my reading. "The other side."

I flip it over. A beautiful sunny scene drawn in crayon covers the back of the advert. Across the top, large block purple letters read: Get Well Soon, Nickie. A stick figure with long brown hair and all black clothes holds a brown stick that is stuck into a frowning stick figure. On either side of his frown are two pointy teeth. The bubble coming out of his mouth says "Ahhhhh!" Three little stick figures are off to the side, two with just stick legs and the third with a long pink triangle skirt holding an even smaller stick figure (with only one eye). These three little ones are all saying "Hurrah!" with big smiles. There's a brown tall rectangle topped with a triangle on the other side with a white circle near the top. Numbers line the inside of the circle.

"See," Rufus says. "That's Big Ben." He points to the tall brown rectangle. "And that's you killing a vampire, saving us." He points to the three smaller people on the right.

"This is beautiful, boys," I say and reaching down to Cassie at my feet, patting her on her little back. "And my sweet girl, too." While balancing the cake on my lap, I examine this lovely drawing. "Did you draw this, Rufus?"

"Me and Edwin did it."

"I helped!" Cassie says, springing up and nearly knocking the cake from my lap. "See? I did the sky." Long, straight, blue scribbles that extended from one side to the other made up the sky in this happy picture.

"Very nice, Cassie! Good work! You're very talented, madam."

"Thank you," Cassie says and curtsies.

"We all signed it, too," Rufus points out the names scribbled at the bottom.

"These are the best gifts ever. Thank you so much!"

"I made you this, Nickie," Franklin says. "It hasn't been properly tested yet, but I think it will help you.

You know, be prepared even if you're not in your hunter outfit. Always be ready."

Edwin returns with the plates and forks, dropping a few forks on his rush back over. He stops, steps forward, then back, and then forward again, wondering what to do about the dropped forks.

"I'll get them," Rufus offers.

"I'll hold the plates," Mrs. Hannon says. "Here." She holds her hands out for the plates and forks, placing them in her lap. "Now take one at a time. Conrad will cut the cake. Did you bring a knife?"

"Ooops!" Edwin says and slaps his forehead with an open palm. "I'll get it."

"Careful now. No running with a knife! The cake isn't going anywhere. It will be here when you get back."

"Anyway, it's not ready," Franklin continues. He holds out his arm, which is now wrapped in a brass contraption in which a sharpened wooden stake is affixed along the underneath side. "See. It wraps around your arm like this and can be worn under your blouse, Nickie. With a flick of your wrist," he demonstrates. The stake shoots out and Franklin lunges over Conrad's head as if staking an invisible being behind him.

"Careful with that!" Mrs. Hannon says.

"Sorry, Mrs. Hannon." Then to me, he says, "When it's dust, you just release this catch and push it back. It locks back into place like this."

"Amazing, Franklin, as always," I say. "Thank you so much. I look forward to being able to work again." My words betray more than I care to give away. Able to work. Like there is something wrong with me. Like I'm not functional. You can do this, Nick. You can do this. You got out today. You walked across London on your own. You can do this, Nick.

"Cake everyone!" Conrad says. He's holding the knife Edwin just brought for him up in the air, reverently.

"Yes, please" the chorus says.

"Yes, please," I say, smiling at Conrad. He smiles back, and there is something different about him. I can't put my finger on what. More grown up, perhaps. He is only a few months behind me, after all. The knife slides through the cake with little effort, and the first piece goes to Edwin. I insist. He drags his finger along the icing. His lips wrap around his little finger and he sucks it clean making an "mmmmmm" sound as he does.

"Ladies first!" Cassie demands.

"Yes, little one," I say. "You're next."

"A big piece, please. I have to share with dolly."

"A big piece it is," Conrad says and cuts a piece the same size as Edwin's. Cassie wraps her little fist around the fork and stabs at the cake. She manages to get a piece to her mouth, losing only a few crumbs back on the plate. Dolly gets to sample the icing-smeared empty fork before Cassie takes another bite.

Once all the boys are enjoying their cake, Mrs. Hannon takes the platter from me and hands me my own plate full of the special treat. Although it's a little heavy and the icing, too too sweet, it's the best cake I've ever had.

Between the apple tarts this morning and now cake, I'll put the weight back on in no time.

After we all enjoyed the sugary goodness (including a second slice), Mrs. Hannon goes to the kitchen to make some fresh tea. Edwin jumps up and runs into another room. When he reappears, he has a sheet wrapped around his shoulders and holds a newspaper high in the hair. On his head, he wears a paper crown, much like mine.

"Hear ye! Hear ye!" he shouts. "The king, that's me," he whispers an aside before continuing in his regal voice, "declares a celebration of Nickie Nick, The Protector of all our people. Gather 'round, gather 'round! Let all hear this royal decree!!"

"This is the best part," Conrad leans over and whispers in my ear. A shiver goes up my arm when he touches my hand. There must be a draft in here. Perhaps I should stoke the fire.

Cassie joins Edwin on one side and Rufus on the other, and the three perform a scene. Rufus walks around, mesmerized, with his arms out in front of him as if sleepwalking. Cassie, the only girl, plays me. They didn't give her a real stake, though. Thank goodness. She holds an old newspaper shaped into a point like a stake, and Edwin plays the part of who I can only assume is Dr. Pilkington. He laughs maniacally and thrusts out his chest and says "WooWooWoo" every so often between sentences to show just how mad the demented doctor really is.

It's simply the most delightful thing I have ever seen. This, right after the most delicious cake and homecoming, I feel joy again, just when I started to believe I'd be sad and broken forever.

We all applaud loudly when they finish their skit, and Edwin takes an exaggerated bow. Then another and another. Pure joy fills my broken heart and I must, again, stifle the happy tears.

I shall be all right after all.

CHAPTER FOUR

IN WHICH NICKIE NICK
SEES THE MASKED MAN

"Come along, Nickie! It's a lovely day," Edwin says. "I wish to play in Temple Gardens. Please?"

"It's too close to dusk," Mrs. Hannon says.

"It's only a quarter hour if we don't dally," Edwin says, eyes bright. "Besides, we'll be with Nickie!"

"We'll come home before it gets dark proper," Cassie chimes in. "I promise. Please?" She clenches her little hands together and holds them under her chin. Her dolly lolls under her arm. Its cracked face mocks my happy mask.

"It would be a nice time," Conrad says. "They could use the fresh air, and I suppose Nickie could as well. We could all go."

"Well, all right, if Nicole's up for it, but it's too cold for these old bones," Mrs. Hannon says. "I'll keep the hearth fires burning and have some hot cocoa waiting when you return."

"Hot cocoa?" Edwin cries. "Truly? We have hot cocoa?"

"We don't have much, of course, but I was saving it for a special night. Tonight qualifies good as any, having Nicole back and all. Be back promptly at dusk, or it will be cold when you get here. Cold cocoa is nowhere near as tasty."

"Oh! Yay! Yay! Yay!" Cassie jumps up and down, and her doll's arms flap about.

"But in order to get your hot cocoa, you must all do as Nickie and Conrad say, agreed?"

"Yes! Oh, yes, ma'am!" Edwin says, blue eyes wide and sincere. Rufus puts a hand on Edwin's shoulder, both their faces beaming.

"Get yer coats and scarves, gloves if ya got 'em," Conrad says. "It's freezing out there."

"It sure is." I bend over to Edwin and Cassie's level and point to my nose. "Still red and nippy even though I've been next to the fire this whole time. Quite cold. See?" I wrinkle my nose and squiggle it around, making Cassie giggle and Edwin roll his eyes. "Feel." Taking Cassie's index finger, I press it to the very tip of my nose.

"It's not that cold," she says in a playful sing-song manner. "Let's go! Let's go!"

"All right. We'll go, but just for a bit. It's getting late." Mrs. Hannon goes back to her crochet after a glance up at me. She shakes her head side to side and smiles widely. It must be wonderful for her to have a family again. It certainly is for me.

After everyone is bundled up as much as possible while still being able to move, we head out. Franklin even joins us. Although we're pretty safe before dark, I still strap his gift to my arm. Plus, Conrad and Franklin and Rufus all have stakes stored in their pockets here and there. A wave of sadness shadows my eyes. These children have known such little joy. These dangers of the world should still be years away for them, but then, perhaps it is best for them to grow up with the harsh realities of life, then they won't be caught unaware later. I only hope it doesn't make them too hard, if there is such a thing in these times.

The air stings my nose and ears, and I pull my scarf up around them. My breath hits the wool and condenses there and back on my cheeks. Warmth for a moment, then colder against the damp. It's barely past tea time and already the skies are dimming.

How I long for the days of summer, the warmth of the fleeting sun. This moment here, however, has the warmth of love and family, so I push those longings, and others, away and focus on the joy before me. Cassie is skipping. She keeps her head down to ensure she doesn't trip over a high cobblestone. At six, she's still learning to control basic movements and coordination.

"Don't get too far ahead, Cassie. We're almost at the park," I say. Edwin and Rufus are talking in low tones about something of great importance, no doubt.

They lean into each other, whispering their plans and schemes. Franklin is fiddling with a gadget as he walks, always focused on his work, that one.

A sense of peace fills my body and stretches my lips into a smile. I glance back at Conrad to find him looking at me. His face lights up with his own smile when our eyes meet, but then he looks away, blushing.

Ashe intrudes on my happy moment, and my body reacts viscerally. A contraction in my stomach, like I might vomit. It goes just as quickly, thank goodness. Strange all of a sudden like that, and I've been having so much fun tonight. A needed reprieve. Don't want that nonsense to ruin it.

"Here are the gardens," I say, hoping no one noticed that strange physical reaction.

"Yay!" Cassie exclaims. She jumps on the soft lawn and runs toward the pond. Edwin and Rufus follow.

"Don't get too close to the water," I say.

Franklin wanders off toward a bench to be alone with his thoughts. Everything is as it should be.

"Everything all right, Nick?" Conrad asks.

He noticed.

"I'm fine," I lie. "I'll be just fine." That's closer to the truth. Eventually, I will be.

Cassie covers her eyes and starts counting out loud. "One. Two. Three. Four. Five." She peeks between her fingers and looks around, trying to see in which direction Edwin and Rufus had run. When she sees me watching her, she chirps, stumbles over a few numbers, and then stomps her little foot. "Drat! One. Two. Three." This time, her voice holds an edge of exasperation, which makes me chuckle. I lean into Conrad beside me, elbowing him at her antics.

He brushes a stray strand of hair off my face. I have never seen him look so serious or tender. Is he going to kiss me?

No. That can't happen. He's my best friend. Like a brother, he is.

But for some reason, I'm not moving. I'm caught in his stare, but he doesn't move in. I don't know if I'm relieved or disappointed. Everything is so jumbled up inside, then another wave of nausea comes over me at the thought of Ashe, or is it my Protector powers alerting me to danger?

I take a step back and breathe in deeply, focusing on my surroundings. Cassie yells, "Ten! Ready or not! Here I come."

"Cassie! No!" I shout, but it's too late. She's already off in the direction of a small grove of trees and a marble bench when I see the shadows. "Cassie! Come back! Boys! Come out! Now!"

Conrad reacts to my panic and rushes over at them.

Another figure dashes from behind us over to the grove as well. It's Ashe. As if an arrow pierces my heart,

I gasp and that same visceral gut feeling from before returns, forcing me to the ground. Folded in two, I gasp and gasp for breath. The grass is cold beneath my fingers. I hear Cassie scream, then Conrad shout, "NO!"

Get up, Nick. Get up now.

Pushing the heartbreak and anxiety and nausea aside, my training takes over. I'm sprinting towards the grove. Conrad holds a screaming Cassie. Ashe stands between Rufus and a group of older vampires, hardly any resemblance to human beings remain. One infernal beast clutches Edwin, who's frozen in utter terror; his wide eyes too scared for tears.

"Put him down this instant," I shout at the grinning fiend. I can't risk an attack with Edwin there. Just a moment. I was down for a few seconds. That's all. Right? That's all.

The vampire does as I ask, but doesn't let Edwin go. Long, spindly hands rest on his shoulders. Grotesque fingers stretch down past his chest, and the beast laughs. No, growls. A low rumbling sound that brings the nausea back.

It nods, almost imperceptibly, and its two friends flank him. One sets upon Ashe who pushes Rufus back and attacks. The two collide in mid-air. The second one rushes Conrad and Cassie, but he's taken down by a man in a mask who appears out of nowhere.

Franklin catches up and is by my side, stake at the ready.

"Let him go, and I'll let you live," I lie again. He's dust. They all are.

"So. This is the great Protector." It says that word with disgust and mockery. "I'm not sure why everyone is so concerned. Look, your lackeys are better at this than you are." He indicates the two fighting: Ashe with the tall, blonde vampire and the masked man with the shorter one. Rufus dashes behind me and Franklin, at least he's safe.

"A message for you, Protector, from my clan. The Old Ones. Pay attention."

Three things happen at once. In the blink of an eye. In a breath.

A solitary breath.

The flap of a butterfly's wing.

I hear a whoosh to my left, and out of the corner of my eye, it registers that the masked man just staked his vampire. A cry from Ashe's fight followed by a ripping sound and the smell of blood, then dust.

Then the third thing.

The moment that will haunt me for the rest of my days.

The beast folds his extended grasp over Edwin's head. Big blue eyes reach for me through those devilish fingers. I bolt towards him. After a quick twist and sickening snap, his eyes go blank.

I catch his falling form and cradle him to my breast, screaming. A guttural wail from the depth of my shattered soul. His neck lolls so much like the arms on Cassie's doll. Limp, disconnected. I howl into the darkness.

"No. No. No. No. No. No. No. No. No."

Hugging him. Squeezing him. Willing him to live.

Another whoosh pulls me out of that hell for a moment. A flash of ginger hair in the fading light, and a black mask. A cloud of dusk followed by silence. No more laughter from the demon. I don't even breathe.

"It's over," the masked man says. "He's gone. I'm sorry I wasn't faster. I'm so so sorry." Then, he goes. A flight away as the others crowd me and Edwin.

I'll never let him go. No. They can't have him. They can't. He'll be safe in my arms. Here. Always. Had I never let him go. Had we not come here. Had I not faltered at the sight of...I can't even bring myself to think his name.

He did this. He did all of this.

Cassie cries silent sobs, her face turned into Conrad's shoulder. Her one-eyed, cracked dolly mocks me again. Looking at me. Telling me it should be me growing cold. It should be me.

She's right.

"Nickie," Ashe says.

"Get away!" I shout. "Get away from him! You monster!"

Ashe puts his hands up and backs away, wounded.

Conrad stands over me and Edwin, holding Cassie. His jaw is clenched and face screwed up in a scowl.

"No. No. No, Nickie. No."

"I'm so sorry, Conrad. I should've been faster. I'm so sorry." My arms crush Edwin against me, and I rock back and forth. "I'm so sorry. My god, I'm so sorry."

Chapter Five

In Which Nickie Nick Cries in the Rain

February 8, 1881

Granted, I haven't seen many coffins, but this one is so small. The size of it alone makes my heart ache. There should never be such a small coffin. Ever. I think of the babies born still. Their coffins must be even smaller. Do they make coffins that small? They must, for there it is.

It sits on the small altar inside the side chapel of St. George's. Edwin wasn't important enough for the main sanctuary, so we're saying our goodbyes in one of the side alcoves. Hard wooden chairs, just half a dozen situated before the small altar holding the smaller coffin. The priest speaks in Latin, and everything seems like a dream. Nightmare, rather. His mouth moves over the syllables, but the sound disconnects and wafts up to the stone rafters. Light spills in from the side windows through saints draped in gold and burgundy brandishing swords to fight some holy battle. Behind the droning priest, a solitary statue of some other saint stands watch over the small chapel. I don't know who it is. The Catholics have so many saints, after all. Who can tell? A deep red curtain drapes the inside cubby behind it, softening the cold, unfeeling white stone walls.

There I sit on the hard wooden chair listening to unintelligible sounds, meaningless. Stone Gothic archways separate us from the main sanctuary with its dark pews stretching from one side to the center aisle, then across the other side as well. When we enter, the length of the cathedral surprises me. At the other end of the long aisle sits the main altar, illuminated by the colorful stained glass behind it. Before we were shuffled off to the small chapel on the right, this one with the tiny, tiny coffin, I remember thinking that the aisle led to peace, but it was at such a distance that no one could ever get there. They would toil and try and crawl through exhaustion, but that beautiful peace always lay just beyond reach. I prefer this tiny chapel after all.

It's real. Small and painful. Cold and forgotten.

Mrs. Hannon weeps in the chair beside me, and Conrad comforts her by patting her on the back with one hand. His other squeezes her hand, the one not pressing a handkerchief to her nose. Conrad's jaw is clenched. I can tell. He's maybe even biting his lip, trying not to cry himself. He believes he must be strong for his mother, as the man of the house.

Me, I cry.

Without a sound.

This day is my fault. That tiny coffin is because of my weakness, my nonsense—because of a boy.

Edwin is dead because of my stupid broken heart.

My entire family mourns because I fell in love, because I trusted a man to be true to his word.

Never again.

I once vowed I would show Ashe that I belonged in the darkness with him. I would prove to him that the sunshine didn't suit me. The darkness which cradles me, embraces me. I believe that still. So much darkness, but not with him. Never again with him.

Now I make a new vow.

Ashe will pay for this.

Edwin's death is as much on his soul as it is on mine. I love Ashe, and I hate myself for loving him. The heart does as it will, so they say, but not my heart. Not The Protector's heart. I must control my feelings.

Fanny's right. I don't have the luxury for love.

We each approach the coffin one at a time, its lid now open. The priest steps off to the side of the small altar and presses his palms together reverently, lifting his eyes to the heavens or just up to the stone arches above. I know not which. He pauses, mouthing a silent prayer to bless each of us after we say our goodbyes to Edwin. Rufus and Franklin go together, but they don't stay long. They just look inside, then at their feet, and return to their seats. Rufus cries. Franklin's expression is blank, one of shock. Mrs. Hannon holds Cassie's hand. Standing on tip toe, Cassie looks within then up at Mrs. Hannon. "He looks funny, mum. Why does he look like that?" Mrs. Hannon can't answer. Conrad picks Cassie up, her doll's arms flapping, and carries her back to her seat. Mrs. Hannon takes another moment and touches the body, strokes its hands, then moves to the side. Her handkerchief is pressed tightly to her nose as the priest blesses her.

My turn.

The thing lying inside hardly looks like Edwin. Pasty white. No, rather grey. Eyelids. Lips. Cheeks. All the same pasty color grey. Its hands are folded around a rosary and placed properly on his chest. A cheap scarf— nothing more than a rag, really—encircles his throat, covering the death wounds. Just along the right side I can see a bit of purple peeking out from under the dark scarf. Must be horrifically bruised under there. Gold and purple and black, like the priest's vestments. Edwin's remains are still. So still, but I half expect him to move. I watch for some time, but he doesn't move. I've never seen a dead body before. Not like this. I touch his hand, like Mrs. Hannon did. Perhaps that's what you're supposed to do.

It's cold and hard like stone, but silky, too. I recoil and snatch my hand back near my warmth, my life. And I cry.

I should've felt the monster near.

I should've heard it coming.

Had I been myself. Had I done my training. Had I eaten and not behaved like a foolish girl in foolish love, he'd still be here.

But he's not. He's there.

He's gone. He's gone. He's gone.

Stiff and grey and dark. Lost. So very small. Even this tiny coffin is too big for his tiny body. I lean down low, my lips just a breath away from its ear, and I apologize to this thing, this vessel—this mound of flesh that used to be Edwin. "I'm so sorry, Edwin. I'm so sorry," I whisper into the coffin.

No more. He's gone to that undiscovered country, *from whose bourne...*

The priest says a few more words of hypocrisy disguised as hope, splashing droplets of holy water on Edwin's body after we're back in the chairs.

He lifts a brass bell and rings it three times. The offensive sound breaks through our silent tears. It surrounds me and worms into my head, glancing off the stone walls, reverberating. I feel it in my teeth, in my bones. Four altar boys, about my age and dressed all in black, make their way up the narrow aisle. They surround Edwin's new home and carry him past us. Each sedate step takes hours. The silence, somewhat peaceful before, now threatens to deafen me with its bellow.

This is pure torture.

Mrs. Hannon sinks down, knees giving way in her grief. Conrad fails to hold her up, but he doesn't let her collapse alone. He guides her onto the hard chair and encircles her with one arm. Cassie is still in the other, resting her head against his shoulder. Leaning his head against hers, Conrad whispers in his mother's ear. Words of comfort, no doubt.

The priest ushers us out and lines us up behind the tiny coffin; the four altar boys are at the mouth of the grand aisle. Gothic stone arches frame the room high overhead and the colorful stained glass behind the altar beckons us forward—calls to us and promises peace. It looks just as far and unattainable as before, more so now. We walk in procession down toward that peace, and I never take my eyes off the window, a splash of color against these dreary walls. With each step, we're closer, and I begin to make out the scene. It's the crucifixion, of course, supposedly a sign of hope, but it has always been rather morbid and guilt-ridden for me. There the Christ hangs in the center of all the blues and reds and purples and yellows, dying. His family and disciples surround him in grief, just like we all surround our fallen son. Angels flank the cross, inviting Him to heaven.

It taunts us with its mournful beauty, its promise of peace. That briefest moment of solace is ripped from me when the men carrying the coffin take a sharp right and disappear out the back door into the graveyard. Before I turn from the false hope shown in that bright scene and follow Edwin out into the grey day, I repeat my new vow in front of the crucified Christ, in front of God, Himself.

Never again.

We weave through the moss-covered headstones until we come to Edwin's open grave. Two straps stretch from side to side over the muddy hole, all that's needed for such a small thing. The four boys, one on each end, hold the coffin steady and lower it onto the straps as our small family gathers around.

The mist turns to rain.

The world cries with us.

The priest's white collar shines too bright among all this death and grief, mocking our sorrow with a white blight of light on this grim scene. I want to leap over the grave and rip it from his throat. How dare he bring such light into this dark moment. The light and the dark, forever pulling me from side to side. At one moment I feel safe in the darkness, the next it's the light that brings me comfort.

Perhaps I am as lost as Edwin.

My teeth bite down on my lip, drawing blood. The coppery taste fills my mouth, and fresh tears burn my eyes. It's my fault. It's my fault. It's my fault. These selfflagellations drown out the priest's words. I only hear: "Ashes to Ashes, Dust to Dust"—and I stop listening.

Ashe.

This is because of Ashe.

Never again.

CHAPTER SIX

IN WHICH NICKIE NICK GOES MUDLARKING

February 9, 1881

"How long do we have before the tide comes back in?" I ask and step around something quite disgusting on the shore. The smell on these south banks makes me want to hold my breath. My only wish is to disappear. A twinge, like death's hand squeezing my heart, stops me quick in the muck. Up ahead, I catch a glimpse where Ashe and I walked together, the tunnels that lead to Blackfriars and the flat in Barge House Street. A lifetime ago. Edwin's lifetime. I avert my eyes and breathe deeply, letting the stench chase the heartache away. The memories of him that play over and over, I would give anything to forget. Forever. To have never met him, and certainly never loved him.

"Nick?"

"Hmmm?"

Conrad looks at me with concern.

"I'm fine," I lie. "It's nothing," I say and trot up next to him.

I shake my head and picture the memories coming out my ears in broken shards. Pushing them out. Clearing my head. Never again.

"How about this?" My toe nudges a piece of rather large driftwood. Twisty and knotty, like my stomach feels when he crosses my mind.

It won't be like this forever, I tell myself. It will pass. Fanny says it will, and I must be strong for Edwin. I owe Edwin. I owe them all.

"It's rotten, see?" Conrad turns the wood over with his boot and reveals a hollow underside. The sole of his boot glides along mine. He snatches his foot back and shoves his hands in his pockets, walking once more. "Pretty sure I picked this place clean the other day, but you never know, Nick. New things wash ashore every day. Normally only come down once a week or so, but..." His voice catches in his throat. Swooping down, he scoops up a small stone and chunks it out into the dark grey water. "I've been down here five or six times already since yesterday morning. Well, I don't know what else to do with myself since the funeral. Anything to keep my mind occupied."

"You blame me," I say, and my voice breaks, too. "I blame me."

"I don't blame you, Nick." Conrad comes close and wipes a tear from my cheek.

"I should've been more aware. I should've done something, felt something."

"Nickie." His voice is soft, and it quivers slightly along with his lips. "It's not your fault. You could've done something differently. I could've done something differently. We could've not gone out that day. We will make ourselves crazy thinking this way. There is only one to blame, and that's the monster who took him from us. That bloody monster murdered a child."

Conrad lets go, finally, and cries along with me. One hand rests on my cheek, and his thumb wipes away each new tear as it falls. His own tears mirror mine. Tear for tear. It's the first time he's cried since Edwin's passing. I feel a comfort with him, and he must with me, as well. My best friend. Always there. Teasing me, keeping me honest, and now comforting me with his own tears. Sorrow for sorrow. Regret for regret. Together.

Stepping away, I wipe my face dry with both hands. Sentimentality does no one any good. What's done is done. I clap Conrad on the shoulder twice. Just one of the boys, Nickie. That's all you are to them, to him. It's best.

Still, before I move past him, with the back of my hand I wipe his tears away, too. He grabs my wrist and holds it before him, keeping me still. I'm thrilled and scared and cross all at once. My muscles tense, so he releases me. As we start walking again, he says, "Edwin would want you to fight, Nickie, like that drawing he made for you. He was so proud of you. And that skit!' Conrad laughed at the memory. We had all been so happy just a few days ago. Laughing, eating cake. Enjoying life. The first joy since Ashe left.

He's gone. He's gone. He's––Good.

Good that he's gone, I tell myself, interrupting the hurtful mantra.

Good.

Conrad might say it's because of the monster that would kill a child, but I blame Ashe, the monster who destroyed me with a lie. The monster that crippled me, distracted me so another of his vicious kind could kill Edwin, and so many others like Edwin.

Never again will I be distracted by love.

Never again.

"What is it, Nick?" Conrad steps closer again, but I back away and continue my search along the shore for treasures. Something up ahead catches my eye, so I motion to Conrad to look. Pointing to a small round brass thing, I wait for Conrad to tell me, yet again, that it's worthless. He knows what to look for. He knows what he can use and what he can sell. He's been a *mudlark* a long time now. Years. It's how he's kept the boys modestly fed and clothed. He's done so much for them all, and he's known so much loss, too.

Now Edwin. So much pain for us all.

"Brilliant, Nick! Great find!" Conrad stoops down to examine it more closely. It's a pocket watch, closed and a little rusty. Conrad's thumb releases the latch and it pops open. There's water behind the glass. "Don't worry. A little water won't hurt anything. The gears inside will still work. Great for parts. We can get a shilling for this, at least! Cheers, Nick! Well done!"

"You would've seen it if I didn't."

"Why do you always do that? Give all the credit away to others and heap all the responsibility on your shoulders. You found it, Nick. You help us, Nick. Without you, we'd be much worse off than just losing Edwin. I don't know what we'd have done all this time without you looking out for us, too."

"You take good care of everyone, Conrad. I'm so impressed at the man you've become." Too serious, and I feel my face flush with feeling again, so I break eye contact and start walking. "To think, we used to play together at the factory, and here we are after all this time. You're my oldest, dearest friend, Conrad. Well, besides Fanny. I might not say it enough, but I'm grateful to have you...and the boys"—Conrad chimes in with a smile, "And girl."

"And girl," I repeat, "in my life. Very grateful."

"Don't get all serious on me, Nick. Too much sombre seriousness of late, don't you find? More laughter, that's what we need." With that, he ran along the south bank, his boots sinking in the dirty, stony sand with every step. Arms spread wide, he ran at life full force. When he turned back to me, his cheeks and nose were chapped and red with the cold. It reminded me of how Edwin blushed that day, and the sorrow threatened to consume me again.

"No use in that," I say aloud so only I can hear myself speak, but the world hears me, too. "No use in that." I spread my arms and run toward Conrad. The cold London air stings my cheeks and freezes my teeth. My wide smile exposes them to the world. Conrad laughs.

"That's it, Nick. We're alive. Remember that. We're alive!"

I laugh along with him and see my childhood friend mixed with a grown man. It's odd to watch him change before my eyes, but the past few days have given me a new respect for Conrad. A new appreciation for him as a friend. As a—

"Great find, Nick," Conrad says again and tosses the watch in the air. I snatch it before he catches it again and run from him, laughing. Inhaling the stench, which suddenly smells sweet, as it is life. Rank, but real.

The sun, something one rarely sees in London (especially in early February), peeks out from behind the clouds. The uniform grey has broken into sporadic puffy clouds of a lighter grey, and the sun shines on us. It makes the murky water of The Thames look...is that blue? It can't be. The Thames?

I laugh again, splashing through the edge of the water, wetting my skirts. I hear the laughter of Conrad close behind. Just as I duck beneath Southwark Bridge, he catches up to me. We both stop, breathless, in the shade of the bridge. Still laughing.

"I got it," I say, holding the watch between my fingers. Taunting him. He tries to grab it, but I pull it away at the last second. Twice. Three times. The fourth, I pull it back too far and lose my balance. Conrad stumbles against me, reaching for the watch, and pins me against the brick underbelly.

Laughter stops. He's a breath from my lips.

Ashe flashes back and my stomach clenches. I bite my lip, ready to push him away, but before I can, he steps back on his own, mumbling apologies.

"Don't worry," I say. "Turned out to be a lovely day. Sun and all." I pretend nothing happened. Nothing did, after all. Right?

He plays along. "Great day. Your hair looks almost red in the sunshine. Did you know? Like cinnamon streaks along your head. I wish the sun shined more just for that."

With one quick movement, while I stand stunned at the compliment, Conrad snatches the watch from my hand and takes off running and laughing once again. In delight, I follow suit.

We spend another hour or two, maybe even three, along the south bank, wandering all the way into the far east side of Southwark, mostly on the cobblestones above, much to my relief. The muck had begun to seep through my boots. The ominous Tower sits on the north bank, and I lean against the wall to contemplate the amount of misery its walls have seen over the centuries.

"It must be awful to be kept locked up. In there or even in Bedlam. Don't you think?"

Conrad jumps up onto the wall, facing away from the Tower. "I don't think about such things, Nick. What's the point of worrying about that? We've enough to deal with."

"I know, but I think I'd rather die than be locked up is all. It must be so cold and miserable, so lonely."

"A lot of people outside those walls are lonely, too. An epidemic, I think."

"Remember what Bedlam was like?" I ask him, then I remember about his mum. "Oh, Conrad. I'm so sorry. Just stuck my foot in it."

"It's all right. Just glad she's out of there now. Trying to forget about it and just find some happiness in our little corner, some contentment. Harder now, with Edwin and all."

"Yes. He's at peace, though, right? I mean, that's what you always hear, but how can anyone know? It's just what we tell ourselves, isn't it? Because anything else is unthinkable."

Shut up, Nick! Just shut up. With every word you're making it worse. Still, I continue, unable to help myself. If I can't talk to my best friend, who can I talk to? "Do you believe in an afterlife? Like, you know, heaven and hell and the like."

"Not sure," he says. "Sometimes I'd like to think there's something better after this, all this struggle and sorrow, but there probably isn't. Just nothing, I suppose."

"What about ghosts? Those dead who aren't at rest for some reason. Unfinished business, some say. Do you believe in ghosts?"

"Nah."

"Really? I do, I think. I mean, I've never seen one myself, but I do love those ghost stories. They're always so horrible, aren't they? Or so very sad. I think that's the worst, perhaps even worse than being in Bedlam or The Tower. At least then there is death—a relief, but if you're trapped between two places, helpless and miserable, no one, or very few, can even see you. That must be hell, indeed. To not be seen or heard. Trapped in your own mind, in a way. Yes, that must be the worst."

Conrad doesn't say a word, just looks off into the distance.

"I'm sorry, Conrad. We can talk about something more cheerful. Sometimes it helps to talk about it for me, but I can see it's distressing you, so I apologize. I, well, I feel like I can tell you anything. You're why I'm not lonely, Conrad."

He snaps his eyes to mine, full of hope. He thinks I mean love, and I do mean love—a kind of love, anyway. I shouldn't say such things, knowing how he feels about me. I shouldn't say anything that can be misinterpreted. "You're my best friend," I repeat, "and I love you. You've always been there for me, and I hope you will always be. I will be for you."

Conrad's expression is one of restraint. He's holding back something. Tears, perhaps. Expressing his own heart. It's harder for men, I'm told. Not me. I feel like I'll explode if I don't at times. "Anyway," I continue. "There I go getting all serious again. These past weeks have just made me think about a lot of things differently. Makes me grateful for what I have."

"I'm glad you're in my life, too, Nick. I can't even imagine it any other way," he finally says, and it seems almost painful for him to say it. "You've got to promise me you'll be careful out there, you know, on the hunt. I don't want to bury another friend. Promise?"

"Now look who's getting all serious!"

"Promise?" he repeats.

"I promise. I'll be careful, very careful, on the hunt and otherwise. We've both experienced enough pain for a while."

"Blimey!" Conrad exclaims. "I've got to go, Nick." He jumps off the wall and turns to face The Thames with me. A huge, rusty barge crawls by and blows its steam whistle, but Conrad looks through it. Eyes focused on nothing in particular.

"Is everything all right?"

"Those blokes back there," he says, then adds, "Don't look!" when I start to turn around, touching my arm to prevent me from moving. "Three of them. I owe them money, and I don't have it. They're bad news. Well, their leader is, anyway. I've got to disappear before they see me." Gears turn behind his eyes.

"All right."

"I'm going underground. You coming?"

He means the sewers. Too many memories there at the moment, so I make an excuse. "Not in my fine dress! I'll be all right up here and I'll see you tomorrow?"

"Very well. Until tomorrow, Nick." With that, he leaps over the wall and lands below in the mucky sand. After a quick wave, he disappears into the sewer tunnel, and I am left alone on the south bank to contemplate The Tower on my own. I turn to see these three menacing blokes Conrad was trying to avoid. The one in the center walks in more of a strut, chest thrust out and arms held wide, as if his muscles are much bigger than they are. The other two, one blonde and one ginger, walk just a step or two behind him. They don't look so tough. I'm ripe for a fight, after all. Would be quite cathartic, but I wouldn't want to rip my dress.

I guess I'll just make my way home and try to stay out of trouble.

CHAPTER SEVEN

IN WHICH NICKIE NICK SEES DEAD PEOPLE

The streets of London feel altogether unsettling this early evening. At every new turn and step, another danger presents itself. First, a runaway cart full of produce nearly runs me off the road. An angry driver shouts, "Watch where yer goin', Missy!" Just as I step out of the way, I collide with a rather horrid looking man who takes the opportunity to grope me. I pull out of his grasp, and he says, "Now, don'be like that, swee'hear'. Come on back over 'ere, sit on me lap. I won'bite ya." I get to a safe distance but keep checking over my shoulder to make sure he's not following. A horse whinnies, and I jump at least a foot off the ground. A group of young men laugh at my reaction, making lewd gestures and comments.

Another sound startles me even more. A gunshot, perhaps, some kind of loud bang. I flatten myself against a building and focus on the hard bricks against my back. Taking deep breaths, I calm myself, but the feeling of danger doesn't go away. My Protector powers have abandoned me. I'm frozen in fear, perhaps the coward Fanny warned me against after all. Will my life be defined by an act of cowardice or courage? Try as I might, I can't shake the terror. The people and motion on the street becomes one mocking smile after another.

Pointing. Laughing. Leering. Snarling.

I'm not safe. It's still easily an hour walk home. How will I ever get there?

Ashe should be here.

He's gone—"No!" I say aloud, stopping the mantra. A group of working girls scowl at me, looking me up and down in disgust.

Up ahead, I see the great square tower of St. Saviour's on the other side of London Bridge. I can make it there. I'll be safe there. Sanctuary. I had felt an odd sense of peace at Edwin's funeral in St. George's. Then, time with Conrad distracted me enough from my grief, but as I walk home—so very exposed and raw—it threatens to consume me once more. I close my eyes and take a deep breath, then make a beeline to the church. I step into the black flint walls of St. Saviour's and breathe easier.

Safe in this sacred sanctuary, I can regain my balance and then make it the rest of the way home. The relative silence soothes me. Although I can still hear the clatter of hoofs and wooden wheels on the cobblestones and hear the shouts and conversations of people outside, this blessed place protects me.

I look around in awe. I've been in the hallowed light that spills into Westminster Abbey. Stood beneath the giant dome of St. Paul's, but I had never set foot in St. Saviour's before today.

It reflects my very soul.

Dark and sacred. Shadowy crevices hiding treasures. A brass Shakespeare reclines in an enclave carved in the stone wall, always watching worshippers coming and going. Even after death, he continues his study of human nature, his examination of the human soul.

The main nave stretches into the daylight that filters through either side, illuminating Gothic arches and muted marble. At the far end, over the altar, a small stained glass window sits atop rows of stone people. Reverently, I walk down the long aisle, wondering if I'll ever get to walk down in a white dress with my beloved. Can he even be in a church without burning?

See. Right there.

Another reason it's good that it's over. He left.

He's gone.

My hands grasp the back of a wooden pew, focusing all my attention on the silence and the hard wood beneath my fingers, willing the panic away. After another deep breath, I continue down the aisle. Besides, my other choice is to go back out into the dangerous night, and I hate feeling so frightened, so weak.

Grief. Regret. Fear. Sorrow. The magnificent sight before me blurs through my tears.

Edwin just had his only trip down a church aisle. Carried there and back. Nine years old and dead. Dead and gone. He will never fall in love. He will never have a broken heart. He will never know the joy of a lover's kiss. He will never know the agony and ecstasy of passion.

Perhaps it's best.

Perhaps it's best if I never do again as well.

Perhaps the next time I travel down a center aisle, I'll be carried down, too. Morbid thought, that, but realistic. Dangerous life, being The Protector. It's more than possible. It's likely, no matter what I promised Conrad, and I find a kind of peace in that thought, like relief isn't too far away.

I reach the end of the aisle. In awe, I stand before the marble hosts of saints that keep watch over the gold leaf altar. Directly above, also in gold, the Madonna and Son, and above her, the boy king. My eyes trace every peak, every crown, every scepter, and every pair of hands folded in prayer. One next to another, holy men and women who gave their lives to God, to truth. Martyrs, many of them.

Yes. Here, I'm safe.

A gold crucifix stands in the center of the altar which is flanked by more gold statues. I can't get close enough to see who they are, but their presence comforts me. I feel less alone here. A wooden carving of the three kings stands to the left and more ornate wood carvings on the right.

Peaceful. Quiet, almost too quiet. Safe. Yes, safe. Yet not. Like a false sense of safety. Something here is not right. Something deep inside me stirs. Familiar, yet distant. Before Ashe. Before the tears. I felt something similar, like inner warnings. My fledgling Protector powers, but surely not in here. It must be something else.

"Good afternoon, child," a priest says. He manifests from the shadows, as if created from the surrounding darkness. Every inner warning gifted to me as The Protector goes wild inside my head, my guts, my broken heart, my fractured soul. They all scream inside me at once. I will burst if I don't let them out my mouth. Unless I let out a shrill scream to shake the very foundation of this holy place, I will explode in a shower of blood and bone and sorrow.

I breathe deeply, clenching my jaw. "Father," I say with as much polite tone as I can muster. This man makes my skin crawl, and I'm embarrassed to even think such a thing. A man of the cloth should inspire peace and safety, not warnings and fear. The too familiar nausea returns, but I contain it. It must be the traumatic occurrences of the past weeks. It's made me overly protective, overly cautious, overly afraid.

I can control this. No one else will die because of my weakness. No one.

It's fine, I tell myself. *He's safe. He's a priest. It's all right.*

"Such a lovely young thing to be out all on your own. Dangerous times. It will be dark soon, child. Many nasties about after dark."

"Indeed. I'll be going then."

"Or, you could stay here for the night, dear girl. You'll be safe here. I'll personally keep watch over you."

I no longer care about the scary London night, the only thing on my mind is getting away from this priest, and I can't say why. He's pleasant enough, I suppose, albeit has quite the Bermondsey Look about him. Tall and too thin, lanky. Hazel eyes sunk into his skull. The entire dark socket surrounding them gives a skeletal appearance. Gaunt face, drawn in the cheeks. Even his hands, folded over a large wooden cross that hangs from his neck, are emaciated. Long black hair pulled back in a ribbon gives me the impression of days gone by, like that of old drawings. Quite old-fashioned and rather creepy, this one.

"How kind of you to offer, Father, but I'm expected home. Good evening."

"Don't go." The words don't come from the priest. They don't come from the old lonely man kneeling in the pew, hunched over his folded hands praying for salvation from his particular torment. I look over my shoulder, but there is no one there. "Don't go," the voice says again. More like a whisper than a voice. Like the wind speaking. Like the gas lamps along the wall hiss the words. "Don't go. Save us."

The priest stands before me as pleasant as can be. He must not hear it or he'd react, but he doesn't. His eyes never leave mine and don't even blink.

"Don't go." I hear it again. I spin around looking for the source, then back to the priest, who's still as pleasant and motionless as ever. Surreal. Am I mad? Is Bedlam for me as well? Will I join Dr. Pilkington soon?

Never.

"Don't go, Nick. Please don't go."

The priest looks at me expectantly, eyebrows raised over his bulgy eyes like black caterpillars. His expression screams, "Why haven't you left yet, silly girl?" but this is what he says: "Is everything all right, my dear?"

"Yes. Going now."

"Take care, child," he says and bows to me. His clasped hands move down to his belt, then just a little further south as he stands straight, proud. A pointy, slimy tongue licks his lips. It darts out one side, then back in and out again before encircling the entirety of his mouth two or three times. A moist trail of saliva extends a good inch around his lips. "Of course, you could stay and pray with me. I can absolve you, child. Yes, absolve you good and proper."

My insides scream again.

"No, I'm going."

"Don't go," the hissing wind says again, but I ignore it. My boots hit the cobblestones in another minute, and I'm back in the dangerous streets of London. Before I head back toward the west side, from the corner of my eye, I see the priest watching me from a window, and I shudder. Another step, and a man stands before me. "Don't go," he says. "You can hear us."

He looks in his twenties, perhaps. Dressed in all brown, a rope belt circles his waist to hold up oversized trousers. Unshaven and pale. Missing teeth. "Please don't go, Miss."

I step around him, but as soon as I do another man stands in my way, a black-haired man, tall and handsome. His face is old beyond his years and his eyes are bloodshot with deep bags beneath them. Grey sprinkles along his temples and in the full mutton chops that hug his jaw. Tears flow from the corners in a continuous stream, falling in phantom drops on his fine suit. "Please don't go, Miss. Please. Help us."

They each reach out for me, trying to grab me. Then two become four, all saying, "Don't go. Please. Help us." I blink and there are eight. Nine. A dozen. More!

Women, haggard and disheveled, by the dozens stand amongst the poor men. Children, too. Please don't go," they waft in unison. "Don't go. Save us! Save us!"

"Save me from absolution," a particularly rough-looking, red-haired woman says. Her clothes are torn in places and her neckline dips scandalously low. "Please, Miss. I can't take no more. Please!"

"Please. Please. Please," they all start up again.

"What's sauce for the goose ain't sauce for the gander. I see that now. Please, Miss. Please save us." Red's eyes plead with me, haunted and filled with horrors beyond imagining.

"Leave me alone!" I scream and back away, hands out in defense, but they keep closing in. Keep coming at me. "Please. Please. Please." I bump into a couple coming up behind me and fall at their feet. The woman, offended, looks down on me and says, "I beg your pardon!"

The man chides me. "Watch where you're going, young lady! Scandalous to be out after dark alone! Scandalous, indeed!"

They stride past me in a huff and walk through the host of pleading people, who all vanish on impact. I hear the woman say, "Rather chilly night, don't you find, dear?"

A solitary "Don't go, Nickie," hangs in the air. Perhaps it's just my imagination, my own guilt, but I swear it's Edwin's voice.

Jumping up and without looking back, I lift my skirts and run. I've never run so fast. Must get home where it's safe. Darting in and out between couples and others strolling in the cold night, I don't stop running until I see the glow of gaslight in my chamber, shining above like a beacon welcoming me home.

My true sanctuary. The only place I'm safe, with Fanny.

I'm never leaving the house again.

CHAPTER EIGHT

IN WHICH NICKIE NICK FINDS A DISTRACTION

February 14, 1881

"Get up." Fanny rips the blankets off me, but I don't look at her. I can't face her. I can't face anyone. My body lies flat against the mattress, but I keep my face turned toward the wall. Why can't I just die? Just fade away. Me. That's who should be in that cold, cold ground. Not him. Not Edwin.

"Get up," she repeats. Her stern voice brings fresh tears. They slide out of the corner of my eyes, yet I won't turn to look at her. "Nicole. I order you to get up. You have a duty. There are many other boys out there who need your protection."

This cuts deeply. She blames me. Of course she does. It's my fault he's dead. It's all my fault for not training hard enough, for falling in love. It's my fault. Turning completely from her, I curl up in a tight ball and stare at the mauve floral print of the posh wall. I'd give all my parent's money and their factory just to have him back. Anything. Everything.

Even my life.

Fanny grabs my arm and squeezes, hurting me. Pulling with all her might, she drags me to the edge of the bed. Limp like Cassie's doll, I don't move at all. "Get up," she says, shaking me now.

"Leave me alone."

"No. Not anymore. You have a duty. People are counting on you. Cassie and Rufus and Franklin and Conrad and hundreds of other children out there. Adults, too. You, Nickie. You can save so many of them."

"I killed Edwin," I manage through sobs.

"You did not. A vampire killed Edwin."

"I should've stopped it. It's my duty. It's my responsibility, and I froze because of a shattered heart. I'm so ashamed, Fanny. I didn't know such depth of shame was possible. How can I face you? How can I face them ever again?"

"Get up."

"No."

"Get up this instant!"

"Leave me alone, Fanny. It hasn't even been a week since the funeral. I can't do this yet, not with everything else. Especially on the feast of St. Valentine. Oh, Ashe! Damn you, Nicole, no more!" The key to Ashe's heart burns against my breast, so I rip the necklace from my throat and hurl it across the room, then bury my face in my arms and weep. "Oh, Edwin! Sweet, sweet boy. No. I just can't. Not today. No, Fanny, not today!"

"Nicole Knickerbocker Hawthorn. Get out of bed this instant or I will march right downstairs and tell your parents you spend all night walking the streets of London with boys. You will never again see the light of day."

"You wouldn't!" I exclaim, looking at her now.

"Well, at least that got through. Of course I wouldn't, my dove, but enough of this. You've two great traumatic events back to back. No one should ever endure such pain, love, but you have no choice."

"There's always a choice, Fanny. You taught me that."

"Indeed. There are choices. The first is to live or to wither away and die. Are you going to let cowardice define your life, Nicole?"

"Haven't I already?"

"It wasn't cowardice that crippled you in that moment, not as you tell the story. Not as Conrad tells it. It was love. Shock, and it was only a moment. Anyone can understand that. Then you faced those monsters."

"Too late."

"Too late for Edwin, but not for the others. Besides, you have no idea if he already had Edwin before you faltered or no. Even at the top of your game you might've been too late to save him, love, but you didn't kill him. The monster vampire did that. Put the blame where it belongs. Put your anger where it belongs as well. Who, or more accurately what, has caused all this trouble in the past few months? Hmmmm?"

My mind went to Ashe. To his soft lips, intense eyes. Then the nausea rose, and I doubled over. The pain that followed his abandonment. Watching Edwin die. All of it. "Vampires," I hiss. "Vampires did this. They did all of this."

"Yes. They did. Seems they only don't destroy with violence and hatred. They also destroy with tenderness and love. Believe you, me. I use that word very loosely in this case, especially on this day. Feigned love, more like, my dove. Feigned love."

Nausea gone, my blood boils.

"Vampires." I growl the vile word. "I shall kill every one of them for what they've done, for what they've taken from me." Sitting now, my fists clenched around my nightdress, ripping it.

"Careful!"

I fling the torn cotton gown over my head. "Get me dressed, Fanny. We've got training to do. Must prepare. Must fight. I will live and eat and breathe hunting, until I can smell them, taste them, and feel them near. Until I trust every sensation, develop and hone every power gifted to me. For Edwin," I say. "For Edwin."

"For Edwin," she agrees and hands me a chemise.

Power. Energy. Electricity. All course through my blood. Anger and hatred fuel my task. That, and focused grief. "I will end them all."

§

"Again," Fanny says. She resets her pocket chronograph and holds it aloft. Sweat pours down my temples after she's had me do nine consecutive five-minute rounds of punching and kicking the vampire dummy. My knuckles are raw from contact with the burlap-wrapped pillows tied around the wooden stand. My hips scream, and my knees threaten to give way.

"Wait," I gasp. "Let me catch my breath."

"Take a break, then. You've been working hard enough."

After the gasps subside and the dagger in my lungs fades to a mere ache, I pull my hands up to protect my face and say, "No. Let's go again. You're right." Using the sleeve of my training chemise, I wipe my face dry and take the stance to continue. "Go."

"Perhaps a break is best, love."

"No. No time for that. I must catch up, be prepared. Go!"

"At least have some water. Must stay hydrated to be strong."

"After the next round. Even ten. Fanny! Go!"

"All right," Fanny says. She clicks the top of her chronograph with an exaggerated motion. "Go!"

Punch. Punch. Kick. Kick. Again, and again. Controlled breath: in through the nose during the punch-punch—out through the mouth for the kick—kick. I count the seconds, focusing my mind on the time passed while my body does what I demand of it. It will learn what to do whether or not my mind is present. No one will ever be hurt again. Punch. Punch. My knuckles scream at me, and I with them. "Tough!" I tell them aloud. "It hurts, but not as much as it will if you fail again. Focus." Each syllable is another punch-punch, kick-kick.

Deep breath in. Punch-punch. Exhale. Kick-kick.

I feel alive and strong. My heart pumps adrenaline and fury through my body, strengthening me. I picture Ashe's smug face on the dummy, and punch-punch, kick-kick even harder. As the five minutes comes to a close, I count: 295-thousand. 296-thousand. 297-thousand. 298-thousand. 299-thousand, and with the last kick, I give it all my strength and anger and hatred and love and shatteredness at once.

The wood splinters, making Fanny jump.

My knees give way, and I collapse to the ground and weep.

"Wilfred can fix it. He'll have a new one ready for tomorrow. A stronger one. It's all right."

"It will never be all right, Fanny. Never again."

"Have some water, love. Here." Fanny hands me a glass, but I push it away. "You must drink. Nicole, I'm serious. Then, something to eat and a rest."

"No rest," I say, taking the glass from her. I gulp it down in a most unladylike manner, water dribbling from the corners of my mouth. "Water, fine. Food, fine. Whatever it takes. Rest. Never. I'll be ready next time. Whatever they throw at me, I'll be ready. The first thing I'll do is hunt down its clan and annihilate them all. Then, the rest. Until every last one is dust."

"Sweet girl," Fanny says with a hint of sadness.

"No. No time for that Fanny. Food. You're right. Food, then hunting tonight after my parents are asleep. I'll take as many of them as I can. Send them to hell where they belong."

"I'm coming with you."

"No. Too dangerous."

"Nicole. I'm coming, at least for tonight. I want to see you in action anyway. There's only so much training we can do with a bit of wood and pillows, as you can see. Must evaluate your technique on the front, to better prepare you."

"All right, I suppose. Come with whatever you need to help me kill them. Magic or stakes or whatever you've got hidden under those floor boards. I won't lose you, too. I won't. I won't! I won't!" Fresh tears. Damn my weakness.

Fanny gathers me up in her arms. My face is pressed against her soft body, and I feel safe. Exhausted, but safe.

"No, my dove, you shan't lose me, too. Never."

I cry and cry into Fanny's embrace. I'll be ready next time. I'll be ready.

§

After the house is quiet, all except for the card game held between the servants, that is. The gaslights are extinguished on every level but theirs. A solitary window glows from our place on the corner of Walnut Tree Walk and shines into the garden below. I look up at the glowing eye looking into the night and wonder what on earth they gossip about each night up there.

Fanny still hasn't made it through the pantry window. It is a rather snug fit. I should've stayed behind and helped push her through. "Can't we use the front door?" she squeaks, half in and half out.

"You know we can't, Fanny. Although, come to think of it, Wilfred probably would've covered for us if necessary. Next time when we leave, but not when we come home."

"All right. Deep breath," she said. With another grunt, expulsion of air, and a quick tug, she was through. "Perhaps I should've waited to put on me overcoat until after I was out. It is rather cold, though."

"Quite, Fanny. I'm ready. Let's go."

"What's your plan? Just head in any direction willy-nilly? Have you no strategy?"

"Strategy? This is about undead demony things sucking blood and killing whomever they come across. This isn't war."

"It's exactly what this is! War! They may not seem like they have a strategy, but they do. It's just instinctual, and so is yours once you learn to tap into it. So, which direction."

"That way, I say, pointing toward north toward The Thames."

"All right. Why?"

"Central London. Much bustling about. Loads of people to eat."

"Yes. Loads of witnesses, too."

"Can't they just erase their memories? Do their mind tricks?"

"They can and they will in a pinch, but do you want to work that hard for your food? Perhaps if they're on the prowl for them they enjoy the chase and the fright and the kill, and don't get me wrong, many do, from time to time. More often than not, they just feed and move on. If they made their existence terribly obvious, there would be a mob hunting them. No. It behooves them to keep to the shadows. No witnesses. Now. Which way?"

"That way," I say and point in the opposite direction.

"You're guessing, lamb. Feel it. Take a moment and quiet yourself. Inside."

"I can't, Fanny. It's not quiet in there anymore. Not after...then Edwin. No."

"I know, my lamb. I know. You crave distraction from the pain, and it's understandable, love. I know all too well, but you must quiet it on your own. Distraction will only take you so far. Distraction will also make you sloppy during your hunt. You must be completely in your body, not dissociated from it. Focus, as I taught you. Feel."

I stopped and focused on my body. It felt strong and weak at the same time. Strong in my Protector outfit. It felt good to be back in this after so long. The bones of the corset a little loose with the weight loss. My long coat wrapped around me, protecting me. I had Franklin's new contraption strapped to my arm, and I would use it tonight. I would get close enough to do just that. The weakness I felt in my muscles, sore from the day's training and after so little food for so long, but I ate well tonight. I am ready for anything.

I focused on my feet in my special boots, anxious to use the retractable stake again. Dust after dust. Ashes.

Oh, Ashe!

"NO!" I say aloud.

"Good. You were focused and your mind wandered. You stopped it."

"I did."

"Now, again," Fanny whispered, after a nervous glance up to the lit window. "Let's walk as we do this, away from prying ears. Just in case. Feel my hand guiding you. Focus on that nauseous feeling. Remember how I said you would have to learn to differentiate it from other such sensations? Shall we work on that?"

"Yes. It all still feels very much like nausea, really. Although I fancy I was beginning to tell the difference before…but now with all the…" My breath came faster and the nausea rose. "I remember feeling it right before the vampires showed up, but Ashe was there as well. It had been my constant companion for those weeks of heartbreak, too."

"I know. Anxiety manifests that way as well as fear. Your power stems from both of these things, but stronger. Focus. Think of him and what he did and notice that sensation."

My stomach clenched and I nearly doubled over. "That happened that night Edwin was murdered, too. This visceral reaction to the pain, or fear of more, perhaps." Memories of Ashe and I together, hunting and falling in love, assaulted my inner eyes, bringing tears to my outer ones. That just made me angry again. That's what got Edwin killed. Sentimentality and unrequited love. Longing for something no more.

Never again.

"Good. You felt that on that horrible night. Focus on the source. Him? Fear? Danger?"

I loved that Fanny knows better than to say his name. His name is toxic to me now. "Memory. Specifically of him."

"Good. Now remember that night, the feeling when you sensed them near, right before you saw the shadows. Where do you feel that?"

"A little higher. Here." I planted my fist just under my ribcage. "And it sort of climbs up here." I slide my fist up the front of my sleek leather corset until it reaches my heart. "Here," I say, pounding on my heart. "Then here," I say, flinging my arms out to either side. "It's a burning, like fire flowing through my arms."

"Very good, dove. That's your body ready to fight, to protect yourself and others. Stop here."

Looking up, I see we've made it down the street, and we now stand on the corner of Kennington and Lambeth.

"Put your goggles on. We're coming into more light and passersby." Fanny herself wraps her scarf around her head and face, hiding her identity as well. I pull the goggles off my cap and obey. Still feel so silly in these. A cadet from the RAN, who I'm supposed to look like, wouldn't have their goggles down at night. So silly.

"Now, focus again. Close your eyes and focus on that sensation in your stomach. The tingling, you once called it, feel how that's different from anxiety or nausea."

"Yes! I remember. I can feel the difference!"

"Just out of practice is all." Fanny's eyes crinkle. She's smiling at me beneath her tartan scarf, but I don't return her smile. Instead, I look at my feet in shame. Fanny touches my shoulder and speaks in a gentle tone, "Don't give into the shame, my dear. It's a powerful emotion, but you did nothing wrong. Horrible things happen, and you can't be everywhere at once. You must first care for yourself so that you may care for others. You must, body and soul, child. Body and soul."

Her words don't soothe me, though. No. I'll hold onto this shame, to the anger, as well. They will protect me; they will protect Rufus and Cassie and the others, too. If Edwin is looking down on me from heaven, I want him to be proud, knowing how very sorry I truly am. Still, I nod my understanding and close my eyes. Past the Ashe-nausea. Past the sickening sinking feeling when I think of poor Edwin. There it is. The tingling. I focus on that sensation and let it fill me. Guide me. The faintest scent of copper hits my nose and I turn my face into the wind. "That way," I say. "Blood." I'm compelled forward. An invisible rope pulls me towards the source of the sensation. "Follow me."

I take long strides down Lambeth, heading away from the city centre. Fanny trots behind to catch up. "I'm moving faster, Fanny, but you once said I would move as fast as vampires."

"Yes, you will, my dove. Indeed. Once you need not even focus anymore, once it's second nature. When you can feel and sense and smell the vermin, you will meet them in speed as you already do in strength. With a clear mind and heart, you will meet them in cunning as well."

"My heart will be clear from now on, Fanny. Never again will I be distracted by such frivolity. There are more important things, after all."

"Oh, sweet dove. Nothing is more important than love."

I don't believe it. I refuse to believe it. To keep others safe, I mustn't believe it.

This is all that's important. The hunt. The kill.

We pass Bethlehem Hospital on our right. No fond memories there, except that Pilkington is where he belongs. A patient now, not the overseeing doctor. Hopefully conditions have improved. Even he doesn't deserve such treatment.

A left on St. George's Road puts us right in front of St. George's Cathedral, where we left Edwin. I stop and feel, extending psychic fingers out all around me. The hunter inside urges me forward, alongside the great church, and the stench of blood increases. "Forgive me,"

I mumble to Fanny, then break into a run. I'll be too late in another moment, no time to explain. A heart slows.

This time, I don't let the proximity of the victim stop me from the attack. She'll die if I don't. She might not if I do. Limp in the demon's arms, a woman's head lolls to the side. It reminds me of Edwin, but instead of feeling sad and weak, it spikes my anger and thirst for dust. It looks up just as I lunge, knocking his victim from his arms, I slap its blood-stained face as I come down upon it. It hisses, and I lunge, thrusting my right arm out in a palm strike to the chest. Just as he designed, Franklin's machine thrusts the stake out. It pierces the vampires flesh and bone, and with a squish, its heart.

Whoosh.

Dust.

Yes.

Fanny catches up and rushes to the side of the hurt woman. "We must get her to a hospital. Straight away."

"He's dead," I say. "I was almost too late. She's still alive for now, and that leech will never hurt another. Who's next?"

"Nickie. Hospital?"

"What's happening," the woman cries. "Who are you?"

"We're here to help. You were attacked, and you've lost a lot of blood." Fanny speaks in soothing tones. She's using her magical powers of calm on her, and I suddenly wonder why she hadn't used them on me all this time. Saved me some pain.

"We're going to take you to a hospital," I say. "Can you stand?"

"Sleep. I just want to sleep. All right? It's so cold. So, so cold."

"The nearest hospital is too far, Fanny. St. Thomas' is at least a half mile away. We'll never get her there on time. What about Bethlehem across the street? They can send word to St. Thomas' to get her proper help while they care for her."

"The asylum?"

"What other choice do we have? They have nurses there. People trained in this. We're wasting time!"

Fanny tries to lift the woman, but falters. "I've got her," I say and take the woman into my arms. "Wrap your scarf around her neck, tightly and quickly." Once done, I hold the grown woman against me, and remember the feel of Edwin's lifeless form in my arms. Such a short time ago, and yet forever. Another life. Another reality. One with him in it. As fast as I can, I run over to Bedlam. This time, I want the night guard to see me.

"Help!" I shout when the swinging lantern comes around the edge of the long building. "This woman is badly hurt. Can we get her inside? Safe until a proper doctor will see her?"

The lantern swings faster as the guard rushes up. "Of course. The new doctor is a medical doctor as well.

You're in luck, Miss." Using a key from a large brass key ring on his belt, he opens the great door, and all the memories of that night with Ashe and Conrad and everything rush back. I push them aside.

Not now.

Much to my surprise, no cacophony of screams this time. I follow the guard up the stairs to the third floor. We make little noise on our way up, but enough to wake some patients no doubt. Yet, there is no shouting or banging on cells and doors. The stench is gone as well. It actually feels like a proper hospital this time. No cages on the floor. No wailing or crying or shouting. The place has been transformed in a matter of weeks.

I breathe a sigh of relief. Suddenly, I know that good can prevail—does prevail—in the end. Just as the thought crosses my mind, right before we turn into the new doctor's quarters, I see the face of Dr. Pilkington peer out his cell window. White hair stands on end everywhere, and his eyes are hollow. Vacant and dead.

Broken, much like Cassie's doll. I feel sad for him, but I must remember that his choices and his alone brought him here. No one forced him to betray nature by mesmerizing innocent people for an army. No one forced him to accost the Queen and try to rule England himself. No one forced him to try to kill us. He, alone, did all that. Here, he can hurt no one else.

CHAPTER NINE

IN WHICH NICKIE NICK TALKS TO A GHOST

Fanny waits for me, still breathless, as I emerge from that horrible place.

"I saw him," I say.

"Again?" She thinks I mean Ashe.

"No, not him. Pilkington." That name makes her shudder. After all, he tried to kill us both. Quite traumatic, as far as traumatic experiences go.

"Oh," she says, trying to appear unshaken, but her hands tremble when she reaches out for my arm, and not from the cold.

"He looked shattered, like he defined the word. Utterly broken, lost."

"Pity," she says through clenched teeth in a tone that meant anything but. Her grasp on my arm tightens.

"Indeed. Miserable place, that. I feel better with each step away from it. Although, the conditions seem to have improved under new guidance. Still, after seeing Pilkington, I wonder if it's not a chemically induced calm. What a fate to be sent to Bedlam. I'd rather die. Please Fanny, don't ever send me there or let my parents send me there. Not for hysteria, not for anything!"

"Never! Oh, never, Nicole! I'd die first, meself. I know I threatened you with Bedlam before, and I apologize. At my wit's end, I was. Didn't know what else to do. Even my magic didn't work, your sorrow was so great. I just felt so...helpless. Still, no excuse to resort to such manipulations. Will you forgive me?"

"Your magic didn't work? You tried to control my emotions?"

"I'm so sorry. I don't normally, Nickie, I promise. It's so invasive, after all. I don't like to do it except under extreme circumstances and pain, really. Lest I abuse the power. Must be wary of that. Still, these were extreme circumstances, my dove, especially after losing poor Edwin. Forgive me for trying?"

"I do forgive you, and I love you for trying to take away my pain, Fanny. I love you all the more!" After all this time, she did try to help ease my suffering. Love swells in my breast and I blink back the tears. Fanny's eyebrows tilt in worry, so I give the best comfort I can.

"I suppose pain does have a purpose, though. Doesn't it? Like physical, tangible pain, somehow more tolerable because it is tangible, but it serves a purpose. It tells us something is wrong. It protects us. I suppose the intangible kind does as well."

"It is a great teacher, perhaps the greatest of them all."

Fanny smiles again, at least her eyes do. All worry and concern gone, so back to the task.

"Where to now, Fanny? We saved one tonight, and taking the demon down felt very good, indeed. Cathartic. I want to hunt more. We have the whole night ahead of us. Come with me?"

"I won't stay out with you all night, but I will stay for another hour or two, at least. Let's see how fast you can find them, shall we? You did so well at finding the last one. He was rather close. Can you feel them further away?"

"Let's find out!"

"Although your execution was rather clumsy, you got the job done."

"Clumsy? My execution was clumsy? Is that so, Fanny? Clumsy?" Playfully, I push her away. "It was no such thing, Fanny. I was the epitome of grace and propriety," I say and make an exaggerated curtsy. "I am, after all, a delicate flower."

We both laugh, then turn back onto Lambeth Road.

"You slapped him, pet."

"I did. Caught him off guard, did it not?"

"That it did."

"So, where to?" I ask on the corner of Lambeth and St. George's again. I can still smell the blood and dust near the cathedral just to our left. That place will forever remind me of poor little Edwin.

"That's up to you. You're The Protector. Where does your sense draw you?"

Closing my eyes, I focus once again inward and outward all at once. It's as if the barriers of my mind and body dissolve, and I become one with London. With every sight and sound and smell. Simultaneously, they are me. Never before has it been this clear, and I like it.

I am London. London is me. We are one.

When I open my eyes again, it's no longer me looking out from them. Well, it is me, only better. Hunter me. Focused me. Determined me.

"Come on," I say, and start walking. My inner compass takes us across Waterloo Bridge into the city, proper, near the warehouse and factory district wherein lies the Hawthorn Textile Mill.

Fanny's breath comes quick, and she braces herself by putting her hands on her knees.

"All right?" I ask.

"Fine. A bit winded, is all. It's good for me, my lamb. Don't worry. Although, I'm thinking of asking Lucian of driving us the next time I go hunting with you. London is rather large, isn't it?"

"I'm being pulled from several directions now." I place my fists against my corset, and then demonstrate the sensation by opening my hands wide, and in a sweeping motion, extend both out.

"Use your other resources, too. Remember?"

"Yes! The compass!" I take Conrad's gift from its little pocket and read the inscription out of habit.

To find your way back to me.

He had gifted it to me for my seventeenth birthday, and I was ever so touched. I turn it over and over in my hand, feeling the cold metal against my skin. Rather a romantic gift from a friend, granted, but Conrad and I are close, aren't we? It's just a close friendship after all.

I feel suddenly lost without him here. Strange, that. These past weeks have really taken a toll on my spirit and my mind. Sad or confused, or distracting myself from the same.

"Where did you get that?" A voice says, causing me to look up and see a dark-haired man standing before me. He looks familiar, like someone from long ago. The memory of a memory of a memory.

"Where did you come from?" I ask him, taking a protective step in front of Fanny. No one will hurt another person I love. They will have to get past me first.

"Who are you talking to, Nicole?" Fanny says with concern in her voice, looking over my shoulder.

"Him." I point to the man not two feet in front of us.

He repeats, "Where did you get that compass? Tell me!" This time, his tone holds more than a touch of anger.

"It was a gift, if you must know. Take a step back, sir. Now."

"Yes, it was a gift. To me, from my love. How did you get it? Give it back to me, this instant! I thought I had lost it, but it is rightfully mine!"

My eyes widen at the realization just as Fanny says, "There's no one there, love. Are you feeling all right?"

"Mr. Hannon?" I step back into Fanny. "Is that you?"

"Nicole, you're frightening me."

"Shhh," I tell Fanny. "It's one from Southwark. You know, a…" I can't say the word ghost because Mr. Hannon quite obviously doesn't know he's dead, and it would be quite rude to tell him bluntly.

"Right here? Now?" Fanny peers over my shoulder, looking from side to side, squinting, as if that would help her see a ghost. "I can't see him. Where is he?"

"Shhhhh," I say again. "Mr. Hannon. I'm Nicole Hawthorn. You worked in my parent's factory, remember? You had an accident there."

"Little Nickie! You've grown so! Just yesterday you were a little girl playing with my Conrad. I can't find him, Nickie, not him nor Laura. Are they all right? Tell me they're all right! I've been so lost, Nickie, so very lost. Have you seen them? Are they all right?"

"They are quite well, Mr. Hannon. Quite well, indeed. Why are you here, sir?"

"I'm not sure." He looks around, frightened and disoriented. His hands go in then back out of his trouser pockets—jittery, jerky movements, afraid of all around him. Wide eyes dart back and forth, then focus back on me before looking off to the right. He squints and points toward the warehouses. "The factory is just down there, isn't it? But I didn't come from there. I came from—" He turns around and around in a circle, looks left then right then left again, and finally fixes his eyes back on me. "I'm confused, Nickie. I don't know why I'm here. Sometimes I'm here, and sometimes I'm there, and sometimes I'm nowhere. It's just black. For years, it seems. Black and empty and lonely and forgotten, it seems. Where is my wife. Can you take me to her? I miss her so much and she must miss me, too. I don't know how we got separated like this."

"What's he saying, Nicole? Is he still here?" Fanny holds onto my waist and gawks over my shoulder, examining the street in front of me, but she sees nothing but the cobblestones and street lamps.

"He's asking about his family. I don't think he knows he's dead," I whisper to her, careful he doesn't hear me.

"Why is she talking to you like I'm not here? This is all so strange, Nicole. I know that woman, don't I? Isn't she your Nanny?"

"Do you remember the accident, Mr. Hannon? The accident with the machinery?"

"Sometimes I remember a horrible grinding sound and then everything went all jumbly. Shaky, like. Then that darkness. For a long time, darkness. Black. All black. Then this. But that black, the first black, it wasn't lonely. It was just there. Peaceful. Silent. Comfortable. But then this. Chaos again. Cold and confusion. Now the black comes and goes and it's not peaceful or silent. It's certainly not comfortable. It's lonely and cold and terrifying. Oh, Nickie! Don't let me go back there! Please! Don't make me!" He laughs then and runs his hand through his hair. Eyes wild and then closed. He's shaking his head. "Forgive me, child. I don't know what came over me. What you must think of me. I'm not mad. I promise I'm not a nutter. Where is my son? My wife? Can I see them? I've been searching and searching and I can't find them. Will you take me to them?"

I reach out to him, but just as I do, he dissolves, evaporates into a vapor. In a blink. There, then gone.

"He's gone," I say to Fanny so she'll stop craning her neck over my shoulder. Her chin pressing down on my shoulder is getting rather tiresome, as she's been holding on to me for balance while she tries to see the ghost. "That was so strange. He doesn't know he's dead, Fanny, nor why he's back here. We have to find out more about the ghosts in Southwark. We have to. It can't be a coincidence, can it? I mean, I've never seen a ghost before the ones by St. Saviour's. He must be connected to them, right?" I squeeze Conrad's gift in my palm, and I wonder how I'll ever be able to tell him about this. I shan't say anything until I know more. This news will just distress him, or he'll think I'm the nutter.

"Mr. Hannon recognized the compass, the gift from Conrad's mum. He remembered a bit of the accident, but he doesn't know he died! How can one not know they're dead! Oh, Fanny! And he was so sad, so confused. How strange. Could the compass draw him somehow? Is that why he was away from Southwark?"

"Perhaps, my dove. This is disturbing, indeed. Why were you able to see him and I wasn't? That's strange indeed. Must have to do with your Protector powers, I'd wager. I've got books back at home on specters and the like. I shall do some research tomorrow. For now, there's nothing more we can do, so let's return to the hunt. I've much to learn about your abilities, clearly. Focus. Still feel pulled in more than one direction?"

"I do, and they're indeed vampires about. Lots of them, from what I can tell. The city is crawling with them." I look down at the compass and open it. The needle spins around and around, but then settles after a moment pointing behind us, towards Parliament. "This way," I say and start heading west along Embankment.

The night is full of scents and sensations, especially the cozy smell of smoke from fires burning in home after home trying to stay warm in the cold night—the grasses and winter blooming flowers in Victoria Gardens, the pungent smell of The Thames. Perhaps my favorite, in the end. Then, the faintest hint of wormwood reaches my nose, mixed with peppermint and copper, as well. Picking up speed, I make my way to the Egyptian Obelisk. There, right on the north bank, I see him again: the masked man who helped us last week, just a moment too late for poor Edwin.

Edwin. Oh, poor, poor Edwin!

No. Not now. I will grieve Edwin later, but I must push it aside now.

The masked man is surrounded by vampires, all of whom have the same bizarre branded symbol on their foreheads. A stake in one hand and a crucifix in the other, he's holding them back, but he's clearly outnumbered. They growl and inch forward.

My turn to repay his help.

"Cheerio!" I shout from across the road, then skip towards them. This cheeky move distracts the monsters long enough for the masked man to spin and stake the one on the far right just as I reach the one on the far left. That leech and the one in the middle lunge at me, simultaneously. I duck under the first one's grasp, spinning into a back kick. My boot-stake activates, and I get him square in the chest.

Crack. Squish. Whoosh.

Done.

The other turns and faces me again, but I no longer face him alone. The masked man stands beside me, stake at the ready, and says, "Hey, Nick. Thanks for that."

He knows who I am?

"No problem. It's what I do."

The last vampire is now the one who's outnumbered, so he turns to run.

"Not so fast," Fanny says, hand out. The monster, now immobile, trapped by Fanny's magic grasp, looks around in terror. Its eyes roll in their infernal sockets like the trapped animal it is. The same brand on his forehead, just as the ones who killed Edwin, infuriates me and stirs my grief and anger all together into a stew of fury. I see red. Vengeance fills my mind. Avenge Edwin. Kill.

"It's them, Fanny. It's the same clan that murdered Edwin."

"Let me go," the fiend says. "I'll not be bested by a bloody witch and two brats like you. Release me, and fight me proper."

We all ignore it.

"Yes, I've been hunting them for quite some time now. Powerful lot, them. Still, I've taken a few down.

I'm sick about your friend. I'm so sorry I was too slow," The masked man says, looking down. His hair catches the light of a nearby gas lamp and for a moment shines the color of cinnamon. I sense something familiar about him, but I'm not sure what. Something in the way he moves.

"The only one at fault for Edwin's murder is the fiend who killed him," I reassure him, echoing Fanny. "Must put the blame on the predators, mustn't we? They are the only ones at fault here. I appreciate your help nonetheless, Mister..." I wait for him to fill in the name, but he doesn't. All right, a more direct approach. "Who are you, anyway?"

"I'm The Protector," he says.

Fanny drops her hand, shocked, and the vampire runs off. She and I turn in unison to the masked man and say, "You're the who?"

Chapter Ten

In Which Nickie Nick Skips Stones

February 15, 1881

"Ghosts, Nick? You saw ghosts?" Concern for my sanity crumples across Conrad's features. I just said "ghosts" at first, not naming any particulars. Must ease into these things, after all. Still don't know how to tell him about his father. I must trust that I'll know when the time is right.

Conrad tosses a rock into The Thames, and it skips three times before sinking beneath the murky surface. Barges growl and hum in the background, and the brown, murky waters lap at the stony shore. A pigeon flutters in front of us and drops a feather. I watch it float down and land on the water's surface beside random seaweed and rubbish. The smell of seaweed and sewage mixes to create an aroma unique to The Thames.

I choose a nice, flat round one from the pile we gathered from the muck below and fling it across the top of the dark water. It skips once, then, with a loud *plunk*, disappears. "There's no other explanation, Conrad. They were there and then they were gone. Those people walked right through them. You've heard all the ghost stories with me, from when we were children. They must come from somewhere. They were there but not solid. I don't know how to explain it. You just had to be there." Conrad regards me with quite the skeptical look. "Look, I'm not mad! Don't start with accusations of hysteria and women overreacting."

"I believe you."

I turn to him and lash out, angry. "I mean, why does it always have to be that women are mad? I suspect it's based on men always trying to control everything we do from what's proper to wear or how to behave—to keep us down, and it's not fair! I know what I saw, Conrad, and I didn't imagine it. It's not because of Ashe"—cringe—"It's not because of Edwin, either. I saw what I saw, believe me or not."

I toss another rock, even though it's Conrad's turn, and it plunks right into the depths. Conrad's next one skips four times. Perfect circles spread out from each place the rock touched the water. "I said, I believe you, Nick."

"Oh. You do? Um." My cheeks burn red. I'm so used to the scoffing, mocking Conrad of our youth…well, of just about a month ago, it seems, but the man before me now is just that, a man. A fine man, at that. Not a child anymore at all. My eyes tear up in gratitude. "So much loss and confusion," I mumble. It takes everything I have not to throw my arms around him and kiss him in my gratitude. "Thank you! These past weeks have just been…it's just that…I mean…thank you."

"Of course."

Awkward silence follows, during which Conrad skips another rock. Four times again.

"How do you do that? Make them skip so much?"

"It's in the wrist," he says and takes my hand, positioning a flat stone between my forefinger and thumb. "Like this." He bends my wrist back and forth, demonstrating the movement. "Keep your hand flat like the water. Watch." Pinching a rock in his hand, exactly the way he positioned one in mine, he flexes his wrist back and forth, back and forth. Faster and faster, so I can get a feel of the motion. He finally lets the rock go, and it skips five times. "You try."

I do, and it at least skips twice this time before the *plunk*.

"From what I've heard about ghosts, they're usually here for a reason. I know I said I didn't believe in them the other day, and I don't much like to think about it. But, since that talk, I have thought about it, with Edwin and all, and my father, a'course. The stories always say they stay here for a reason, like because they were murdered or looking for revenge. Is that what you believe, too? What do you want to do now? I mean, you're a vampire hunter, not an exorcist. We'll need a priest for that, to release them."

"I am a vampire hunter, true, but I'm The Protector. It encompasses much more than vampires. They, from what I've gathered, are the most damaging to us humans, actively hunting and feeding and killing us. Plus, there are many more of them than say a demon possession, but I suppose this falls under my duty. Spiritualism or anything clairvoyant is supernatural. Perhaps we should find out what Fanny discovered first. Or, I don't know, contact a medium or psychic? I see them advertised in the newspaper all the time, but as frequent are the reports of fraud."

"What do you think you can do for them, Nick? You can see them and hear them, and you said they sounded surprised at that."

"They did. So odd."

"That's likely some of your Protector powers, but can you release them? Give them relief or peace of some kind? I mean, how do you think you can even help them? "

"I know, but I'll find a way, with Fanny's help, to give them some peace. I'm sure of it. At least find out what's going on so I know what I can and can't do. I sure don't need any more confusion right now, and I can figure this out. It will give me a sense of purpose again.

Keep my mind occupied." I toss another stone across the water, and this time it skips three times. "Hey! See that! Not too bad!"

"Much better! See, it's all in the wrist." Conrad chucks another and it skips five.

"It must be awful roaming around year after year without being able to be seen or heard, without touching anything or anyone touching you. No comfort, no solace. How utterly horrific, Conrad! Oh! Those poor souls!"

"Wait, Nick. Don't get upset yet. You don't know if they're in pain or not. Maybe the first step is to see what they want. See why they called out to you."

The memory of all those pitiful faces comes back to me, and I shudder. Overwhelming sorrow rises up my throat, and I choke on my grief. The last voice I heard, so much like Edwin. If Edwin is with them, I must do everything I can to help them. Mr. Hannon, too. If for no one else but them.

"They begged me not to go, Conrad. Begged me! They weren't happy. Suffering, they were. In agony. Pleading with me to save them. Those aren't the words of beings at peace. I saw it in their faces and felt it in my heart, a tugging sensation. They need me, and I can't turn my back on them. So much pain, Conrad. Even after death, it seems. Does it ever end?"

"Listen to us, Nick. We're only seventeen and already we're talking like hardened old fogeys. Isn't this supposed to be the time of joy and dreams and love?"

A rat scurries on the mucky beach beneath our feet, sticking close to the stone wall so as not to get its teeny paws too wet. Another follows, then another along with three baby rats, a family out for the day.

"Not for us. We've seen too much already, haven't we? Our innocence already lost." I reach for his hand, and he laces his fingers around mine. His touch triggers something warm and calm inside me, like having my hair stroked. His eyes meet mine, and I see his sadness. "You losing your father and your mother being taken away. Living on the streets and losing Edwin. I have a charmed life by comparison, but I've known sorrow, too."

"Don't knock sorrowful experiences, Nick. They serve to make the joy that much more joyous, knowing sorrow. It makes people kinder."

"You think so?"

"I know so, Nick. I know so." He pulls my hand up to his lips and kisses the back of it. Sweetly.

"Thank you, Conrad. You always know how to make me feel better. By the way, *we're* not seventeen. I'm seventeen. You're still sixteen, for another month, and don't you forget it!" I laugh and yank my hand away from him, only to shove him playfully.

"Hey! Close enough!" Conrad laughs with me. "Ready," he says. "On three." He gets a nice big flat stone and gives me one as well. "One. Two. Three!" We both toss the stones out over the water, and they hit at the exact same time. His skips four times and mine, six!

"Wow! Did you see that? Six times! Six skips! Yes! I'm the best stone skipper ever! In the history of skipping stones!" I say and throw my arms up in victory.

"Lucky shot, nothing more."

"Lucky nothing! I'm the champion of tossing stones. I've been fooling you with my clumsy throws this whole time—for your own good. Can't be shown up by a girl, now can you?"

"Luck—you can't fool me, Nick. Do it again, if you're so clever."

"All right, you got me." I'm mesmerized by the laughter and light in his eyes, which reminds me of Rufus, leading me to Edwin and back to the ghosts. "So these ghosts." The joy in his eyes fades when I start speaking again, and I curse myself for bringing it back up, but it is rather important. "We can't do anything about their state of existence. We didn't put them there, but perhaps we can release them. I'll see what Fanny discovered, at least that much is decided."

"I'm surprised you didn't pester her about it this morning. She already knows what you're like when you get your mind set on something. You can't talk about anything else. She is your confidante, after all."

"Every bit as much as you are." White caps crest as a boat cuts through the green-brown water in front of us. Full of tourists, this one. Quite a strange time of year for a river cruise. Steam billows from its stack and joins with the rest of London's smoky air. The crisp wind caresses my cheek as the chimes from St. Paul's drift across the river. Conversations of passersby fade into a faint hum behind us as I focus on the bells, the flapping of a pigeon's wings as it takes flight, the low mumble of another barge, the whisper of the wind in my ears, and the splashing of The Thames against Bankside.

In the peace of this moment with my best friend, my thoughts suddenly return to Fanny's pitiful tale. "But, I don't know. I suppose since she told me her story—the one I can't tell you without breaking her confidence—I suppose I feel more protective of her, like I don't want to bother her with anything else. She's suffered enough."

"She loves you, Nickie. Plus, she's your mentor. Teacher, or whatever. Training you and all. I mean, she's the very person to talk to about this, especially with her powers. She has the most experience in all this, more than the rest of us put together. Perhaps she knows some secrets of life and death the rest of us don't know."

"True. We haven't done much training yet, between you-know-who and losing Edwin. We just started again yesterday, as I wasn't in much...Well, you know. Perhaps that's best. You're right. I'll talk with her about it tonight. Perhaps that will get me refocused and give some answers."

"Give it a go, Nick. Can't hurt."

"Still, I'd like to get more information from the creepy priest before I go back to pester Fanny. Would you come with me? I mean, not inside, but nearby. Or if inside, at least separate from me. He comes across as quite unscrupulous, and I want to hear just how much so. I will have to appear as bait, I'm afraid." Conrad's neck muscles tense in protection, no doubt, but before he can protest, I continue, "I can take care of myself, Conrad. You know that. I'll be fine, albeit distressed at the confirmation such creatures exist. I mean, one hears stories, of course, but one doesn't want to believe them, certainly not of a man of the cloth."

"Nicole, please. Talk to Fanny first."

He called me Nicole. Must be quite concerned, indeed. "It will be all right. We've faced harsher realities, haven't we? We're survivors, Conrad. You and me. Fanny, too. Rufus and Franklin and even little Cassie. Your mum. We're all survivors. He can't hurt me. I'm stronger than him, than most any human, no doubt. Plus, I shall have the strength of will as well. He scared me out of there once, but I shan't give up until I know the truth. He's got something to do with this. I can feel it."

"Onward, Nick. Lead the way."

"Brilliant."

I swing my legs over the wall, making sure my skirts all follow without getting snagged on the stone, and hop down. The moment after Conrad's boots hit the street, I feel his hand on my waist. Then I see why. Three boys approach. Ruffians. Street urchins, more or less. Dirty, much like Conrad and my boys back at the flat. Harmless, I'm sure, so why the protective stance? Then I remember last week after Edwin's funeral. I only saw them from afar, but perhaps these are the same Conrad was trying to avoid then.

"Conrad, m'best mate. Got that shilling ya owe me, do ya? I've been patient, I 'ave. Patient as the day is long. Time to pay up."

Yes. The same ones, all right. The one in the middle, obviously their leader, speaks to Conrad in the most condescending tone I've heard since the last time my mother took me shopping and commented on my fashion sense.

"Hey, Buck. Not on me, mate. How's about we meet later this afternoon, round the banks. I'll have it fer ya then. All of it. Then we's square. All right? It'll be done. Once and fer good. Deal?"

This Buck chap makes a tsk tsk tsk sound between his teeth then wipes his mouth with a dirty sleeve, leaving behind a clean-ish smudge across his mouth, which only serves to accentuate its astounding size. He smiles and half his face disappears in yellow-stained teeth. One in the direct center is chipped. He tongues it, pink flesh comes and goes with each tsk.

"I fink I'd rather 'ave it now, if ya don' mind. Right about now, mate."

He's quite sure of himself, this Buck. The other two with him, one very tall and the other medium height, stand behind him. I assume they are back up, but they look as if they really don't want to be there. Perhaps they're forced to be. That's the sense I get from this Buck chap. He gets people to do what he wants through force, a bully in the current sense.

The one on the left, messy blonde hair, wears a patch over his left eye. A deep scar extends both over and beneath it The one on the right, red mop with downcast eyes, also has a scar, pencil-thin, that starts in his left eyebrow and circles around the outside of his eye and down his cheek, almost like a question mark. Rough life down here. Red's eyes dart up to see me looking, and he turns his face away as if to hide the scar. His cheeks darken to the shade of his hair.

"Or," Buck continues, running his eyes from the top of my hat to the bottom of my skirts, "we could make.... other arrangements for repayment."

Conrad's hand tightens on my waist, and he pulls me to him. I'm not sure if I'm more cross with Conrad behaving as if he owns me or has to protect me when I've proven more than once I can hold my own, or this

Buck chap for suggesting such impropriety as debt repayment. Revolting!

"Now look here," I say, pulling out of Conrad's protective grasp. Face to face with Buck, who stands a few inches taller, I plant my hands squarely on my hips and look him in the eye. It's important to show bullies they cannot intimidate you, that's what Fanny taught me. I hope she's right. Or, rather, I might hope she's wrong. I could use a bit of cathartic violence at the moment. "The man said he'll meet you this evening. I'm sure that will suffice. It would be wise for you to turn around and leave our company this instant."

"Oh, my. This one's feisty, Conrad! You've found yourself a live one 'ere, mate. Good on you! 'ear 'ow she called 'im a 'man'? Simon? Pete? Conrad, a man. What a laugh? Ain't it Conrad? Ain't it a laugh?"

Pete, the blonde, laughs a bit nervously, but Simon just looks down at his shoes and kicks at a loose cobblestone.

"Address me, you buffoon, not him. *I'm* talking to you, and I'm giving you a way out here unscathed. You may conduct your business with Conrad later. Stay here and you'll be limping home."

"Mmmmm." He licks and smacks his lips, leaving another break in the generous amount of dirt covering his face. "You'd be tasty, you'd be. Righ' tasty, I'd wager." His filthy hand strokes my cheek. The sensation of this bully touching my flesh sends a charge through my body, and not the nice kind. In a blur, I grab his hand off my cheek and twist it around his back, thrusting him against the stone wall. Bent at the waist, the bully looks over the side onto The Thames.

He's not smiling now.

But I am.

"Is this what you had in mind, Buck? A bit of rough play with the lady?" I whisper in his ear. He struggles, but I'm far, far stronger than him. Eyes wide in shock or fear or anger or all of the above, he averts his gaze from me now. His nostrils flare, and if he was able, he'd be breathing fire right about now.

"Let me go," he spits between his teeth, pink tongue flickering against the chip.

"First, swear you'll behave like a gentleman, even though you are clearly not one."

"Nickie," Conrad says from behind me. "Not here."

"You need a woman to fight your battles, do ya, Connie?" Buck yells over his shoulder. I put more pressure on him until he can't breathe. He coughs and gasps for air, but I don't let up.

"I've had a really hard month, Buck, and I'm not in the mood for your petty, childish games. Conrad will meet you later, as he suggested. He will pay you in full, and you will not bother him ever again. If I see your ugly mug any time from this moment forward, I will be the last thing you see in your miserable life. I've killed before, Buck, and I have no problem killing again, especially river filth like you. Understand?"

Buck nods, nostrils wide. I even see a waft of smoke.

Begrudgingly I release him after one last push against the wall that will surely leave a bruise. He backs up from me until he's behind the other two. Pete looks at me with fear. Buck, with fury, and Simon with a hint of amusement. In fact, there's a faint smile on his full lips as they turn to leave.

"One hour," Conrad shouts after them. "by Blackfriars."

Buck throws up a very rude hand gesture, but doesn't turn back around.

"Guess you'll be going to St. Saviour's on your own after all, Nick. You all right with that?"

"Like I said," I say, straightening my skirts and smoothing my hair back after donning my white-gloves, "I can take care of myself."

"You can, indeed. Next time, though, would ya try not to embarrass me in front of me mates?" Conrad says, but he's smiling as he does.

"Mates? You call them mates?"

"Well, Buck is a pain in the arse, a'course, but Pete and Simon, they're good blokes. Good fer a laugh, ya know. Buck, well. He's a pain, is all. Rough life an' all."

"Yes, well many people have had a hard time of it. Doesn't mean they have to bully and hurt others. Yes, that's where my compassion for them ends. He will either learn to be a decent human being, or he won't leave unscathed next time. There is no excuse for such aggressive behavior. To anyone, but especially a lady," I say with a curtsy which give Conrad a chuckle.

"I got to find the coin I owe Buck. Guess I'll be scouring the banks again."

"Here," I say, taking a crown out of my reticule, "Next time come to me if you need something. All right? Please." As I place the coin in Conrad's palm, he looks down, brows furrowed in shame. "It's nothing to me, Conrad, and I hate that it's nothing to me. I hate that my family has so much and you and others so little. Please take it, settle your debt, and get something nice for your boys...and girl. Perhaps some sticky buns or chocolate. Bring your mum a pansy or two from the flower girl wandering Borough Market. All right?"

"Nickie," Conrad says. His face holds something between shame and, I think, love. He closes his hand around mine. "You already do so much for us."

"Enough," I say and push him away. "Don't worry, Conrad. You're like a brother to me, after all this time. You and the boys and Cassie, you're my family much more than my family is. I'm happy to help. Anytime. I mean it. I really mean it, Conrad."

"Brother," he says. "Of course. Look, Nick. I've got to meet ol' Buck and you've got a priest to investigate. Right? So, let's leave it here."

"Right. Tomorrow, then? Or even later tonight? I can check in and tell you what I've found before I go hunting."

"Tomorrow. Tomorrow is good," he says, turning away. "See ya, Nick. Thanks again." He holds the crown in the air between pinched fingers before pocketing it. Without another word, he walks away.

CHAPTER ELEVEN

IN WHICH NICKIE NICK GOES TO CONFESSION

I can't believe I'm going back there alone. Perhaps I am mad after all. My pulse races as I get closer to St. Saviour's, and panic rises at the memories of the ghosts. An overwhelming feeling of dread trickles up my throat and down my arms. My skin tingles and my stomach rolls. No, lurches, more like.

Each step I take is more uncertain than the last. My pace slows until I come to a complete stop. I must look ridiculous standing still on Bank Side while London bustles around me, continuing their daily business, but I don't care. I wrap my overcoat tightly around me, turning its collar up against the wind, and I pinch my legs tightly together beneath my skirts, trying to make myself as small as possible, compact. Searching for a feeling of safety.

Please come. I can't curl into a ball on Bank Side.

It takes all my will not to turn around and run home.

I truly don't know what I'm doing. I'm no Protector of the people. I've barely been able to get out of bed for the past month. How am I going to save anyone, let alone ghosts that might very well be part of my imagination? It's looking more and more like I'm mad after all.

To my left, a group of men load large sacks of something onto a docked barge. One after another, the largest of them grunts, lifting the heavy pillow-shaped sackcloth off a cart and hands it off to another, who, in turn, hands it to another, who hoists it up to the man on the barge. Masts of docked boats spring up along the south bank as far as the eye can see. Wooden soldiers awaiting their orders. Soon, they'll sail down The Thames and off to exotic lands all over the world delivering their cargo and gathering some more.

I'd like to travel, I think. See the world. There must be so much wonder and beauty to discover.

"Hello, Sweetheart!" a gruff voice burps from my right. Startled, I turn to see three men pulling a cart full of crates. They lean into the weight, grasping tightly to the ropes with gloved hands. Their feet are wrapped in cloths and tied with twine. They don't even have boots. "What's a pretty little thing like you doing 'round these parts. Come for a ride? I'll give you one, darling."

Perhaps Conrad is right. This is too dangerous. Sure, I can take care of myself in a physical confrontation, no problem, and Fanny's amulet protects me from supernatural mind control, but psychological mind games and creepy feelings might just be more mental trauma than I can handle now. So much loss in a short period of time has made me quite vulnerable, I fear.

State the obvious, Nick.

I force myself to move again, outpacing the men heaving the cart forward and ignoring the foul things they're shouting at me. They're right. I don't belong in this part of London. Such unsavory types in Southwark, and I can't cope with any more suffering. It's as if it's cumulative and another drop of torment, mine or someone else's, will cause me to rupture.

Edwin's little voice echoes in my mind, "Don't go, Nickie."

No. Find a way to gather the strength of character needed, for Edwin's sake. Too much misery already. Just look around. Too many bad people hurting others. Supernatural or no, those bad people must be stopped.

And I'm the one who will stop them.

I failed Edwin when he needed me in life. I shan't fail him in death. No matter how scary they are, I'm scarier. I'm a vampire's worst nightmare, and if I can stand against the super-stong undead and their treacheries, certainly I can handle a human and a few ghosts. Look at how well I did with Pilkington. Well, with Fanny and—*cringe*—Ashe's help.

Still. I can do this. I can do this. I can do this.

With a more determined gait, I pick up my pace. The sound of each footfall on the cobblestones strengthens my resolve. I did so well hunting last night. I saved the masked man. I saved that woman. She's alive today because of me. He is, too. I am powerful and strong and capable, and I can do this.

I turn into St. Saviour's, already more comfortable out of the misty chill. The colored window panes soothe me, along with the overall reverence of the place. The bard reclines, smiling at me, watching over me, and the silence of this sacred place, even one that has been infiltrated by evil, resets my calm.

Just as the thought passes, a chill ripples up my back making all the hairs at the nape of my neck stand on end.

The priest.

No need to turn around. I feel him there, and a moment later, his voice confirms it. "You're back, sweet, sweet child. Welcome." Internally, I tell my tumbling stomach to stop already. I get it. He's dangerous. "Welcome back to St. Saviour's. We didn't get a chance to introduce ourselves before. I'm Father Benedict, the head vicar here, and you are?"

Who am I? I'm not going to give him my real name. No. Not on my life. Quick, Nickie! Think! Shakespeare.

William Shakespeare. What's the feminine of William? Wilomena. No. A play. Any play.

"Miss Juliet Nichols. How do you do?"

"Quite well, Miss Nichols. Much better now I've made your acquaintance," he hisses. "What brings you into this place of worship today? Confession? May I lighten your load, child?"

"Um. Yes. Confession. That's why I've come." I finger Fanny's pendant beneath my blouse, looking down in mock shame and innocence. "It this a good time, or do you have hours for private confessions?"

"Whenever I'm here and free is a perfect time, Miss Nichols. The set hours are everyday between four and six in the afternoon on weekdays and Saturdays. Saturday evening and Sunday mornings we have group silent confessions during the service, of course. Now, however, is fine, as I am your humble servant in Christ. It is what I do. What the Lord, thy God gave me the honor and power to do for my flock. Give absolution to the repentant. Take on their sins and offer them deliverance. It's the most important part of my calling, dear child. Come, come into the confessional and let me absolve you. You are repentant, are you not? Of course you are, sweet, sweet girl"

He touches my shoulder and strokes down my arm. Snakes against my bare flesh would've been more pleasant. Even spiders or other nasties are less creepy.

His eyes linger on the bodice of my dress then drop down to my waist, and linger there as well, then a little lower. I suppress a wretch. "Follow me," he purrs.

Even if he wasn't a priest, he's revolting. Even if he wasn't revolting, such behavior is always revolting, but he is especially revolting.

Have I mentioned? Revolting!

Tall, at least a head taller than me. Bulgy hazel eyes that look more green today in the afternoon light and a scruffy beard, as if it hasn't grown in all the way. I suppose it looks like that naturally. His breath is rank, a mixture of spirits and garlic, I think. Ugh. Horrible. He's as thin as I've ever seen a man. The harsher light today accentuates it even more than the growing shadows did before. Lanky to the point his limbs look rather comical when he walks, much like a puppet with jerky motions as its master pulls its strings.

I follow him to the confessional. It looks like a giant wardrobe made of ornately carved wood. Two openings, each covered by a heavy red curtain, give the confessor and priest privacy from the rest of the church. Between the two rooms inside is a wall with a small window so that the confessor might confess their sins through a muted screen, designed to distort visibility for ostensible anonymity, if so desired.

Believe me, I would very much like to never see his face clearly, nor he mine. Too late for that.

He shows me behind the curtain on the left, and as I draw it closed once inside the dark closet, I see his hand grasp below his belt.

Ugh, again.

Another moment and the shade that separates both sides slides to the right. Father Benedict's form is shadowed on the other side. I'm in the dark, too. The heavy red velvet curtain separates me from the rest of the church. Light filters from beneath my curtain and his, giving just enough to make out human features. Just enough to see that twisted grin distorted by the screen.

"Bless me Father, for I have sinned," I begin, knowing the routine even though it has been longer than I care to remember. Still, not long enough. This is one of the few instances having parents who spend so much time working is beneficial.

"How long since your last confession," he asks.

"Three weeks," I lie. "I'm quite distressed, Father. There is a boy, and I'm thinking rather impure thoughts about him. My mother doesn't know. Neither does my father. He would disown me!"

"Go on," he says. A stroking, scratching sound in a constant rhythm emerges from the other side of the screen.

"Well, my parents would never approve. I sneak out to see him sometimes, Father. He works at the butchers and we pass notes without anyone being the wiser. Then, last week, he gave me a note along with our cuts to meet him after work, and I did. Oh! I'm so ashamed! He tried to kiss me, Father, but I didn't let him."

"Good girl. Oh, yes. Oh. Good girl." The pace of the scratching increases.

"Since then, though…" I pause until I infer an appropriate amount of shameful silence. "I've wanted to see him again and let him kiss me this time. Oh! I'm so ashamed. Is that wrong, Father? Is that a sin?"

"You're a naughty girl. Oh, yes. Oh. Oh. Naughty indeed. Lust. You lustful girl, you. Yes. Oh, yes. Yes. Yes. It's a sin, all right. A cardinal sin. You naughty, naughty girl. I will absolve you. Are you penitent? Oh, yes. I will absolve you of your lust." Each time he said the word 'lust,' it sounded more like a growl from a hungry dog than a spoken word.

Conrad was right. I can't do this without vomiting. People trust this man with their deepest darkest secrets, and he's gaining pleasure from it.

"Go on, child. Go on. Be right in the eyes of the Lord, thy God. Oh! Oh! Yes. I will absolve you, sweet, sweet girl. Absolve you over and over. Go on. Tell me everything."

My suspicions about his character were obviously correct. It's time to find out about the ghosts. Not my imagination after all, I'd wager. I change the subject to catch him off guard.

"Then last week, when I was leaving here, something frightened me so, Father. It made me wish I had stayed here and prayed with you."

"Oh, yes, child. What. Tell me everything."

"I fear I saw....well,....a ghost, Father. I saw a ghost. Is that possible?"

"Oh, my," he said and the steady scratching sound stopped abruptly.

"I mean, is it even possible that spirits can be here and not in heaven or even hell. Also, not just one ghost, Father. I saw several. They tried to stop me from leaving here at first, which is why I was so eager to get away. Then they accosted me outside. They terrified me, Father. I was so, so scared. Please tell me I'm not mad, Father. Please. It took so much courage to come here today. I was afraid to come back, but I simply had to. Father? Father, are you there?"

After the rattle of a belt buckle and a shuffling about, followed by a distinct clearing of his throat, the priest says, "Ghosts? You have been taunting Satan, girl. Your lustful thoughts have plagued you with these images. That is your punishment."

Honestly? "So Satan filled my thoughts with these images because I'm so evil for wanting to kiss a boy?"

"That's exactly right, child. What you speak of is an abomination of the Lord, thy God. You need a right good absolution, you do. Deep, cleansing absolution. There are 'angels up in heaven above and demons down under the sea,' but there are no such thing as ghosts, child. No such thing at all."

Astounded that he just quoted Poe, father of supernatural and psychological horror, while lecturing me on sin and piety, I had to cover an outburst of laughter with coughing. "Truly, Father. You find me mad? You've never seen a ghost in these halls? With all the dead buried here, you've never seen anything you couldn't explain?"

"You spawn of Satan! You question a man of God about such abominations? You must do ten Hail Marys and an Act of Contrition each night for eight nights. Return here for your proper absolution, after you've done your penance. Yes. Pray to the Lord, thy God to wipe such evil thoughts from your mind, child. Pray to save your immortal soul. Pray with me now, girl. Pray with me. Our Father, who art in…"

Before he could finish the first line, I slip out from behind the curtain and get out of that church as fast as I can. He either can't see them or he knows much more than he's letting on. I'd wager the latter. His behavior is that of the guilty covering their tracks, spewing accusations and the like to take the light off themselves.

Yes. Something is not right with that priest, that much is quite clear.

"Don't go." Again the voices come as I reach the edge of the church yard about to ascend the steps to Borough High Street. I stop, one foot on the stairs and will myself forward. Don't turn around. Please.

Of course, I do turn around, and I see the same crowd of ghosts as before. "Please," they say all at different times, in different pitches. Women, men, and the wee voices of children, too. Each voice breaks my heart anew.

"What do you want from me?" I ask. "Please, just tell me." Making eye contact with each man, woman, and child, alike. I recognize Mr. Hannon, the woman with the red-hair, the man in brown, and the black-haired man, all of whom spoke to me before. The rest are strangers. No sign of Edwin after all. My heart sinks with the lost hope of seeing my little brother again. The black-haired, well-dressed man, still cries. The young, filthy man reaches out to me, grasping at nothing. Conrad's father steps forward. "Help us, Nickie. I think you're the only one who can. Please."

"Who are all these people, Mr. Hannon?"

His face goes blank. "What people?" he asks and blinks a few times. "Who are you?"

"I'm Nickie. Conrad's friend. You just called me by name a moment ago."

"Of course, Nickie. Have you seen my son?"

This again.

"I saw him earlier today. He's just fine, Mr. Hannon. Tell me why you are all here, please. What can I do to help?"

"'e gets confused, that one does. Still too new." The haggard red-haired woman from last week speaks. "Most of us 'round 'ere 'ave been 'ere for a long, long time. Too long. It's Benedict, it is. 'e's the one keeping us 'ere."

I knew it! "Why would he do such a thing?"

"To absolve us, well, me, anyway, again and again. I can't take no more absolution, Miss. No more!" She grabs her messy red locks with both fists and tugs, pulling out clump after clump. "'elp us, Miss. Only you can 'cause you can see us. You can see, so you can 'elp. Please, Miss. No more absolution. No more!" She shrieks up into the grey day. Head thrown back and fists full of matted red hair, she howls to the heavens.

All the rest around her, including Mr. Hannon, all start saying "Help us, Miss. Please, don't go. Don't go," creating a cacophony of noise mixed with all the sounds of the busy city and the nearby dock. The bells in the tall tower of St. Saviour's ring out the hour, and I cover my ears and crouch down to protect the remaining shreds of sanity.

"No more!" I shout.

Then, silence. I look up, and all the ghosts are still there, quiet as a church mouse. The red-haired woman has all her hair again. The bald patches from where she had so recently yanked it out were full of messy locks again. She smiled sweetly at me, as if none of that had just happened.

"Well, 'ello, Miss," she says, pleasant as the day.

"Don't I know you?" Mr. Hannon says.

The black-haired man says, "Please, Miss. Please get a message to me bonny lass. Tell her I'm sorry. Tell her I know what I'd done was wrong, vile even. Don't go, Miss. Please help me."

A very deep voice speaks from somewhere in the ghostly crowd. "Treachery is afoot. Don't trust those close—"

The toothless man from last week, the one dressed in baggy brown trousers held up by a rope sweeps off his sixpence and bows before me, interrupting the deep voice. "'enry Mayhew at yer service, Miss. Would you need any help today, Miss? I'm a 'ard worker, Iyam. Right 'ard, Miss. I'll work for a loaf, and I'll work 'ard, too. You won't find a 'arder worker than 'enry Mayhew, no ma'am!"

The rest behave similarly, and the noise rises again. This time I shout, "Quiet!" Passersby stop and watch, pointing and whispering at the mad girl talking to no one. Whispering out of the side of my mouth after nodding and waving to those who had stopped to look, I say, "Tell me about the priest. How can I help? Please, focus. What is Benedict doing to keep you here?"

The sound of his name sends them scattering in all directions. I hadn't even finished my sentence, and they were gone.

"Well, well, well," Benedict says, standing in the doorway of St. Saviour's. "Slipped out from under me, didn't you, my sweet, sweet girl? I must have a more firm grip on you next time. Yes, indeed."

With that, I run away as fast as my legs will carry me.

Chapter Twelve

In Which Nickie Nick Devises a Plan

"Where have you been, young lady," my mother scolds me as I come through the front door out of breath. What timing. She mustn't have been home long, and I had to catch her just as she came downstairs.

"At church." It isn't a lie. "Praying for Edwin's soul. You're home early. Slow day at the factory?"

She ignores my question and walks into the library, still talking to me, so I have to follow. "Really, Nicole. Alone? What will people say? We need to find you a husband and fast. I'll not have any old maids in my family. No, sir. No spinsters in the Knickerbocker family. You only have three good years before you'll be too old. I don't know what you did to chase away Lord Godwyn. He hasn't called on you since he left here on Christmas Day! Although it was quite rude for him to stand you up for New Years, I was willing to forgive him. He was your best chance at a happy life, Nicole. What did you say to him?"

"A man with Lord Godwyn's charm must have many options," I say, as I can't tell her the truth: that I told him to leave here and never return. I won't marry, certainly not the likes of him.

"So true. You can be charming when you want to be, Nicole. I do wish you would take these things more seriously. You can't live with us forever. We'd be the talk of the town!"

"Of course, Mother. I'd like to change for dinner, if that's all right."

"You're not getting away that easily, Nicole. You've been very strange since your Yule birthday ball, and I want to know what's going on with you."

"If you must know, mum," Fanny says as she enters the library and stands behind me, placing a soothing hand on my shoulder. Mother sits by the fire already, but I stayed close to the door, hoping I wouldn't be here long. "She has been ever so lost since Lord Godwyn hasn't called. It rather broke her heart, I'm afraid. Forgive me, Nicole," she says. I have to bite my cheek to keep from laughing. "She was too embarrassed to tell you, afraid she had let you down."

"Oh, Nicole! So you didn't say anything to ruin it after all! Well, perhaps we can gain his interest once again! No one throws over my daughter!"

"Forgive me, mum, but I've just heard of Lord Godwyn's engagement to Miss Jopling yesterday from my friend Eliza. She's their head maid, you know."

I gasp and bite my knuckle, playing along, and mold my face into one of utter despair. This is rather fun!

"Miss Jopling? You mean Bertha Jopling? He threw my daughter over for Bertha Jopling? Why, she looks like a horse! That man has no taste. You're better off, Nicole. Good riddance, I say. I always knew something was off with that boy. Always did know it. No matter, Nicole. You still have three years! We'll host a ball once the weather warms up and you get some color back in your cheeks."

I sniff and wipe my eyes, playing it up. "Yes, Mother. Thank you, Mother." I curtsy. "Might I change for dinner now?"

"Of course. Go. Go, you two. Dinner is in an hour, Nicole. Do be on time today, will you?"

"I'll make sure she is, mum," Fanny says.

Fanny and I leave the library, and I burst into laughter halfway up the staircase.

"Shhhhh," Fanny says, "She'll hear you!"

Once we're safely in my chamber, I hop onto the bed and gather my skirts close around me. "That was brilliant," I say to Fanny. "I really needed that laugh after what I just went through."

"Surely no vampires in the daytime, my dove. You didn't see...*him*, did you?"

"No, nothing like that," I say. I had gone so long without thinking of him with everything else going on. I don't appreciate the reminder. My smile falters a bit, but I smile again when I realize it truly faltered just a bit. No clenching gut. No nausea. I'll be all right after all. "The ghosts! I saw them again, and Father Benedict, that's his name. Something's quite wrong with that man. Very wrong, indeed. What did you find out about ghosts from your books, Fanny. Anything useful?"

"I'm afraid not, my dear. The usual...a specter having unfinished business, something that's keeping them here. Nothing about spirits en masse like you've described, but then I don't have any black magic books. I have heard of some powerful and awful books, most lost to antiquity, they say, that supposedly have rituals outlining how one can summon and control demons en masse. Perhaps they have rituals that can do that with ghosts as well."

"Can we find one of these books?"

"I wouldn't even know where to begin. Rome, perhaps."

"Controlling spirits, you say. Like controlling demons? Would a powerful witch or wizard be able to control vampires? Like, a sort of necromancy?"

"That is indeed possible. Are you thinking of the clan?"

"Yes. Father Benedict had an amulet with the same symbol as that burned into those vampires' foreheads. What would burn a vampire like that, Fanny? Why wouldn't it heal like their other wounds?"

"Holy water?"

"That's what I was thinking. Have you ever seen that symbol before?"

"I didn't get a close look at it. Some kind of circle?"

"It looks like this," I say and draw the shape with my finger on the bed quilt. "It's a circle within a triangle."

"Are you sure it's not a triangle in a circle? That is a representation of the holy trinity."

"Why would vampires have a Christian symbol burned into their heads?"

"For absolution?"

"That word. Benedict kept saying that over and over, how he wanted to give me absolution again and again. Still, I'd think that a Christian symbol burned into a vampire's skin with holy water would destroy them, or at least make their lives very painful indeed. Wouldn't you think?"

"Rather. There is an old Pythagorean symbol, if memory serves," Fanny says. "A circle within a square within a triangle within a circle." She traces the shape on the bed as she speaks. With her little added magic, the symbol appears in thin gold lines and remains a moment before disappearing. "Is that what you saw?"

"No. It wasn't that intricate. Just a circle in a triangle. That's all."

"Well, I don't know, my dove. We'll have to keep thinking. I'll write to my coven for help as well."

"I saw Mr. Hannon again. Strange he's there. Then with the vampires from that same cult and the mysterious masked man. How can he be The Protector, Fanny. I thought I was the only one."

"You're not the only vampire hunter, my lamb, as I told you before; however, you are the sole Protector, as far as I know. That boy was mental, no doubt. The prophecy said a Hawthorn born on Midwinter Night would have the powers. That's you, love. You felt the change on your seventeenth birthday and you obviously have inherited the powers of The Protector, so I'm not sure who that cove is. Whoever the chap, he saved your neck last week, and your friends', too."

"Yes, and I saved his last night. We're even."

"You are indeed."

"Still. I want to know more about him. Strange how he was scared off like that. There and then gone. Come to think of it, that's exactly how he appeared last week. He came out of nowhere, and tonight, disappeared the same way. Disappeared, like the ghosts." My eyes fly wide open and I gasp! "Oooooh! Do you think he's a specter as well? A vampire hunter ghost? That would be astounding, Fanny! Maybe he's a Protector from the past. You said there have been others, right? Before me, years ago."

"Yes."

"Maybe he's a ghost!"

"I saw him, too, remember, but I didn't see the other ones. Something is truly strange here, and we must learn all we can about the ghosts of Southwark as well as this fellow who claims he's The Protector. I'll definitely write to my coven."

"That will take too long for the letter to get there and back. These ghosts are in a lot of pain, Fanny. So confused and lost!"

"All right. All right. I can conjure up something tonight to contact them through the aether, get the supplies tomorrow, and do the ritual tomorrow night. Better?"

"Yes. You can do that?"

"Of course, my dove. I'll send a telegram first thing in the morning telling them when to expect me. That should give them plenty of time to get the receiving end ready. Ooooh! I am rather excited about this. I haven't made a call across the aether for some time, and it is ever so much fun," Fanny says, clapping her hands. Then, her face falls. "That means you must return to the cathedral, I'm afraid. Can you do that?"

My skin slithers up my back as I think of that horrid priest. I do not feel at all safe there. Not one bit, but, I suppose, I must. "Of course. I'll go back tomorrow. Although, he was not forthcoming about the ghosts. I know from his reaction he saw them, or he at least knows about them. So defensive, and he stiffened at the mention. Denied everything and started accusing me of being the spawn of Satan. What more can I find out from him? Plus, I really don't fancy being alone with him."

"Conrad. Perhaps we can enlist his assistance in the matter. Didn't you say he takes confessions and gives absolution in the afternoons?"

"Yes, four, he said. Or anytime he's free. He really likes absolving people, it seems."

"Four? Tea time? What! What! How rude!"

"I thought the same thing, actually, but I get the feeling that most of his clientele don't have the luxury of afternoon tea. Southwark and all."

"Yes. Dodgy place. Do you think Conrad would go to confession, just to ensure—Father Benedict, was it?"—I nod—"Father Benedict remains occupied while we snoop around his rectory and see what he's hiding? Are you up for an adventure, my lamb?"

"Always."

"Now. Onto this business of The Masked Protector. Come with me." Fanny leads me into her chamber and lifts the floorboard beneath which she hides her magical tools and such. First, she removes the black satin bundle containing her amathe and other tools. Then bundles of herbs, a handful of stakes, and a large bottle of holy water. The wooden floor devours her arm as she reaches way, way under. Her tongue sticks out in concentration as she fumbles beneath the wooden planks. A moment later, she pulls out two books: a large leather-bound book with parchment pages, and an ancient tome, small like a prayer book with a worn leather cover. "My notes through the years and our coven's book of prophecy. Let's have a look, shall we?"

"Did you see how fast he moved, Fanny? Like just disappeared. Why aren't I that fast? Perhaps he is the actual Protector and I'm the impostor." My heart falls a few inches in my chest. I'm not sure I want all the danger and trauma all the time, but it does make for a meaningful life. If I wasn't really The Protector, all I'd ever be was Lord FussyPants's wife, and I want more than that. Even if I'm not The Protector, I shall travel at least. Mother cannot make me marry anyone.

Fanny soothes my worries: "Don't be silly, Nicole. You're THE Hawthorn. You're THE Protector."

"Yes, well, perhaps he's a Hawthorn, too. It is a fairly common name, after all. Well, at least not uncommon."

"True. But the Hawthorn of the prophecy must be a descendant of John Hathorne, remember? What are the odds of that. Honestly!"

"All right, but something is off with him, Fanny. He has some sort of supernatural power. That's obvious. If not a ghost, maybe some kind of demon. Maybe he's a vampire, too! That would be my luck! What's it with me and vampire boys?" Thankfully Fanny didn't hear that comment or she's ignoring it because I think I just admitted that I fancied this masked man and I know nothing about him. Really, Nickie, I chide myself. You should know better after learning your lesson with Ashe. No more dark, mysterious boys. They're exciting, but they're trouble. A few hours of ecstasy and thrill is not worth the weeks of agony. Remember, that level of elation has a cost.

"Ah, here it is," Fanny says. Yes. Definitely ignoring my questions about boys. Just as well. She reads, "The Hawthorn Legacy. A child shall be born on Midwinter Night, and it shall grow to become The Protector and, on its seventeenth birthday, inherit the powers of the damned to fight and defeat them, driving them back to the darkness."

"Yes? And?"

Fanny flips the page to the next one, then the next, looking up and down the parchment on each one before going back to the first. She reads the passage again, and then a third time. "That's all it says, my dove. Just says 'a child,' not a girl, but my coven foretold of the event on that Yorkshire moor. They had visions of a female Protector dating back generations. Of course, it's you. It must be you." Fanny continues reasoning through it. I'm not sure if she's trying to convince herself or me. "You have all the powers. You were conceived on Beltane! The original coven who laid the curse said The Protector would be female, to avenge all those witches harmed by your ancestor. They dreamed it, but"—she flipped the pages back and forth again, as if something would magically appear on them in the past few minutes—"but there's nothing about that here. Nor does it say only one, which I knew. There have been others, of course, but not for generations! Is it possible there are two of you now? That would be indeed interesting!"

"It would be rather nice not to be alone in this, to have a brother in arms, as it were. More of my friends would be dead if it weren't for him, and he might be if it weren't for me. We could watch out for each other. Help each other fight this war. Enough vampires and the rest of the baddies roam the earth to go around. Supernatural and human, it seems. We must find all we can about this Masked Protector."

"Yes. Yes, indeed. We must. I shall send a telegram to my coven first thing in the morning about the aetherial call tomorrow night. It's too intricate to telegram it all, not to mention costly and rather sensitive, as well. Can you imagine me at the telegraph office telling them to send a message about vampires and ghosts and the like? Ha! They'd take me straight to Bedlam, they would! So, yes, telegram with the time to be ready for the aetherial call. After your parents leave for the factory tomorrow, you go talk with Conrad about the confession plan. We'll meet near St. Saviour's to see what we can find. I bet we'll discover some interesting things in his rectory."

"Perfect. Let's get me dressed for dinner. We'll go hunting again tonight for at least a few hours. Still so full of energy, Fanny. I'll see if I can track down some more members of that vampire clan. See what information I can get out of them."

"Yes, I think that's best. Not to Southwark, though. Not to St. Saviour's."

"Oh, no. Like I said, I don't fancy being alone with that man again."

"You be careful, my lamb."

"I will. I'll also continue to hone those skills, practice what we went over last night. I fell weeks behind in my despair, but I'm back now. If this masked man is a Protector as well, he's exhibiting skills that exceed mine. That will not do. You did once say I would be able to move as fast as a vampire. It's past time that I was able to do so, and I'll be pushing myself tonight.

"Thank you, Fanny," I say and kiss her temple.

"What's that for?" she says, holding my kiss against her cheek. Her eyes are all misty with emotion.

"For everything! For not giving up on me. For being here for me when I needed you. For training me and pushing me just enough. I'll be a remarkable woman because of your example."

"Oh, my dove, you are already a remarkable woman."

Pulling my goggles out from under my pillow and down over my eyes, I take a comical heroic stance and exclaim, "Off to hunt vermin, my dear. Watch out leeches, here I come!"

Fanny giggles at my antics. "Yes, my love, right after your supper."

It's nice to make her laugh and to be silly again. I sit down at my dressing table so that Fanny might fix my hair for dinner. Then, I've much work to do.

CHAPTER THIRTEEN

IN WHICH NICKIE NICK
IS SURROUNDED BY BONES

February 16, 1881

"Here's the plan," I explain, keeping my voice low even though it's not necessary in the bustling afternoon. Habit, I suppose.

The Borough Market adjacent to St. Saviour's is especially busy on Wednesdays, it seems. I've never seen so many people in one place before, save that time outside Westminster Abbey when I saved the Queen from becoming a mesmerized zombie. That already seems like someone else's life. So much has happened, and I've changed, I think. Grown. No longer the same girl who saved the Queen. Now a woman determined, wiser from loss. Hardened by despair. The wicked will pay for every tear.

So many carriages clutter the street that one can hardly maneuver through on foot. The smells are horrendous. Mounds of horse dung piled up here and there while boys in bright red shirts dash to and fro, trying to scoop it up and out of the way before the next carriage comes and runs them over.

Hordes of people, all carrying baskets or buckets or sacks. On foot or with wagons, some riding, others pulling. Some horse driven, others on horseback. A mother scolds her child for stealing an apple, shouting that they can't afford such things. Grimy, thin waifs go from person to person, group to group with their hands out, hoping for a penny or a crust of bread. Dapper gentlemen pose in their fancy new duds, careful to stay out of the way of the splashing horse manure. Prompt clerks rush to and fro with pencils behind their ears and tablets in their hands, counting shipments as they're rolled in off the docks just a block away, marking down number and figures in their record books. The dirt smudged cheeks of the flower girl hold a plastered smile as she displays her pretty pansies for sale.

Fanny, Conrad, and I do our best to muddle through the crowds, avoiding the street as much as possible, stepping into it only when a vendor's cart is pushed too far out, then making sure we're stepping on only cobblestones and not anything the horses dropped behind them. Of course, the ghosts of Southwark are mixed in all these people, and I can no longer tell which is alive and which is but a specter.

We make it into the church's courtyard and are finally able to talk. Thankfully, the villainous vicar is inside and not loitering out here. Absolving his flock, no doubt.

"Right. You'll go in for confession, Conrad, and make it good, believable. It will be horrid, as I've warned you, so lead up with some more benign sins first. Remember we're nearby if it's too dreadful. Leave if you feel like you're in danger, of course. Keep alert and safe. Fanny and I will sneak into the rectory and see what we can find. Give us at least fifteen minutes. Can you keep him busy for that long?"

"Easy," Conrad says. His eyes twinkle, and a blush rises in my cheek, which then transfers to his.

"Excellent," I say, shaking that off. "Something is really off with that vicar, aside from his buggering innuendos. His entire countenance changed when I mentioned the ghosts. He knows something. He's doing something, and I want to know what it is."

"Are you sure about this, my lamb?" Fanny asks. "This is so dangerous, and you've had quite the time of it lately."

"Fanny! They're in pain! You know we have to do something if we can, right? You're the one who said we had to come back here, remember? You and I both know we have to help these poor souls."

"Yes. I know, and I applaud your strength. Please, let me do a spell to help protect us, at least until I can talk with my coven tonight. Please. Something.."

"No, Fanny. You said yourself, if magic is afoot then he might feel that, like a rift in his magical field or something. Then he'll know something is amiss. For now, he knows nothing about me or us. This is as safe as houses."

"You have your amulet of protection on all the same?"

"I never take it off. You know that." Grasping it beneath my blouse, I smile warmly at her. I feel absence of the key to Ashe's heart, as well, and I'm really glad it's gone. What's done is done.

§

After parting ways with Conrad in the main nave, surreptitiously watching while Benedict led Conrad into the confessional and disappeared behind the second red curtain himself, Fanny and I tiptoe past the candle stand and donation bin and make our way along the north wall of the glorious sanctuary and stopped just before John Gower's memorial in its bright reds and greens, whose effigy draws the eye in this otherwise grey chamber. Dressed in robes of red and gold, the celebrated poet presses his wooden hands together in prayer for all eternity. Angels watch over him from above, hovering in fields of red and green. Gower's head rests on books and beneath his feet, a black lion protects the poet's resting figure. To the left of this and almost directly across the nave from my beloved bard, a wooden door set inside a Gothic arch stands ajar. The sign reads: Private Vicarage.

"This must be it," I whisper to Fanny. We slip through without notice, as the few inside the church on a Wednesday afternoon are focused on their own prayer. I expect to find a hallway leading to another part of the building, or even an adjacent building, but on the other side of that heavy oak door is a small empty alcove with the top of a stone staircase leading down into darkness. Since there's no other choice, we descend. I haven't been in many rectories, granted, but I thought they were separate quarters—and not underground. The walls are wet and furry, covered in moss. Sounds of trickling water fill the otherwise-silent descent, and my hands trail along the soft, damp stone to keep my bearings. It's not even updated with gaslight down here, which might be just as well. One wouldn't want the underside of a church filling with gas if the flame goes out unattended. It's so dark, I can't see anything besides blackness and tiny points of light from periodic candle sconces situated about ten feet apart. The candles burn so low they only illuminate their waxen perch and a small spot of stone behind them, and then more darkness. My toes feel the edge of each step before proceeding to the next one. No telling how far this goes down. It's like we're descending into hell. A chill ripples through my entire body as some kind of draft drifts up from below, making the sparse candlelight flicker. For all I know, it was one of the ghosts out for a stroll.

"Strange place for a rectory," Fanny says to me, but this is where the worn, wooden sign above pointed.

I only hope Conrad can keep the villainous vicar busy long enough for us to find something. We shan't be too long once we find his vicarage. I hope. I wouldn't want to be in this place one second longer than necessary.

"Are you sure this is the way?" I ask, a little nervous about how far we've already descended, and they just keep going down. "Perhaps we're heading to the catacombs."

"I know as much as you do, my lamb," she says in a voice almost as shaky as mine.

Not reassuring.

We finally reach the bottom of the stairs and, sure enough, the walls are lined with open graves. Macabre grins mock us from every angle. Their vacant eyes dance in the dim, flickering candlelight to which my eyes must've finally adjusted. There is no more light, but I can make out more detail. I rather wish I couldn't with these deathly grins surrounding us. Stacked four high, the thin, rectangles dug out of the wall each contains a complete skeleton. Some wrapped in decaying strips of cloth, while others have clumps of hair here and there on their skull. In between each column of graves is a large cross made out of human skulls set into the dirt wall. Unsettling to say the least.

The entire circular room is lit with two solitary candles, one at three o'clock, if the staircase is twelve, and one at nine. On the opposite side of this strange chamber from the staircase, at six o'clock, is another wooden door, cracked open ever so slightly.

We don't waste a moment. If we're caught down here, there will be no explaining it, and it took far longer to get down here than I ever would've expected.

Fanny pushes the old door open. Its hinges squeal, scaring a family of rats out of their dark cubby. The piercing sound and sudden movement sends them scuttling over our toes and across the floor. We both hold our breath, waiting to be discovered. Nothing.

A few moments more. Nothing.

We're so far beneath the church we probably could scream and no one would hear.

That's a disturbing thought.

We slip inside Father Creepy Face's quarters, which are quite sparse. Perhaps a condition of his order. The room feels dirty. Vile, somehow tainted. I push images from my mind, as they're pelting me one after another. Images of his sins and transgressions. The screams and moans and pleas for mercy. My stomach turns, but with all my will I push them out and focus on the job at hand.

A copy of *The Bible* lays open to Leviticus on his nightstand, which is nothing more than a three-legged milking stool. There's a single bed, more like a straw mattress on a wood platform, low to the ground. Burlap pillow and sheets, used, no doubt, to deny the flesh comforts and punish oneself for original sin and others. I've read about the priests who whip themselves and purge the flesh. Mortification of the flesh and self-flagellation, it's called. Popular among church radicals about five centuries ago, if memory serves, but judging from these surroundings and the black leather whip leaning in the corner, I think this priest practices it often. At least, I hope he uses that to punish himself and not others.

I move to get a closer look, and my boot scrapes the stone floor. Brushing the dirt aside with my toes, more stones are hidden beneath the prolific dirt. Billows of dust waft up, and I cough and wave my hand in front of my face to disperse the cloud.

"Shhh!" Fanny scolds. "Don't leave tracks!" She points to the cleared-off space on the stones beneath my feet, brows furrowed. I cover my mouth and with my toes arrange the dirt evenly back over the stones.

A leather-bound journal sits open atop a simple desk in one corner. Piles of paper and parchment and more journals and bound books surround it. Quite cluttered, and in such low light. I find it difficult to imagine anyone reading or writing in these conditions. An unlit candlewick peeks out from the top of a wax mountain growing on a silver chamberstick. We can't risk lighting it. Luckily, just enough light filters in from the cata-comb room to read the words on the open page.

"Fanny," I call out, "look at this!"

She had been looking at the books on his makeshift bookshelves: wooden planks fit into a dug-out cubby, much like the graves outside, only larger and filled with books instead of bones. This whole place is morbid. "Fascinating reading material for a vicar," Fanny says.

"Leave it for a minute. Have a look at this diary. It's open to the latest entry, from this morning, looks like. It's about me, Fanny!"

That gets her attention. She joins me and looks over my shoulder.

"*16 February 1881*

Strange but beautiful girl came to confession yesterday. Second time I saw her in the past week. Strange, this one. Strange and very enticing. Yes, indeed."

Pausing, I shudder. "Ew!" Shivers run down my back at the thought. This man thinks about me in that—I can hear him licking his lips as he wrote this. Ugh! Although, it doesn't come as a surprise, especially after the way he behaved during confession yesterday. One does wish one was wrong about these things. One tries to excuse it away, understand. He's a man of the cloth, after all. He's to be trusted—revered, even—but even as I think these thoughts, I recognize them as the lies of innocence, thoughts of a child. Things that parents tell children because they desperately want to believe themselves. They tell their children that those in such position are true and trustworthy. Safe. But they know, as I do, that their station and the belief of piety masks their true nature all the better in more cases than anyone cares to admit. One just needs to pick up the newspaper. Always a vicar or trusted politician or an esteemed professor or other respected leader—scoundrels. Power hungry, lustful brutes, all.

Poor Conrad. I wonder how he's faring upstairs. I never should've subjected him to such a vile creature. The sudden urge to take a long, hot, cleansing bath comes over me, just to wash away this sense of filth and violation, if nothing else.

Ugh!

"There's a power about her. A power that is somewhat magic and somewhat supernatural. I can feel it, and before long I shall truly feel it in every conceivable way. She's full of sin and lust, this one. I can feel that, too. I shall absolve her again and again, purify her. She is in desperate need of a good, hard cleansing. She saw my angels and had the audacity to call them ghosts and even ask me about them in the confessional. Spawn! I foolishly froze, but I don't believe she noticed. Must keep a close eye on her. She mustn't learn about BESSIE. Yes, a very, very close watch until I can absolve her good and proper. Must keep her mouth shut,

and I know just the thing to stuff it. I shall ensure she never speaks again. Yes, indeed.

"Must keep an eye on me? Ew! And threats, too! This isn't fun, Fanny. Mad psychiatrists are one thing, but Pilkington was at least honorable in his most dishonorable and psychotic way. Not improper, at least! Oh, for a vampire to kill. That's simple. Clean. Easy by comparison. This is far too complicated and sordid, and I don't want to be here anymore. Let's get out of here. Now."

"I couldn't agree more, but there is more to discover. One more minute, dear. There's a book here worth studying." She moves back to the bookshelf and takes a large leather-bound tome from the bottom shelf. Judging from its worn and torn skin cover, ancient. Gold leaf lettering says something in Latin, I believe. *Legmegeton.* As soon as Fanny opens it, a rush of cold air brushes by my cheeks, and I catch my breath. "Oh, my!" Fanny exclaims.

"Did you feel that, too?"

"Certainly. This is a powerful book about necromancy, raising the dead. A grimore of the darkest, blackest magical arts. Controlling the dead and demons, and maybe even ghosts. This isn't the only one, but this is by far the most dangerous. The lost book of Solomon if I'm not mistaken."

"Who's Solomon."

"My, that's a long story, love. King Solomon of Israel. Prophet to some. Heretic to others. Magician and alchemist. Rather a scoundrel, as it's said he had 700 wives and 300 concubines, not to mention authoring the Song of Solomon or Song of Songs, a long, rather disturbing, erotic love letter to his God, Yahweh. Additionally, through magic and alchemical practices, he wrote texts outlining all the demons by name and had detailed rituals on how to conjure and control them to one's will. The practice of which is known as exorcism, so not the same use of the word as we know. Dark, evil stuff, my dove. Strange book for a vicar's collection, no?"

"Quite. Let's leave. Please. I do not wish to be caught in his quarters. Now even less than before."

"Couldn't agree more. He's a dangerous man, my dove, in more ways than one. We must get out of here now."

"I'm right behind you."

Fanny snaps the book shut and tucks it under her arm.

"You're taking it with you?" I ask. "What if he notices it's gone?"

"Even so, he doesn't know we've been here. We must learn more if we're to help those poor spirits you keep seeing, and more importantly, stop this man from whatever evil he's up to. There's no doubt anymore, love. None whatsoever. He's up to no good, indeed."

"Fine. Let's just hope we get out of here alive and unscathed so we can."

We slip out the door, and I pull it closed to the exact place it was when we arrived. The squealing iron pierces the silence again, but we don't wait to see if anyone heard this time. Decorum alone keeps us from sprinting up the stairs.

After a quick peek into the main nave, we slide out and stand reverently in front of Gower's memorial, heads bowed until we're sure it's safe to make our way out the front. We cross over to my beloved bard, reclining in peaceful dreams, and make our way along the south wall with our backs turned to the confessionals.

Conrad storms out of the confessional, shouting, "You're a real sick bugger, know that?"

He dashes out of the church, which tells me we haven't much time. Fortunately, the front doors aren't too far off, so we follow Conrad through the tall wooden door without a moment to spare. Just before the door met with its brother, I glance over my shoulder to see Father Benedict step out of the confessional and buckle his belt.

The smirk on his lips will haunt me for the rest of my days.

CHAPTER FOURTEEN

IN WHICH NICKIE NICK
FIGHTS IN HYDE PARK

February is a miserable time to be The Protector in London. Well, February is a miserable time to be anything in London. It's bitter. It's cold. It's grey. The wind is relentless. When it rains, which, let's face it, is almost constant, it feels like tiny icicles pelting my cheeks. I wrap my long, leather coat around me and face tonight's hunt.

Still, with each passing night I enjoy the hunt even more. After a few moments, my rage warms me and flushes my cheeks, and I no longer feel the cold rain. I smell the vampires, and as revolting as they smell, it is sweet to me because of the rush that follows. Even now, with so little sleep, I feel energized. Since Edwin died, the only solace I find is in work, the hunt to stop these vermin. Another innocent will not die because of my negligence. Every waking moment I prepare mentally, even while playing the part of the dutiful daughter to my parents, even when physically in training sessions with Fanny. It all turns visceral out here on the hunt.

I sleep only as I must to stay fresh, a mere four or so hours last night. I need so little with the powers of The Protector. If I must appear as a perfect daughter, albeit still avoiding posh parties as much as possible, train in the afternoon while mother and father are at the factory, and discuss pleasantries and frivolous matters over dinner and dessert, there is no time for sleep anyway. The catnap by the fire in the evening after I had my fill of apple tarts helped a bit. Mother doesn't even scold me for my sugary indulgences since I lost a good stone in my former despair. She encourages me. Father and I read together in the parlour after dinner, but I nodded off over my book. Father nudged me and whispered, "It's time to sleep, my peach. Go up to bed, and I'll see you in the morning."

Father thought I did exactly that, but here I am while they're cozy in their beds. That catnap empowered me to hunt for the night, to eliminate the kind of rubbish that killed my friend and broke my heart.

Every time I feel a stake break through that skin and bone barrier, I hear that satisfying squish sound as wood meets dead heart. The whoosh following the explosion into dust is an opiate to me. It's as if I absorb their power and it merges with mine. The sensation is as exciting and addictive as a first kiss, more euphoric than fine dark chocolate. One that I can control.

I not only accept my fate and my duty, I revel in it. My focused anger finds an outlet between their ribs. I will kill every vampire in London. Then England. The Europe. Then the world.

They cannot hide from me.

They will hurt no one else.

I will make sure.

I will not stop until every one of their kind is *ash*.

As if my thought was sent out as a beacon to the undead of London, challenging them to cross me, around the next corner I turn I catch their retched scent. There in the alley, hiding in the dark like the cowards they are, a revolting leech tosses aside a limp form. The smell of blood, which used to make me nauseous, now just fuels my fury.

The monster growls like a rabid dog. Flesh caught in his teeth. Blood dripping down his chin. His fierce eyes lock me into its predatory stare. He's confident—arrogant, more like—as he's just fed. But he has no idea who he's up against.

"Up for an after dinner snack," I say, never blinking.

He growls again.

"Good doggie. Fancy a game of fetch?"

I am getting quite cheeky, aren't I?

He rushes me, but I don't move. At the last moment, a quick step aside has him face-first into the stone corner behind me. His howl echoes off the walls of the buildings.

My laughter does the same.

I run, goading him, and head toward Trafalgar Square.

Best. Game. Ever.

Fierce footsteps come ever closer behind me. I can feel his proximity, his presence. In another instant, too brief to register in a human mind, those footfalls stop at once. He lunges, jumping to tackle me.

Lucky me, so young and spry, I duck.

He sails over me and hits the ground with a dull thud. Somersault after somersault, as our speed was so great, he rolls over and over until the base of a Laneer Lion stops him. This time, before he can recover, I'm upon him. Flinging my coat open, its long tails billowing in the relentless wind, I grab a stake from its loop on my corset and dive into a forward roll. On my feet again, lunging with the momentum, I plant the stake into his heart.

Ahhhh. That crack. That squish. That whoosh.

Three of my favorite sounds.

"Nice work, Nickie."

His voice.

I spin around to see Ashe. Watching me.

My gorge rises. Anxiety takes over in something between fear and anger and hatred and confusion. It was here we shared our first kiss. That perfect moment in time, when everything stopped. Now, after everything, how dare he come back here of all places. How dare he.

"What are you doing here?" I question cautiously.

"I check on you from time to time." He steps closer to me, and I step back. Not even in physical proximity will he get close to me again. Never again.

"Well don't. You're not welcome," I say and put my palm up between us, illustrating that point. To come back to the place of our first kiss, to accost me here. The nerve.

"Nickie," he says in a wounded voice. Quiet, barely more than a breath. Shame sits on his brow, and he looks down at the ground. The image of him kissing me returns, and I angrily push it away and replace it with the image of his cowardly goodbye letter. I replace it with the image of my bedchamber, the only thing I saw for weeks in agonizing heartache. In fact, I've had enough. I turn to leave, but he continues, "I'm sorry to hear about Edwin."

I stammer. "You—you—you're sorry? You're sorry to hear about Edwin? Edwin is dead because of you! Get out of here now before you face the same fate as your brother of dust there." I will not give him an inch, not after what he did. Not after what I endured, and now with losing Edwin, too. Ashe will be held accountable if by nothing else than my words.

He shoves his hands in his pocket and kicks a stray stone across the square. He doesn't look at me but rather over to the left, to the place he kissed me, and says, "I was hoping we could talk."

"Talk! About what?"

"Well, about us."

The absurdity of that statement forces a laugh from my wrenching gut—a bark of sound in the relative silent night. Shocked, I step a few paces back. "There is no us, Ashe. You left, remember?"

"I was rash, a fool." His eyes find mine, and they plead with me for something. Mercy, perhaps. Forgiveness. Understanding. I have none of those things to give, at least not to him.

"That's quite true," I say. "Excuse me." I turn to leave again, but he's in front of me—in a blink—stopping me with his body. His hands square my shoulders, and his eyes penetrate my soul. They violate my sense of safety, my space, my clear indication that I wished him to keep his distance.

But I don't look away from those intense black eyes. I clench my teeth and shoot daggers back at him with mine.

How dare he touch me.

"Please, Nicole," he says and pulls me closer. "Just a few minutes."

My palm pushes against his chest, keeping him from getting any closer and telling him to move away. He doesn't. "I have nothing to say to you, Ashe. Nothing you say can change what you've done. Nothing can change what's happened since."

"Forget us, then." He throws up his hands and turns from me, pacing back and forth. "There's something else. Danger. Conrad told me about the priest,"—another betrayal. How dare Conrad speak of me to Ashe.—"and I checked him out. I'm worried about you. He's dangerous, Nickie. Really dangerous. You can't be toying with that kind of power."

"Dangerous? Please, Ashe. I kill vampires, like you. I fight demons. I take down mad psychiatrists, and you're talking to me about danger? This is my job. This is my duty, my calling. I was born to do this, and I'm well equipped and trained to do just that. What am I to fear from a creepy priest?"

"You couldn't have taken down Pilkington alone. I was there, remember? Fanny, too. Remember how it was?" The tenderness on his face almost makes me falter, but I clench my jaw and hold my ground.

"Actually, all I remember is the agony of the past two months. Unable to eat. Unable to think. Wanting to die. Forcing sleep for momentary reprieve. No one will make me feel like that again. Especially not you."

Shaking the nostalgia off, he says, "Fine, but that vicar is playing with powers that you cannot comprehend?"

"Is that so? Well, I have help, even without you, Ashe. I have friends—people who love me who, you know, didn't leave me for weeks in agony. People I can count on to not abandon me when times get tough or scary."

"Nickie," he starts, but he says it to my back, as I'm already walking away. After a few steps, I'm actually running away, the fury rising with each new step.

§

The nerve. Any remaining pain over the love lost turns into fury. My boots hit the cobblestones in angry strides, and I pull the goggles off my face, propping them up on the bill of my flat cap. I don't care if anyone recognizes me tonight. What are the odds, anyway? I storm toward Westminster and my beloved clock tower at first, but then turn north. Heading somewhere, anywhere, dark and isolated.

I breathe fire. My head is an ocean of confusion and fog, and I walk.

I walk and walk and walk, without direction. Without a goal. I just walk. Turning here. Avoiding a galloping carriage there. Without thought, just second nature. London whips by me as I stride. Lights and people and carriages and horses blur around me. Ignoring cat calls and shouts about my Protector outfit and the shape of my legs and ankles and the like.

Somewhere in the back of my mind I decide the next man to say anything similar will have a stake right through his heart, human or vampire or whatever flavor of monster he is.

I'm done.

Stars, hide your fires…

Before I know it, I'm on the banks of The Serpentine in Hyde Park, and all is quiet. Away from the bulk of after-dark movement in this vast city, few people are in the park at this time of night, especially in the cold of February.

The tip of my nose is likely frozen. My ears hurt, chilled to the cartilage in the frigid wind. My lips and cheeks chapped. I watch my breath exhale into a vapor. Breathing in, the crisp air fills my nostrils, throat, then lungs, and I feel each breath as if it were my first ever. Finally calm and clear-headed, my Protector warning system deep in my gut calls, pulling me north. Further north. I welcome this new focus, this new goal pressing me forth. Killing a vampire or two is exactly what I need tonight.

Lead me forward. Lead me on.

Next to the Palace Gardens, lovely even in February, I stop and listen on the northwest edge of Kensington Gardens, right before Bayswater Road. A rat scurries from one side of the path to the other. The groan of an indigent man follows. The rodent disturbed his slumber in the shrubbery. Such poverty literally on the doorstep of Kensington Palace's opulence gives me pause, but then I hear it. The faint hiss of a leech, a gasp of its victim, the smell of wormwood and, then, copper. Blood. I rip out the compass, and the needle spins around and lands pointing southwest towards the center of the park on the far side of the pond. Turning, I sprint toward it, every ounce of focus on that scent.

There it is. Feeding.

"Ahem." I clear my throat and stand, hands on hips, tapping my foot. "Pardon me," I say. "Terribly sorry to interrupt, but I rather fancy a fight. Don't you?"

The vampire looks up and snarls at me, still grasping tightly to its prey. Blood covers its mouth and chin and neck. Ugh. What vile creatures, indeed. How did I love one?

"Let him go," I say. "I'm much tastier fruit, don't you think?" Craning my neck to one side, I expose my neck, taunting it. It's rather fun being so cheeky.

"Please! Help!" The man says. "Please!"

"Silence," the vampire snarls then casts him aside. "Stay there," he commands the man, now seated in the grass holding the fresh wound in his neck.

"All right," the man concedes, glassy eyed. Compelled, it seems. Indeed.

"You do look rather sweet, my dear." He licks the blood off his lips, wipes his chin, and then sucks the blood from each finger one at a time. "Come a little closer. I'm safe. I'm a gentleman. I won't hurt you." He's trying to force his will on me as well. Once again, I'm thankful for Fanny's amulet. He's rather human still, so he must not be that old. The faint moonlight reveals the symbol burned in his head.

Lucky me.

"So. A member of the same cult that killed my friend, I see. Perfect," I chide and reach into my coat for a stake. The feel of wood in my palm is one of comfort, protection. With a stake in my hand, I know I am The Protector. With every fiber of being, I know. "You're going to answer some questions for me, you are."

"Is that right?" He steps closer to me with a quizzical look, wondering why his mind games aren't working on me, no doubt. "You're she, aren't you. I've heard about you. Yes, my master has warned me."

"I'm all fluttery inside," I say, twirling my long braid through my fingers. "Your master has been talking about little ol' me? Stop it! I'm blushing." Then to the man on the ground, "Go. Now."

"No. Stay," the vampire contradicts. "I'll save you for dessert after I have this succulent main course." He lunges at me, and I step out of the way causing him to tumble a few times beside me. That move works far too well, really.

I could've ended it right there like I did back at Trafalgar Square, but I fancy more of a fight now. It will be cathartic, I think, especially after the run-in with Ashe.

He jumps to his feet, more nimble than a cat, but not more than me. These leeches haven't been trained to fight, as they normally just lurk and lunge and feed and kill. He comes at me, and I let him get his hands around my throat, for an instant.

Two quick jabs to the face, and I feel his nose give with the second one. His hands tend to his broken nose instead of my throat, and I smile.

Yes. This will be quite cathartic, indeed.

"My nose," he cries. "Ow! You'll pay for that!"

He swings with his right. Sloppy and relatively slow. I duck and come up with an upper cut to the jaw with my right. While his head is thrown back from that, I spin on my stake heel and kick with the other foot. It lands square in his stomach. Doubled over now, I finish with a jump kick to the jaw, sending him reeling back into a group of gathered goslings, who take flight, squawking as they go.

In that moment, crumbled in pain, he loses his hold on his dinner. "What's happening?" the man cries, then looks at the geese floating away peacefully on the glass water of the Round Pond, mesmerized by their tranquility.

I whip my head back to him, hands still up protecting my face in front, and say, "Get out of here. Quick, before he gets back up. Find a doctor for that neck wound. Now! Go!"

After a moment frozen in a fearful stupor, the man scampers away, and I turn back to the vampire just in time to jab as his charging form, sending him sprawling to the ground. "You're making this too easy, really," I say. "I can do this all night. Do you want me to keep this up or are you ready to talk?"

He wipes fresh blood off of his face. His blood. He's not used to being smeared with his own blood.

"What's that symbol on your head? Who put that there?"

But he doesn't speak. He growls again and charges. This time when I throw a punch at him, he ducks and grabs me around the waist. I hit the ground hard beneath him, his form pinning me down. He's heavy and strong.

"Not so cheeky now, are you, Missy?" he says. He's got my legs pinned. His knees dig into my thigh muscles, which scream in pain. Huge hands hold my arms at the wrists rendering me utterly immobile.

He laughs over me. Blood from his nose drips, drips, drips onto my face, and I fight the urge to be sick. His twisted face, scarred not only by the symbol on his head but also now with the damage I just caused, delights in my helplessness, and I admit to myself that I might have been a bit too arrogant in this fight.

One moment can change everything. One decision can define one's life. Perhaps not cowardice for me, but definitely foolishness.

"So, you're The Protector," he hisses. "Pretty little thing, aren't you? I bet your blood is exhilarating. I've heard stories, of course, but I've never had the pleasure."

"What's that symbol?" I repeat.

"You're about to die, foolish girl. Slowly, too. I'll just drink enough to make you weak and me strong. Then,

I'm going to take you back to our place. You'll like it there. Deep underground and peaceful. Well, for us, anyway. I don't suppose it will be too peaceful for you once we have you down there. Plenty of lonely vampires would love a go at you, along with your powerful blood. I suspect we can keep you alive and kicking—oh yes, the kicking—for at least a month. If we're really careful, maybe two."

"What's that symbol?" I don't know what else to do but stall and hope for an opening, for something to distract him. It's my only chance. "If you're going to kidnap me and eventually kill me anyway, you can tell me. Right?"

"It's part of our duty to Father. He marks us after we demonstrate our loyalty to him. He promises us power and ultimate absolution if we do his will. Immortality is ours, of course, but our kind of immortality can end, as some of my brothers have discovered when you and that other one got hold of them. Then, we have a chance at peace, since most weren't given a choice for this life. Now we have one–through Father. He reconnects us with our lost souls, pulls them from the aether and ties them to us through this." His eyes cross rather comically as they point up to the symbol branded on his forehead. "He absolves us, so when we die, we will sit at the right hand of Satan, ruling over heaven and hell."

"Satan doesn't rule over heaven," I say. That's right. Be argumentative. It doesn't matter what you say, just stall and hope for an opening.

"God and Satan, foolish, naive girl, are one in the same. Now. Dinner." His lips pull back from those pointed teeth, even more than just the two canines. They're all pointed at his age. He must be at least a century, maybe two, judging from his state of transformation.

All my muscles tense at once, and I thrust up my hips, hoping to buck him off, but he just laughs at me. "Yes! Oh! Please keep gyrating like that. Oh. Definitely taking you back to our lair." Then with a ferocious snarl, he rears back and strikes like a cobra. I shut my eyes tight, willing this moment to end, hoping he kills me here and now. Then, it will be over. No more heartache. No more struggle. No more pain.

No pain.

Wait, there's no pain.

His teeth don't pierce my neck. Instead, I hear: Crack. Squish. Whoosh, and I have a face full of dust. I spit the vile stuff out of my mouth and wipe it from my eyes, as I'm suddenly unencumbered and free to do so. Looking up, I see him.

The moonlight catches an auburn lock, and the masked man says, "Hey there, Nickie. Nice to see you again."

CHAPTER FIFTEEN

IN WHICH NICKIE NICK
TALKS TO THE MASKED MAN

"Why did you disappear the other night?" I ask the masked man and take his proffered hand. After I'm back on my feet, I brush myself off and wonder if I'm supposed to feel embarrassed at being caught about to die. In fact, I'm rather shocked I don't feel embarrassed. I feel oddly calm with him. He doesn't answer my first question, so I try another, "And why do you wear that mask?"

"Same reason you wear those goggles, I suspect." At least he responded to that one. How very mysterious.

His voice is deep, like a soft cello. Not growly, gravely deep. Not gruff baddie deep. Just lovely. Perfect. A cello, yes. Like a Bach cello. Like hearing his Suite for Solo Cello No. 1 in G Major, my favorite. The sound of joy and sorrow and love and pain all wrapped up in a single sustained chord.

His hair is the color of a cinnamon stick and smells like the faintest hint of heather. A few ginger locks fall over his mask, almost reaching his eyes. That black mask accentuates his piercing green eyes, and I feel at once captivated. A glorious rose blossoms in my heart, at least that's what it feels like. An opening, of sorts. Perhaps an invitation for love to return.

No, I chide myself. Not again. Turning away from those enchanting green eyes and the way his inviting lips turn up into a half-smile when he looks at me— not too full, but not too thin either...they're perfect—I begin walking away from him, determined to focus on anything other than him. I take note that the vampire's original victim got away. Good. Hope he found the medical attention he needed.

The masked man walks beside me and doesn't say a word. I can feel his eyes on me, and I so want to look back into them. Instead, to be safe and protect my fragile heart, I talk about work. There are a few things I want to know anyway. Best not get all fluttery before I know him. Remember how that turned out last time. "You said you were The Protector. That's rather odd, actually. How is that possible, since I'm The Protector? I fulfilled the prophecy, The Hawthorn Legacy. Fanny and I, we checked and double-checked. No mistake. I'm The Protector." I test him, knowing full well there is a remote—albeit unlikely—possibility. Really, what are the odds?

"I fulfilled the prophecy, too."

"You were born on Midwinter Night?" My voice is full of disbelief and perhaps a touch of mockery and absurdity, for this is just that. This is absurd, all just ridiculous nonsense. I stop and face him, square on. Now his eyes don't captivate me at all. I look into them and challenge him with a rather harsh stare.

He doesn't falter.

"Yes. Just over seventeen years ago," he says and blinks. His expression is that of not, like there is no emotion there, just blank. Rather odd, really.

"So was I." My eyes search and study his face, trying to read what's behind that empty look. What's behind that mask?

"I know," he says and his full lips turn up into that half smile again. Now his face is full of expression, that of amusement or affection, perhaps. Hard to tell.

Our ambling walk has taken us out of Kensington Gardens. We're now in Bayswater, walking amongst the tall white buildings in this area. They glow aethereal, ghostly between the gaslight below and moonlight above, like huge white cliffs along Leinster Gardens, shining in the darkness.

I find it rather unsettling that he knows about me and I don't know about him. In fact, that's just the thing to ask. "How do you know about me if I don't know about you?" He looks down and shuffles his feet to and fro. Something about that movement is so familiar. Something about him, too. "What's your name?" I ask, since, he, again, doesn't answer my first question. Curious.

"I must keep my identity secret."

"Who am I going to tell? All this mystery, and for what? How am I supposed to trust a man who wears a mask?"

He's hurt by my words. Something in his face changes, and he turns it away from me, then continues, "I am a descendent of Hathorne, and I do fulfill the prophecy. I am The Protector, or, rather *A* Protector, as it were."

"You're a descendent of John Hathorne as well? So, we're related?" My heart sinks a few inches, despite my resolve against loving again.

"Quite distantly."

It rises again, and perhaps swells just a touch. *Stop that*, I will my heart, my hopes. No good can come of it. Focus, Nickie. Work. Duty. Those poor trapped souls. Vampires. I bring the conversation back to the thing that brought us together in the first place. "So, you've been tracking this vampire clan?"

"Yes, they're called the Clan of Ashen."

My gut clenches in momentary panic. "Ashen? Does this have anything to do with Ashe Tanner?" My stomach turns at his name and the memory of his hands on my shoulder, those violating eyes. Why does everything have to do with Ashe? Ashe this. Ashe that. Ashe Tanner? The Clan of Ashen? Ashes to ashes, dust to dust. Enough Ashe! I'm sick of Ashe!

"The vampire who fought with us last week? No. Nothing to do with him. Why is a vampire fighting with us, by the way? I mean, I've heard of him, some kind of vampire who's not happy he's a vampire so has vowed to kill them or something. Do you know him? Friend of yours?"

Now it's my turn to ignore some questions. "Look, I can't keep calling you the masked man. What's your name? You know mine. It's only fair after all. We're both vampire hunters—apparently both Protectors—so please just tell me. It would make things so much easier. Your secret is safe with me. Again, who would I tell?"

Exasperated, he says, "Simon. All right? My name is Simon." I can hear the blush rise in his cheeks.

"You mean Simon from the south bank? The one I met the other day? Conrad's friend Simon?"

"That's right. See. You do have someone to tell. That could spell a lot of trouble for me by the light of day. I expect you to keep your word."

"But," I say, processing this revelation, "you were with that bully. Buck, was it? How can you be fighting against the forces of evil and darkness and the rest at night if you support a bully like that during the day? Doesn't that just drip of hypocrisy off every side, Simon?"

"I know. Buck and me, we have a history."

"He hurts people, Simon." There is no excuse for supporting a bully, no matter what other good deeds he might have done. None whatsoever.

"When I was growing up, he protected me, in a way—as much as another child could—before he became so mean. He saved me, helped Roger find me when he came looking on the south docks. Roger, my guardian and teacher, taught me about the Prophecy and The Hawthorne Legacy. He knew my father. Julian, Roger said his name was. Told me how they changed the spelling of their name from Hathorne to Hawthorne to distance themselves from the cruel judge, but Julian was also horrible to women. Well, at least to me mum. Story goes, to spite his strict father, Julian lie with me mum, a whore, on Easter, the holiest of days. Me mum couldn't keep me and keep working, so she left me on the doorstep of a church on that cold Midwinter Night in 1863, a newborn babe. I'd rather not talk more about that, though. Roger told me how he cared for me mum when syphilis took her because he had been in love with her since their youth. Her family fell on hard times, Roger said, and she turned to the streets when he was off at University. He never stopped loving her, despite her profession. She told him all about the pious author's son, the one who sired me, and how he bragged about his lineage. How he was sticking it to his father by sticking it to her." Simon's voice catches in his throat as he says the crude words.

"The scoundrel was the great great great grandson of that infernal Judge Hathorne, so I inherited the prophecy. Roger put it all together, then took me in and taught me how to fight, to protect myself, long before the change came over me." He stops for a moment and wipes his eyes. I remain silent, as I don't know what I could say in the face of such a tale. Fanny told me of the writer ancestor, and here is his bastard grandson. No one knew of it.

Simon clears his throat and forces a smile. "I have no doubt I'm alive because of Buck and Roger. So, I feel indebted to Buck now, but he keeps getting worse and worse. I don't want to be around him anymore. I try to minimize the damage, but there's just no talking to him. I'm completely inept. I loved watching you give him a what-for, by the by. That was brilliant!"

"Saved you from what?"

"Not what. Who. I—I'd rather not talk about that." With these words, he turns away as if to hide his scar, although it's covered by his mask. Explains the mask, actually, a recognizable mark like that. From whatever or whomever Buck saved him must have to do with how he got that scar.

"All right," I say. My voice gentle now. Everything else fades away. The mystery. The desire. The curiosity. The only thing that remains is sadness, empathy and compassion for this poor man. "You don't have to tell me."

There is so much pain, and far too much of it is caused by other humans, not these vampires and monsters of nightmares. Human monsters. Evil, violent men. Even if done out of their own pain, I don't understand what there is to gain from hurting another so deeply.

"It's all right, Simon," I say again, and I place my hand on his shoulder in comfort. "You don't have to tell me." Simon sits down on the curb in the darkness, far enough away from the nearest gaslight that his entire face is veiled in shadow. This conversation must've upset him, and he's trying to hide it without being rude. I decide to trust him, and I try to get his mind off his past pain by enlisting his help. "Listen, seeing as how we're both vampire hunters and all, I'd like your advice on a side project."

"Side project?"

"Yes. There is this vicar, Father Creepy Face."

"Father who?"

"Well, his name is Father Benedict, but he is the creepiest person I've ever met. He's the priest at St. Saviour's. He…"—how can I put this delicately—"seems to have a penchant for children."

Simon gasps, veiled in darkness.

"Exactly. Thus, the moniker Father Creepy Face. Plus, he also seems to be controlling a number of ghosts, but I don't know how and I don't know why."

"That's odd," Simon says.

"Yes. These ghosts have spoken to me and pleaded with me to help, but I don't know how. Fanny—my governess, also a witch, you see—is doing some research and consulting her coven up north. Who is your teacher? Roger, did you say? Does he have any experience with ghosts?" After all, he does seem to be far ahead of me in some aspects of vampire hunting and in honing his powers. Perhaps his teacher knows other things, too. He sure filled Simon in more than Fanny did me before I turned. Simon had a great head start in his knowledge and training, no wonder he's so far ahead of me.

"My teacher died long ago." Just as his cello voice held such beauty before, sorrow and loss now fill his song. Every syllable, heavy with tears and regret. So similar to mine when I speak of Edwin. So much pain. The thought of losing Fanny terrifies me. After Ashe and Edwin, I can't imagine losing her. She's been more a mother to me than my own, and it sounds Roger was the same for Simon, especially after being saved from whoever hurt him. He must feel so completely alone. Well, I hope not, now that there are two of us. Neither of us will have to be alone again.

I search for wise words, anything to give him some comfort, some peace. But there are no words to soothe this kind of loss. The silence hangs between us, as loud as the chimes of my beloved Big Ben. "I'm so sorry to hear," I finally manage just before another moment of screaming stillness would've burst my eardrums.

"Yes, thank you." His words sound as hollow as mine did. One says what one can when there is nothing to say. Perhaps for no other reason than to avoid being swallowed whole by the vacuum of silence, forever lost in nothingness or agony, or the black void Mr. Hannon spoke of. Just as that fiend threatens to consume us again, Simon speaks, "You are no stranger to loss. Are you, Nickie?"

"I want to help these specters," I say, not wanting to tell him about Ashe. He already knows about Edwin, but he doesn't have to know about Ashe. I'm ashamed of falling in love with a vampire. I'm ashamed of falling in love, like a naive fool, expecting some romantic outcome. Instead, I got a broken heart. Ashamed of that, too. Still trite compared to whatever Simon faced that gave him that scar. Love. Ridiculous. Serves me right, no doubt. Really, after all the books I've read. After Poe. I should know better. Another question goes ignored between us, and I answer the question I wish he had asked instead, "It falls under our domain, does it not?

I just don't know how to help. Have you ever seen a ghost?"

"Well, I actually saw one the other night," he responds and stands back up, moving into the light. I find I'm much more comfortable being able to see him again, and not just because of his green eyes.

"You did? Where? What was it like?" His validation feels wonderful, like my entire body fills with light. Every time I bring up the ghosts, I fear being carted away to Bethlehem Asylum for hysteria or some other kind of madness. He saw one, too. Perhaps he really is a Protector like me.

"I'm almost afraid to bring this up with you." He looks at me with pity for a moment, and then consults his pocket watch. "It's late," he says. "Better head back south." His long strides carry him away from me, back toward the park.

My heels clatter on the cobblestones as I scuttle up next to him. "Why are you afraid? We must stick together, you and me. We're the only two like this in the world, after all. That's what Fanny says."

Simon is quiet for a long time again. I find he's a man of few words, really, not like the chatterbox I tend to be. Men do have a tendency to be more reserved, vocally, don't they? Well, Lord Fouffypants Godwyn didn't, but he just so enjoyed hearing himself speak and ramble on about frivolous nothings. Honorable men, however, are rather quieter, I find.

Walking rather quickly now, hands shoved deep into his pockets, he finally finds his voice. "Well," he stammers, "Well—it was—um—your little friend. The one from last week." The shoulder nearest me rises towards his ears, as if he's bracing himself to be hit, but hitting him is the furthest thing from my mind. It's all I can do not to throw my arms around him and pepper his masked face with tiny kisses.

"Edwin? You saw Edwin!" I exclaim. "Edwin! Oh, Edwin! Really? You saw Edwin?" My hands close around his arm, tugging it over and over, partially in my excitement and partially to urge Simon to tell me more.

"Yes," Simon says, looking rather aplomb at my reaction. "And—I mean, *but* he looked very frightened and lost."

"Oh! Poor Edwin!" Now it is I who sinks to the ground, hands covering my face. My head feels full of clouds, thick and mushy. I shake it and shake it side to side, willing it to clear, unwilling to accept Edwin is in pain. "Wasn't it enough that he had to die terrified? Now he cannot even rest in peace?" I fall to the side, just wanting to lie down, to feel safe, but Simon catches me. All that I've pushed away comes rushing back, choking and suffocating me with its dense magnitude. "Will this ever end, Simon? I give it all back! Take the power, take the duty, just give me Edwin. Give me simple things like mudlarking with Conrad and apple tarts and stupid frivolous balls with stupid frivolous suitors. Take it all back, and give me my Edwin back! Please! I can't bear to think of him so cold and alone and scared. Oh, Simon! The darkness! The nothingness that Mr. Hannon spoke of. No! It won't take Edwin, too." I wail into the London night.

"I'm sorry, Nickie. I didn't mean to upset you. I'll help you with the ghosts. We'll figure something out." Simon kneels next to me and keeps a gentle hand on my shoulder. "I understand loss and grief all too well. It will be all right, Nickie. I'm right here, and I won't leave your side. Here," he says, patting his own shoulder after sitting down beside me. "Rest for a moment. It's rather a lot to take in."

Maybe just for a moment. I will gather my strength again, for now. Perhaps for a few moments, I can be weak and sad for myself and for Edwin.

My mind races with questions. Will I see him, too? What is he afraid of? Is he part of the ghosts of Southwark? He did live near there and was buried near there. I'm not sure how it all works, but I know he's scared, and I don't want him to be scared. Oh, Edwin! Poor little Edwin is scared and all alone. Still, I'm rather glad Simon saw him, as I should be able to as well. I'll find him, and I'll make sure he doesn't feel alone. Ever

since I've become The Protector, accepted my destiny—
or more accurately, had it thrust upon me without
choice—my life has been one trauma after another. This
is the darkness I so longed to be a part of. Not so romantic, in the end. Byron and Poe can keep their death and
pain and loss. Ashe can certainly stay in the darkness
alone. I want the light. Despite all the loss and grief,
tiny points of light keep me going. The love of Fanny
and loyalty of Conrad. The hope of seeing Edwin again.
In this moment, I find nothing else matters except that
I will see Edwin again. Soberly, with resolve and relative
calm, I ask, "Where did you see him? Take me to him."

"Around Southwark, now that you mention it."

"Do you think that horrid man is controlling poor
Edwin as well? I didn't see him with the other spirits,
and I looked for him. Half hoping and half fearing I'd
see him, but he wasn't with them. Maybe he's here for
another reason, Simon. Maybe to help us. Oh, please say
that vicious vicar isn't hurting him, too! Please!" I wail
into the London night. A window slides open above us
and a rather cross man sticks his stocking-covered head
out and says, "Shut it! It's before dawn!"

"We better go, Simon says, helping me to my feet. As
soon as we're walking again, he answers my question, "I
don't know if the vicar is controlling him, too. When
I first saw Edwin, I didn't know he was a ghost. I tried
to speak to him, but he just cried and said 'Thank you!

Oh, thank you, sir for talking to me!' Then he ran to me. I opened my arms to embrace him, protect him, but he ran right through me! Quite unsettling, that. Don't wish to repeat that experience again. Ever."

"We must find a way to help him and the others."

"We will, Nickie. We will. Together, we'll find a way. We'll remember how. Just like it was when the powers overcame us. It was the same with you, too, wasn't it? I know it was, yes. We're the same, me and you. You've been learning since the change, but it's more like remembering, isn't it? Wisdom from the ages, as it were."

"Yes! Exactly like that!" I welcome this change of subject. Besides, I can't do anything for Edwin at the present moment. I must regain my strength or I'll be no good to him or the others. I clear my head and concentrate on The Protector inside me. "I have learned so much, leaps and bounds over the past few days now that I'm focused again. I'm not as far along as you are, though. I had, well, an interruption in training, so to speak."

"Yes. Loss, right? Edwin."

How do I tell him that I fell in love with a vampire and was so heartbroken over this man I barely knew that I couldn't function for weeks? He will surely think me a hysterical woman and send me to a padded room in Bedlam! Right next to Pilkington. It's best not to tell, so I keep it general and avoid the specifics.

"Yes, Edwin, and, well—" I stammer. Even in my head it sounds pathetic. "Someone I loved very deeply, and I lost him, too. Back to back, they came. Devastating. You must think me such a weak woman."

"Nonsense," he says and flaps his hand through the air like he's swatting a fly. "I don't hold with all that nonsense about hysteria and the like. Balderdash. In fact, I find women to be incredibly strong to show that emotion everyone says makes them weak. It takes much more courage to do so than to hide it away. Quite cowardly, hiding things away behind a mask." He lowers his head and turns his face away. "I understand how shattering a broken heart can be, Nickie. All too well. Once someone is in our hearts, even for a short while, their loss can render us quite useless for a time." With those last words, he looks at me again, stopping beneath a gaslight, and I think he might kiss me. I wonder if he will. I wonder if I would let him, but he doesn't move to do anything of the sort. His eyes search my face for something. With sadness and regret, he turns away again, then concludes, "Such is the nature of grief."

This man has had much, I'd wager. Such wisdom and kindness shine in his eyes. Yes, that's what I saw there. He removes himself even further from me and looks away, his brow crinkled in shame. His legs stride forward, and he shoves his hands back deep into his pockets. I welcome the silence and reprieve from the upsetting conversation. Yes. Enough of this. No time for sentimentality and such. "Edwin," I say, composing myself and looking forward to what can be done, for dwelling on the past—that which has already happened—is pointless. "We must find a way to help him and the others."

"We will. Fate has brought us together, Nickie, right at this time for a reason. Together we will find a way to stop the Clan of Ashen as well as release the ghosts of Southwark, including Edwin. I promise you that."

Chapter Sixteen

In Which Nickie Nick Learns About Aether Calls

February 17, 1881

Dawn breaks as I slip through the basement window, exhausted. Too much so for the physical exertion of the evening. Must be emotional, indeed. The run-in with Ashe. Learning about poor Edwin. The long conversation with Simon. New, scary feelings. It's all rather draining, isn't it? The worst of which is Ashe's interference, his presumptions. Ashe. Pffft. He left, why won't he just stay away? Keeps popping up here and there, and it's never good.

My toes find footing on the countertop and I turn to greet Fanny like I do every morning, but I'm alone. Nothing and no one is down here but me and piles of dirty laundry. That's odd. She always greets me as I come in, then I regale my tales of conquest and annihilation over a tart or two before I catch a few hours of sleep. That's the new routine. Actually, that's the way it was at the beginning back in December, too.

But today, she's not here.

This concerns me.

I tiptoe up the servant stairs and disappear into my chamber just as I hear the help coming down from above. Close call. I'll have to start getting back a little earlier. I suppose I was thrown off by both Ashe and Simon. Boys, again. Too distracted by boys. I'm better off alone.

After peeling off my Protector outfit, I dip yesterday's washcloth into the basin. The water is ice cold. Fanny didn't even leave me fresh linen or hot water, which is really unlike her. I could use a good washing, but I've been in the cold all night. The only thing I want now is comfort and warmth for a few hours. I'll wait until I wake up in a few hours to wash, then at least I can do so with warm water.

The sheets will get dirty, but I don't care at the moment. That's why we have a laundry, after all.

Bed. Sleep. Perchance to dream.

The cotton nightdress nurtures my skin, which sings to be out of leather and lace and steel. Comfort. The best moment of every day, besides that lovely whoosh, is when I settle into bed. The soft pillow cradles my head and caresses my cheek as I curl up on my side, hands tucked safely beneath my chin. The silky softness of my bare feet slide against one another under the covers. Mmmmmm. Safe in my down fortress, protected from the slings and arrows of the world. My body warms quickly under the blankets, and I take a deep, cleansing breath before drifting to sleep.

Usually.

But, alas, not today. Fanny's absence keeps me from relaxing. My mind reels with questions and possibilities, making it impossible to sleep. She's always here, attentive and kind. With the strange events of tonight, as well as with the vicious vicar and all his mischief, I'm not taking any chances, so I jump out of bed back into the cold world. My bare feet pad into Fanny's chamber to check on her.

This isn't good.

Her bed is still made. Its lace-trimmed day pillows and handmade quilt wait for her arrival, their white illuminated in amber by the dim light. The gaslights are turned to low, and her hairbrush and nightcap sit untouched on her dressing table. Fanny is nowhere to be found. By the looks of things, she hasn't even been in her chamber since she set everything this morning.

Now I'm really worried, but there's no time to panic. Think. Where could she be? Not here, obviously. Not in the pantry. Did she go out looking for me? Did Father Creepy Face follow us home and do something with her? Question after question bombards my mind, each fresh one scarier than the last. The whirlwind of images and fears and options in my head are all things I don't want to consider, but I have to make sure Fanny is safe. That means facing the truth, no matter how horrible that reality might be. It certainly can't be worse than what I'm imagining.

Who am I kidding? Of course it can be. The last six weeks has taught me that a few times already.

She must be safe, and if she's not, I will get her to safety. Nothing is more important now. Nothing.

No one else will be hurt because of my negligence.

No one, especially not her.

I sneak back through my bed chamber and out into the hallway, ensuring the door closes without a sound, for my parents are likely already stirring. Mother is brushing her hair, counting each stroke, as she prepares for breakfast, and Father is putting on his suit for the day, listening to the sounds of the waking house. They truly have no idea what dangers lie just outside the front door. How could they, as they see only the factory, money, and their place in the ton. Little else matters to them, including me.

Other things matter to me, however. Conrad. The boys...and girl. Fanny. People matter. Relationships matter. "Oh, Fanny! Where are you?" I ask the empty room. "The only other place I could think is the attic, our training space...OR!" A scandalous thought crosses my mind, and I hope beyond hope it's true!

Maybe she's with Wilfred!

I giggle to myself, thrilled and rather tickled that she might be enjoying a night of passion with her secret beau. After a couple of decades, she deserves it!

Still, as quickly as the happy thought comes, it goes once again. I'm not convinced. I continue up to the attic hoping to find her there. If she's not, and she's not with Wilfred, which, let's face it, is a long shot—especially after all that talk of keeping distance and such and digging up the pain of Peter—that means something terrible has happened.

No. I won't believe it. Not yet. She's here. I know it. I can feel it. She's here, and she's all right. As I reach the top of the staircase, the glow of candlelight sends a wave of comfort through my heart, validating my wishful thinking.

I breathe a sigh of relief when I see Fanny hunched over her desk, a table she had set up for herself so she could study and scheme away from others' prying eyes. She made it so any servant wondering up here for a stolen kiss or a moment alone wouldn't suspect a thing or see what shouldn't be seen. The practice dummy, she has explained to them, is for her to work out stress, and they believed her. The image of Fanny punching the pillows in anger forces me to suppress a chuckle. She hid her workspace quite well. Arranged behind crates, an old rocking horse, and my broken baby crib, no one would be the wiser unless they really starting moving things about. Tonight, however, the candlelight gives her away.

Fanny's so immersed and focused in her work, she doesn't even hear me approach. "Fanny," I whisper, maybe a little too loudly.

She starts, coming a full three or four inches out of her chair then crashes back down on it. Its joints groan under her weight. "Oh, my! You terrified me! What are you doing home so early?" she chides, as if I'm neglecting my duties.

"Fanny! It's past dawn!"

"Nonsense! It can't be."

"I assure you, it is. I've had quite an interesting night, thank you for asking. Whatever are you doing up here? Have you been here all night?"

"It's this book, my lamb. Fascinating. Horrific, but fascinating. Just…astounding, really. I must've been so engrossed in it that I didn't even realize the night had come and gone. It's bewitched me, I'm afraid." Fanny pulls her reading spectacles off and bolts out of her chair.

Looks like someone had far too much tea through the night.

"What's the time?" she continues, flustered and smoothing down her skirts. "Dawn you say? Oh! Heavens! I just can't believe the night is over." She turns around three times, like a dog chasing his tail, and then looks intensely at me. Her eyes are wide with fear or excitement, or maybe both. "Nickie, she says, "This isn't good!" After plopping back down at her desk, she jabs the book over and over with her index finger, poking it to emphasize her point.

Yes, far too much tea.

"He's dabbling with dangerous, dangerous magic. Dangerous powers! He's playing with forces we cannot comprehend!" She grasps my hands in desperation and shakes them for a moment then dons her spectacles and pours over the book once again.

Déjà vu. "Huh. That's the second time I heard that tonight."

"Second time?" Fanny looks up from the book and her eyes appear twice their normal size through her spectacles. She blinks at me waiting, and I'm caught between loving her so much at that moment with her owl eyes, so pleased she's safe, and remembering the unpleasant encounter with Ashe.

"Yes. Second time. I'll give you three guesses as to who showed his pallid face while I was out hunting tonight."

"Not the priest."

"No. Not that pallid face, but almost as bad."

"Oh, Nickie," she says, pulling her glasses off her nose. "I'm so sorry." Her hand reaches for mine, and I happily take it. When faced with tragedy, what's really important becomes undeniably clear. It feels good to squeeze her soft fingers. She slathers her hands with lotion multiple times a day, so her hands are silk.

"It really wasn't that bad this time, surprisingly. I didn't faint or go into a panic like before. It didn't even hurt that much. No. Just made me very, very angry." My grip must've gotten a little too tight for Fanny as the fury returns, for she jerks her hand away and flaps it in the air a few times.

"Anger's good," she says, pressing her bruised fingers to her lips. "It's the first step in saying to ourselves, *we deserve better*. Good for you, Nickie. Don't ever stand for a man, or anyone, tossing you aside or treating you with anything but the utmost respect. If they're not wise or aware enough to recognize the jewel that is you, Nickie, best they stay away. Far, far away."

"I get that now, and to think I would've done anything to get him back such a short while ago. To prove myself worthy. It is he who isn't worthy; he who is the coward. Thanks, Fanny. Angry. Yes." I stop for a moment, wondering just how to put this next bit without making her overly concerned. I do have a handle on things now, no doubt. "Well, there's more. He's following me, it seems, and I don't like it much."

"Following you! Is he dangerous?"

"He's a vampire, so I suppose, you know, by definition. Funny, I would've given anything for a single kind word a few weeks back, but now too much has changed.

I've suffered too much. It's like he's tracking me, and I don't know how to stop him."

"You are a vampire hunter, love." She turns back to the book on her desk as nonchalantly as if we were talking about the weather. After she pushes her glasses up on her nose, she turns a page. On it are a lot of strange symbols. Still, I'm not ready to end this conversation yet, so I respond, "I know that's what I do, but he is fighting on our side."

"So he told you."

"You really don't trust him, do you? Even after he saved your life? My life?"

"Sweet girl," she says with a condescending lilt to her voice and turns back to me. After pulling her glasses down to the edge of her nose and looking up at me over them, she continues, but it's not condescension I hear anymore. No. It's pity, perhaps regret. "When you've lived as long as I have and suffered, enduring the treachery of men, you will find that trust is a very rare commodity. The grand majority of people, of either gender, are not trustworthy. They're not even worth knowing, really. You can trust so and so for a time, but each person's reliability and accountability has limits. You've already found his limit, too soon after you met. That says something."

"You've been hurt so badly, haven't you, Fanny. Shattered, by the sounds of it."

"Indeed, but it was long ago, as I've told you." She turns back to her book again, situating her spectacles halfway up the bridge, enabling her to look down at her book and up at me. "What did doe-eyes have to say?"

"Doe eyes!" I laugh at her nickname. Such mirth all of sudden, bursting out of me. Something definitely has changed inside me. Maybe Simon has something to do with that. "Doe-eyes said he spoke to Conrad. Not at all happy about that, by the by. I'll have to have a word with Conrad about the company he keeps and where his loyalty lies, I will. I feel rather betrayed after everything."

"Go easy on him, dove. He's in a difficult place. Doe-eyes gives him a home, remember. Conrad's loyal to you, through and through, but he has a family to care for as well. This can't be easy on him, my dear. He never liked doe-eyes even when you did! In Conrad's eyes, Doe-eyes went from competition to the man—or thing—that broke your heart. I'd say Conrad would like to stake him given half a chance." Through all of that, her eyes never left the pages of the book. Page after page of symbols and strange languages, from what I could see over her shoulder.

"True," I say about Conrad's desire to stake Ashe. Since there's no keeping her from it anyway, I ask about the book, "What did you find out?"

"Dark magics, Nick. Darker than I've ever seen in all my years. I was right in my guess. This is the lost book of Solomon. The Lesser Key, some call it. Very dark, indeed. Quite out of my league, I'm afraid."

"Nonsense. I don't believe a word of it, not for a second. I've seen your power, Fanny."

"Yes, but there is something about black magic, especially this kind, that trumps the power of white magic. Evil, mixed with magic, mixed with abomination. The hatred, wrath. The power of hell captured in our realm. Dangerous, dangerous, dangerous."

"What can we do?"

"For starters, I've made lots of notes," she says, turning back to her desk and grabbing a handful of papers. "To address with the witches in my coven, up in Yorkshire. I'll need everyone's help for this, so when we know what he's up to we can stop him. We'll need a very powerful circle. Yes, at very least. Good thing I sent that telegram. Tomorrow night—oh, dear, I mean tonight. I still can't believe the night's gone. Tonight I'll speak to them through the aether, and I'll be prepared. Yes, I will." She waves the handful of pages over her head, then slaps them back down onto the desk.

"What do you think he's playing at, Fanny?"

"There is so much evil in this book that it could be anything; however, I think I've narrowed it down between what you've seen and based on some of the other books in his library. He's definitely playing with dark forces, toying with the dead. A type of necromancy, I believe. It does have to do with magic, but more than just magic. Evil, pure evil, fuels this. Plus, he has some help. Of that I'm sure. No way a man can do this on his own, no matter how evil. He has a partner, some kind of assistance."

"Bessie, maybe? Perhaps she's a lover he keeps hidden for propriety. Perhaps she's his partner in all of this."

"Perhaps both. I wouldn't put anything past him at this point, my lamb. Find out what you can, and I'll do the same—tonight. I'll talk with them tonight, and you shall return, hopefully not alone. Conrad?"

"No. Too dangerous. Simon would come, I bet."

"Simon?"

"Yes, you know The Other Protector. I saw him last night as well. He, well, saved my life, as it were."

"NICKIE!" She jumps up and crushes me in a bear hug, rocking me side to side. "You promised you'd take care! What happened?"

"It's all right, Fanny. I'm all right," I squeak.

"What happened? Were there a group of vampires again?" She holds my shoulders at arm's length. I want to turn away from her and go back in time about thirty seconds, but I can't. Shouldn't have opened my mouth. She'll only worry more, and what's done is done. Too late now.

"No. Just one," I say, embarrassed. "I was being foolish and cocky. I admit it. I could've killed him straight away. Direct stake to the heart, but I was angry and I wanted to use him to work out some stress, as you say. Hone some skills and try some new moves. Long story short, he got the best of me, and if Simon hadn't been there…"

Fanny makes a clucking sound with her tongue, but more concern than disapproval shows on her face. "Promise me you will never be so foolish again, Nicole. Promise!" She gathers me into a crushing embrace. "Promise, my dove. Promise!"

"I promise, Fanny."

"Perhaps you shouldn't go back to the church tonight, even with Simon. Wait until after I consult with my coven, then go. In fact, we'll go together."

"No. I'll be all right. I can take care of myself, and Simon will protect my back, and I his. We have to find out who and where Bessie is and what this horrid vicar is doing with these poor ghosts."

"No, Nick. I don't want you anywhere near this priest, not after all this."

"Believe me, I don't want to be anywhere near him either, but the people—"

"Yes! The people! The spirits! The ghosts of Southwark. I believe you saw them, Nick. I know you did, now."

Fanny releases me and sits back at her desk, so she must feel comfortable that I won't die here and now.

"I hope you believe me, Fanny! Didn't you before?"

"Well, pet," she says. "More or less. I mean, you have had a rough time of it, but I trust you. Plus, I have no doubt now, and that's something. Right?"

I feign comical offense at her doubts by crossing my arms and tapping my foot with the utmost impatience. Still, I can understand why she had those doubts, after all. She winks at me and turns back to her books. "Have you seen them again?" she asks.

"I haven't, but that vampire who almost got me tonight. He was part of the Clan of Ashen."

"The who?"

"Long story, but the same who killed Edwin and the ones Simon has been hunting. He had that same symbol and said they were controlled by someone he called 'Father.' Do you think it could be Benedict?"

"It's possible. I did find something in this book about calling on the forces of heaven and hell, a ritual to summon both specters and demons, alike."

"A vampire is certainly a demon," I say. "Every single one of them."

CHAPTER SEVENTEEN

IN WHICH NICKIE NICK FOLLOWS THE VILE VICAR

Simon keeps close behind me as we approach the church, and I find myself wishing he was a little closer. Now's not the time for such things, of course. I must keep my focus on what's important tonight, and that's finding and saving Edwin and the others. At the very least, we need to gather the information to do so as quickly as possible. Matters of the heart can wait. Tonight is about matters of the soul.

St. Saviour's dark flint stonework looks even more ominous at night. Since there's no way in or out of his vicarage, save that singular scary staircase within, we're hoping to find Father Creepy Face somewhere on street level, either on the grounds or through a window. We must figure out what he's up to and see how he's tied to these ghosts, not to mention the vampire cult. Could he really be the Father to whom the leech referred? According to Fanny, it's more than just a little possible.

Just as I start across Montague Close, Simon grabs my arm and yanks me back into the shadows. He clamps one hand over my mouth and uses the other arm to hold me tight against him. I tense up and struggle, but his supernatural strength matches mine. Plus, he's a bloke, so I can't break free. Something about all this is most unsettling.

"Shhhhh," he hisses in my ear and tingles go down my back. "Look there."

With his head tucked deep inside the hood of a sackcloth robe, Father Benedict exits the courtyard and walks right towards us. I hold my breath and sink into Simon, who's also holding his breath. We stand very, very still, thankfully well covered by the shadows against the building. Benedict comes so close I can see his beady eyes peering out from beneath the hood. Once the priest passes by us without notice, we once again breathe freely. Yet, we stay pressed against each other for another moment, just to be extra sure. At least, that's what I tell myself.

Simon releases me and apologizes. "Sorry about that, Nickie. There was no other way, I'm afraid. Short notice and all. Forgive me?" Even in the dim light of the night, I can see the blush rise up his cheeks and disappear beneath his mask.

"Of course," I whisper back, careful to stay hidden in the shadows for now. "Just don't make a habit of it."

Although, part of me wishes he would pull me close to him again. And, this time, kiss me.

Not now, Nickie! "C'mon," I say, forcing my thoughts back to the task at hand. "We can't let him get too far ahead. He's up to no good. I can feel it." Sliding along the shadows against building after building, we follow Benedict at enough distance to remain undetected, but close enough to not lose him. He turns on Southwark Street, then again on Redcross Way, ending up at the Cross Bones Graveyard.

Another place I had never been. Seventeen years in London, and there's still so much to discover. It looks quite small. Dirt and headstones, not much else. Creepy place. Perfect for him, of course.

"What's he doing in a cemetery this time of night?" I whisper back to Simon.

"Especially a closed one."

"Closed? What do you mean?"

"It was closed before I was born, the story goes. Overrun with the dead. Room for no more, so they say. Known as a dumping ground for the wicked and poor. The Pauper's Cemetery, they called it, I believe. Paupers and 'single women.' You know? Working girls. 'Winchester Geese' they were called."

Geese? Ah! That poor woman's comment about sauce for the goose. Perhaps she's one of these working women. Her haggard look and clothes would suggest as much. "How can you possibly know all of that?"

"I read a lot," he says.

"You can read? Impressive," I tease. Both my respect and attraction to him increased ever so slightly with this new information. Simon, it seems, is full of surprises. It will be lovely to talk literature with someone other than Fanny and Father. Truly. My heart beats a little faster when his green eyes lock with mine and he gives a blushing half-smile. *No, Nickie. NO!* "Still," I say to break my own distraction more than anything else. "What's Benedict doing here?"

"Let's find out." He slides his hand in mine and that shiver ripples through my body again. Hand in hand, he leads me to the iron gate. Once there, he doesn't let go of my hand, nor do I let go of his. Instead, he wraps his arm around me and hold me in front of him with both our hands up against my right shoulder. My entire body sings.

Careful not to make a sound, from our embrace, which I convince myself is for the purpose of protection and discretion, we look around from headstone to headstone, through the low lying fog, until we see a light flash. "There," he says, pointing with the hand not holding mine. Father Benedict stands between two rather large headstones. He has taken off his hood and he's now wearing a pair of dark goggles, the lens of which caught the gaslight on the street corner. It serves as a reminder to remove mine, so I slip them off my cap and put them in my coat pocket to ensure the same doesn't happen, giving us away. If I had my way, I'd stay right here in Simon's arms for ages.

A burst of light interrupts my daydream, then a steady flickering. Apparently, Benedict just lit a lantern, as it now illuminates his creepy, sallow face. Yes, we see him much more clearly now, and I find myself wishing again for the darkness. The pleasant shivers from being so close to Simon turn into shudders of disgust as I look upon the skeletal wraith-man. Goggles with translucent blue lenses make him quite insect-like in appearance. Apropos, that. The right lens extends out further than the left, rather like a mini-telescope or even a microscope set in the center of the blue glass disc. In a flourish, Benedict swings off his sackcloth robe and twirls it into the air, fanning it out in a wide circle, then spreads it out on the ground. He kneels upon it, and we lose sight of him beneath the headstones.

"Closer," I say and take the lead, but I don't let go of his hand. I'm not sure if it's because I fancy him or if it's for comfort at this point. Simon doesn't let go either and follows right behind me as I carefully weave between the moss-covered stones until we can see Benedict again. We squat down to remain hidden, and I'm again protected by his strong arm.

On Benedict's spread robe, he's laid out the lit lantern, an old tome open to a page full of strange symbols and scribblings (much like the one Fanny took home), and a wooden box with brass dials on the top. Spiral copper wires stretch out one side of the top end and back into the other side. Then, on either side of the coil, two other copper wires stand straight up, much like bunny ears. He takes a long, flexible wire dangling from each side of the wooden box and attaches the ends to sides of his goggles, connecting the metal tip on the box to metal nobs on the goggles.

Simon's breath is on my cheek, and I force myself not to think about how close his lips are to me. I force myself not to think about how warm I feel inside his one-arm embrace, but the distraction is too great. I shift to the right and let go of his hand, putting more space between us. What happens next I wouldn't have believed a few weeks ago. So much of the impossible is actually quite possible. Still, Simon and I both watch the spectacle in awe.

After Benedict flips a switch and manipulates one of the dials, a buzzing fills the air. Blue lightning bolts—I don't know how else to describe them—travel up between the two copper bunny ears, then dissipates at the top just as a new bolt starts from the bottom. Turning the dial to the right makes those bolts emerge and disappear, climbing the ears faster and faster.

I mouth the word "Wow!" to Simon, and he gives a curt nod before his eyes fix back on the magnificent contraption. Not wanting to miss a second of it, no doubt, and I don't blame him.

"Rise! Rise! Rise, ye Angels of Vengeance, Specters of the Sinful. Rise and commence God's work. Rise!" the priest says. My gut screams those internal, infernal warnings, urging me to immediate action, but I'm determined to see what happens next. Here's hoping Fanny's amulet will protect me as it's meant to, for I find that I can't look away.

Hissing and popping noises mix with the buzzing sounds. Spirit after spirit rises from the surrounding graves, and I find myself back in Simon's arms without really knowing if I moved to him or him to me. I'm just glad we're close again. Two Protectors together: protective and protecting. Something very right about this.

The ghosts, which by the expression on Simon's face tells me he can see them, too, hover above their respective graves for a moment then, upon Benedict's command "Come," move to him in unison. Some struggle against the call, their vapor faces mangled in resistance or even pain, but they all go to him regardless. He speaks words in some language I don't understand, although it sounds like a strange dialect of Latin. Then the ghosts disperse one by one in all directions. "Find them," he says, again in English, as the ghosts fly away. "The sinful. The lustful. The adulterers and coveters. Bring me their stories and their sins to that I might save their souls, so that I might endure their treachery and lechery, rescuing them from damnation. Bring them to me for absolution! Yes! Absolution! Sacrificing my own immortality to suffer in their stead, and then purge! Purge, I say!"

He sets the wooden bunny-ear box down and rises up on his knees. His hands run up and down his entire body, grasping and clutching and caressing. I suppress a retch as I watch his hands focus on some areas much more than others. Revulsion comes over me, and Simon, too, I think, for he looks away from the priest and away from me, but we don't let each other go, not during this horrific moment. Not ever again, I hope.

The last specter, a thin, rather emaciated woman, turns to leave like the others, but her wandering eyes find us hiding in the darkness. She swoops down on us and wails. Her face transforms from full flesh to skeletal horror. Strands of decaying skin dribble off her bones and she shrieks the most horrendous sound ever known to human ears. Bloodcurdling and soul shattering. Hovering over us, her bony finger points directly at us, and she shrieks again.

I'm frozen in place. Unable to move. All I can do is look down the never ending gulf of her throat, open to the world. Shrieking. Shrieking.

Then I'm pulled away. The cemetery is behind me and I'm running, running. My feet move on their own while my mind is still in the gullet of that ghoul. London is a blur around me. The next thing I see are lights, tiny points of light far below and a silvery snake reflecting moonlight, winding its way through the lights. Then, another dark place, my feet hit hard ground. Then, warmth. Then, whispers. "It's all right. It's all right, Nickie. We're safe. It's all right."

Shaking, I turn to see Simon, green eyes wide behind his mask. Breath coming fast. Mine. His. Together.

Chimes fill the air, healing the damage to my ears and filling my soul with joy. Those familiar, glorious bells ring out, and I know I'm safe. Miles away from Cross Bones Cemetery and that horrid priest, my beloved Big Ben sings to me, and I'm safe.

It's midnight, from the count of the dongs, and I'm safe in Simon's arms.

"How did we get here, Simon, and so fast? We just left him at about midnight across the city, miles away. How did we get here?"

"Speed of the supernatural. Plus, this helps." He steps back from me, reaches into his coat, and then disappears. Again. He does it again, just like before. There, then gone. I turn around and around looking for him, but he truly disappeared. "Up here," his voice shouts, and I look up. Silhouetted by the light of the great clock face, Simon hovers in midair.

"Simon," I call to him, then laugh and spin around at the miracle of it all. "It's no wonder you're so fast!" He floats back down to me, and I must use every bit of restraint not to rush into his arms. So much is my gratitude and admiration and care for this young man, I can think of no other way to express all that emotion than with a kiss. Still, I know where that leads, so I do, indeed, restrain myself. "You can fly?" I ask him when he lands in front of me, cinnamon hair wind-blown and beautiful, toothy smile.

"Not really. Not on my own, anyway. This helps," he says, shrugging the overcoat off his shoulders to reveal a small pack around his waist. Like a belt with suspenders extending up over his shoulders, as well as holster-like straps around his thighs, the contraption has a brass bell-shaped thing on either hip. Wires run up the right suspender and down his right sleeve. My eyes follow the wire down to his hand, which he turns over when he sees me looking. There, emerging from his sleeve, is a handle, of sorts. On it, two trigger mechanisms.

"What is it?"

"My teacher made it for me before he....well, before he was murdered by the Ashen Clan." His eyes flash a moment of rage. "Brilliant inventor, he was. Utterly brilliant. The invisibility bit really is magic mixed with science. They're two sides of the same coin, Roger used to say. The levitation bit is pretty much pure science, but it's sporadic. He's not around to tinker with it anymore, so I'm afraid it's usefulness will wear out soon. I only hope I'm not airborne when it does."

"Invisibility? Are you serious?"

"It's more illusion than anything. An interruption in perception for just a moment or two. It allows me to use my supernatural speed, which you have as well, I've seen, or The Levitator here. Sometimes both. This time, I got us out of there with a bit of both. You froze."

Hanging my head, I say, "I know. I'm sorry." My boots became the focus of my attention. His came toe-to-toe with mine, and I feel him lift my chin until I'm looking into those striking green eyes.

"No need to apologize, Nick. It happens with trauma and shock. After Roger died—was murdered—I was useless for months. The slightest noise made me jump and I was always looking over my shoulder. Still am, I find. Not sure it ever goes away. You've had a rough time of it. I'm only glad I was there when you froze. The thought of that bugger with his hands on you." His entire body shook in anger. "Well, I'd forget myself and my oath not to harm humans, I'm afraid. I'd make him an exception and an example."

"How long ago?" I ask, not stepping back from the close proximity, even though all my will told me to step back. I did not want to love again, not when it promised so much pain. I don't know this man. I've only just met him, but I found myself utterly captivated by him.

"Just under a year now."

"But, you've only just gotten your powers in December, right? Same time as me."

"Yes. He never got to see me as The Protector. My full potential, as he always called it. He taught me so much for the past ten years, ever since he saved me from..." His voice fades away, and he steps back from me, turning his head to the left, hiding his hidden scar even further.

"What happened?" I ask. Now I reach out to him, touching his face and sliding my hand over his brow and temple. Over his cheekbone and down his cheek, all covered by the black mask. "Is this why you wear the mask? You don't need to, you know." I stop before telling him how beautiful he is.

"It's hideous. I know I'm revolting, and I will never be whole. It's a reminder of just how broken, just how much damage...but never you mind. Past is past and all."

My heart aches for him. So much pain. It's something I've noticed with those who've suffered, though. They're kinder. Much kinder, as if they know how a harsh word or raised hand can wound, destroy, even without making contact. All that much more if it does, as it must've with him to leave such a scar. Oh, poor Simon.

I love him in this moment. So much like me, and worse. So much like me, and better. So much like me, and more. I love him. Pure love, it is. Not tainted with expectation and desire and longing and jealousy and the rest. Not ownership. Not demanding. Not fearful or anxious or insecure.

Just pure love.

Like I love Conrad. Like I love Edwin and Cassie and Rufus, Franklin, Fanny. A familial love, yet with potential for a deeper love, more romantic, perhaps. I feel a flush burn my cheeks.

"It's all right, Simon," I say and stroke his face again. "You don't have to tell me anything, but you can if you'd like. You can tell me as much or as little as you like, and I will believe you. I will be here. We're in this together, after all. It's not terrible, you know, the scar. It's not hideous at all. It's hardly noticeable, really." I don't stop this time. "You're beautiful regardless."

With that, he grabbed my hand and yanked it away from his face. Anger filled his eyes, then tears. "I am not beautiful. Never say that to me again! Never!" He turns away and takes a few steps, distancing himself, but the distance I feel between our hearts is so much greater than a few feet.

"I'm so sorry, Simon. I didn't mean to offend. It was intended to soothe you, not make you angry. I'm so sorry. Forgive me for misspeaking?" I can't understand how what I said could offend, but that didn't matter, as it quite obviously did. "Please. We have to trust each other, and you can trust me never again to call you that. It must mean something different to you, Simon, and I'm here when you want to share that with me."

"He called me that." His voice trembles. "His beautiful boy."

"Who? Roger?"

A scoffing laugh. "Oh, no. Not Roger. Roger saved me from him. To this day, I don't speak his name. He... did things. Then marked me so that no one else would want me. Marked me as his. I was six when it started, nine when it ended—when Roger rescued me. I can't believe I just told you that. Please, Nickie. I don't want to talk about it."

I feel sick, knowing this. Sick at the sickness. The sick people, the sick men. No other word comes to mind other than sick. Evil, perhaps. Evil and sick. Like Benedict. How difficult this must be for Simon, knowing who Benedict is, what he does. I don't know what to say, but I refuse to say nothing. I refuse to offer some platitude to minimize this hell. I refuse to make this normal, something one can forget or get over or ever fully heal from. The damage is too, too great. The inner scar a chasm compared to the outer.

"I'm glad Roger took you away from that monster. I'm glad you're here with me now, Simon, and I'm honored you told me. So honored you trust me enough to tell me. We are two sides of the same coin, like magic and science. The Protector. Both of us. We're like family now, nothing can come between us. We can count on each other, can't we? Our experiences bind us. Our duty binds us together as well. Don't you find?"

"I do, Nickie. I feel safe with you and not alone for the first time since Roger was murdered. The Ashen Clan." His eyes form angry slits when he says their name. "We have to stop them from killing again. First Roger, then Edwin. I think they're tied to that blasted priest. Did you see the amulet he wore? It's their symbol. He's behind it all."

"Yes! I thought the same thing! There must be a connection. What did he call those spirits he summoned? Angels of Vengeance? Fanny said the book we got from his rectory names a bunch of demons and has spells and rituals to control demons and the dead. Maybe he's in control of the Ashen Clan, too. Is that possible? Demons to punish the wicked?"

"He said his angels were to report back sins to him, like they're his spies. We have to find out more, Nickie. We have to go back and learn all we can, so we can stop this monster from hurting anyone else. So we can stop them all." His fists and jaw clench all at once. He's shaking in anger, but his eyes focus on nothing, just empty space over my shoulder. Hard, cold. He turned off any tenderness to survive. I understand that. .

Indeed, I understand that.

CHAPTER EIGHTEEN

IN WHICH NICKIE NICK
RUNS VERY, VERY FAST

*February 18, 1881, just after midnigh*t

"Let's head back to Southwark," I say, happy to change the subject to something more pleasant. "I've a friend near there who would be interested in your levitation device. He made my boots and this." I demonstrate the retractable stake by thrusting my arm out and pulling it back.

"Brilliant!"

"And this is what my boots do," I say. "Watch closely." After moving a safe distance away from him, I kick directly to his face, the spike activates, springing out about five inches from his nose. Simon jumps back and takes a defensive stance out of habit, then laughs.

"Utterly brilliant! Who did this?"

"His name is Franklin, and he's a genius. Merely fourteen and a complete and utter genius. He will love me forever if I bring this to show him. Are you game? Along with Fanny's magic, I'll bet they can duplicate one for me. Then we can fly all over London together, but for now, no unfair technological advantage. I'll race you to the south bank of Blackfriars. Supernatural speed only. Ready...set..."

I take my first step as I say "GO!" and he says "Hey!" and starts a step behind me. London whizzes by us. There is no feeling like running, even in these boots, because of which I have a serious disadvantage. Still, I hold my own. After all, I'm not lugging around two brass bells on my hips, but then, he's not wearing a corset. Our handicaps are quite even, methinks.

Even without his contraption, we fly. I've never run this fast in my life, easily as fast as a vampire. Simon stays a few steps ahead of me the entire way, pushing me to move faster and faster. My legs pump at full speed until the muscles start to burn, then I push even harder, maximizing my own potential as The Protector. This demonstration of speed taps into those powers cursed onto me, but today it truly feels like a gift.

The lights reflected on The Thames become a blur as we zip along Victoria Embankment. Fortunately between the cold and the time of night, very few people are about, for we should be more careful about who sees us behaving this way. But we're not. Not tonight. Not now.

Now, we're just us. Young adults with amazing abilities. Together, we're alive and free and powerful—

and fast. I leap over the corner of Blackfriars Bridge, taking the lead. The heels of my boots hit the cobblestones at such a pace it sounds more like the tapping of a telegraph than footfalls. Simon lags a few steps behind, and I get the distinct feeling that he fell back on purpose. Breathing hard, I say, "You let me win," with a sideways, distrustful glare.

"I didn't, actually. It was close though, wasn't it? I almost had you there."

His smile lights up all of London. Beads of sweat trickle off his hairline, wetting his mask. Locked together in that moment, our breaths slow to normal speed. We don't even blink, just drink in one another.

"It's just around here," I say and force myself to look away from his captivating eyes. "Follow me. Conrad lives there, too. Is it all right he sees you, that he knows?"

"Will he be discreet? I mean, can I trust him?"

"I trust him with my life."

"If we're to work together, he'll find out sooner or later, I suppose. Might be time to let others in."

"You can trust my friends. They're like family to me, and they have talents of their own." Without another word from either of us, we turn on Barge House Street. Simon follows me through the street-level door and up the inner staircase. That queasy feeling is back. I must be nervous for some reason, and I'm not sure why. Perhaps he is, too, revealing himself. Maybe I'm picking up on that. After a deep breath, I knock on the door. Conrad answers and his face first lights up when he sees me, then falls when he sees the masked man beside me.

"Who's this?" he says with a scowl.

"A friend, in more ways than one, and not what you're thinking," I add when his scowl deepens. I'm not in the mood to deal with his suspicions tonight. "May we come in?"

"It's late," he says coldly. "The children are asleep. We just got Cassie down after hours of struggle. She's been whining about Edwin and ghosts and the like. So, it's not a good time, Nickie." I feel him pull away from me, and it pains me to have him do so. We had become so close of late, bonding over Edwin's death. I don't want him to be surly and jealous, especially when there's nothing to be jealous about! All these romantic feelings and notions and expectations ruin everything!

"We'll be quiet, Conrad. Really. It's important. I wouldn't trouble you at this hour if it weren't. We came for Franklin's help and advice, as well as to talk with you about what we saw tonight. If Cassie's been talking about Edwin, I want to know what she's been saying. Simon, here, has seen him, too."

"Hey, mate," Simon says with an awkward wave and downcast eyes.

"Simon? From the docks? You mean Buck's Simon?"—then to me—"What are you doing with this bloke, Nick? What are you playing at?"

"Please, Conrad, just let us in. I'll explain everything."

Franklin doesn't stop bombarding Simon with questions and examining his levitation device for over an hour. I don't think I've ever seen Franklin so animated and full of excitement. He's usually so focused and all work. It's lovely to see his face light up again and again from across the room. When he does, he looks very much like his age, which makes me happy. These boys have had their childhood taken from them, so even fleeting moments of inspired innocence are moving. After a while, two conversations at once, even in hushed tones, becomes overwhelming, so Franklin leads Simon into his kitchen workshop to continue.

I talk with Conrad during that time and fill him in on everything, including the mask, pleading with him not to make a thing out of it. He, of course, is as shocked as I am about another Protector, but he swears he won't tell anyone. He says he trusts me and my judgment. I touch his arm when I talk to him, and he seems more at ease with me. Reconnecting with him usually does that, I find. Everyone he's ever loved has died or left him, so I can understand his fear at losing me, too. I have a similar fear of losing him, my best friend. He's had a rough time of it, but at least his mother is back now.

I still haven't told him about seeing his father. I feel so close to him right now, so comfortable, like I can tell him anything. Perhaps it's time.

"There's one more thing," I say and I pull my hand back from his arm. "I'm not sure how to say this, and I'm so sorry I didn't tell you about it straight away. I just didn't know what to say, or perhaps I was afraid of what you would do or think of me or something. I don't even know what. It's just, strange things afoot, Conrad, and with as painful as this time has already been, I didn't want to stir up something else. I hope you understand. Besides, I can't have you rushing off in anger. You have to promise to wait until we can do something properly, Simon and me. You have to promise not to do anything rash. All right? We have to take this man down right and proper. All right?"

"Yeah, yeah. All right. What is it already?"

Just then, Simon comes out of the kitchen with Franklin in tow, still hounding him with questions about The Levitator, then pleads, "Leave it with me for the rest of the night, Simon. I will work out the kinks."

"I'm not sure. Nickie says you're a genius, but it's about all I have left of the inventor, who was very dear to me. You understand," Simon says, looking at me with an expression that says "save me!"

"One hour. Just one more hour." Franklin doesn't relent. "You can stay here with it. Watch me. I won't hurt it, I promise. I know I can fix it to work properly, even build a better one for you and for Nickie, both."

"What did I tell you," I say in a sing-song-I-told-you-so manner. His big smile responds to mine.

"You weren't joking," Simon says. "We've got to get back to the church, Nickie. It's getting so late, and we can't let him..."

"Agreed, but we also have to stay safe or we won't be able to help anyone, and, like you said, it's so late. Perhaps it's best left until tomorrow when Fanny can come. She's talking with her coven now, so we'll have more answers then, perhaps even a plan. We can use all the help we can get."

"It must be tonight," Simon says. "I can't stand knowing he's out there another minute, Nickie. I can feel it, here," he says with his fist against his stomach. I know how he feels. That sense in my gut has been growing stronger by the minute. "We have to do something, now."

"Hi, Nickie!" a small voice says before I can respond to Simon's sudden demands.

"Edwin!" I exclaim when I see my lost dear friend standing by the fireplace as if to stay warm on this cold winter night. "There's my sweet boy!" I rush to him to hug him, but I move right through him. A thousand huge icicles pierce my skin and force themselves all the way through to the other side in the briefest instant. I turn back around to find Edwin still standing in the same place, only facing me again. The fire warms my bum quite quickly.

"Edwin?" Conrad says to me, angry again. "What are you playing at? That's not funny, Nickie. Not now, not ever!" His cross expression pains me. He can't see Edwin. Poor Conrad. He must be so confused.

"He's here, Conrad. Right here. It's part of what I had to tell you. I've seen him and your—"

"Nickie! Nickie! Who's that man in the mask? He scares me, Nickie. This all scares me," Edwin says. "I'm so cold all the time, ever since the park. What happened? Why can't I hug you? Why can't anyone see me but you and Cassie and that man in the mask and that skinny vicar? Why can't Franklin or Rufus or Conrad or Momma Hannon see me? Or anyone else in the streets? Except some other people can see me, too, but no one else but me and the priest can see them, so it doesn't count. Why can't anyone else see us, Nickie? That priest is a bad man. A big, big baddie. He does stuff and makes people do stuff, watch stuff and then tell him all about it. I don't like him, Nickie. Please don't make me go back. I'll be good. Please! I'll be good!"

All while Edwin is saying this, Simon is urging me to leave and Conrad keeps questioning me about what's happening and why am I looking at nothing. Franklin stands with his arms crossed trying to put it all together.

A piercing scream stops everything. Cassie stands at the bedroom door holding her dolly out before her, screaming. Silence while she takes a deep, deep breath, and then she screams again.

"It's all right, Cassie. It's all right." I run to her and scoop her and her one-eyed dolly up in my arms. "Shhhhhh. Shhhhhh," I hiss into her soft chubby cheek, rocking her back and forth, but my efforts don't serve to comfort her one bit.

"Why is he here, Nickie?" she screeches, and I'm suddenly glad the rest of this building is just full of postal machinery and not other tennants. "Why does Edwin keep coming here? I tell him to go away. I tell him he's dead and to go away, but he tries to hold my hand and it hurts, Nickie. It's so cold it burns, and he cries and then I cry. No one believes me! Why? You see him, too, Nickie, right? You see him, too?"

"I do see him, Cassie. Simon sees him, too. Don't you, Simon?"

"Yes. Cassie, is it? I'm Simon. I can see Edwin, too. He doesn't want to hurt you or anyone. He's scared, just like you. Can you understand that? We're all scared." He turns to me and says, "Nickie, we've got to get back and stop this straight away. Let's go."

"Even you, Nickie," Cassie says and puts her little index finger against my nose.

After a very pointed look at Simon for being insensitive and trying to rush us off when Cassie and Edwin are so scared and everyone is so confused, I say, "Even me, Cassie. I'm scared, too."

She pulls her dolly up from where she had been dangling by one arm and hugs her tight. I remember how much she and her dolly helped us with Pilkington. She can see things through her dolly, so it's worth a shot to ask this time.

"Cassie, has your dolly been talking to you again?"

"Yes. She always talks to me."

"Does she talk about Edwin?"

"I'm right here," Edwin says. He waves his hands wide from side to side and jumps up and down. "Please talk to me! See me! Hear me! I don't want to be invisible anymore! This isn't fun! I don't want to do what that priest says!"

Cassie covers her ears and says, "La la la la la," so she can't hear Edwin. Mrs. Hannon comes out in her nightdress and then ducks back into the room when she sees the strange man in the house. Peeking her head back out, she speaks over Cassie's La-la-la-las and Conrad's scolding and Edwin's pleas, which only Cassie, Simon, and I can hear, and she says, "Can we just all be quiet for a moment please!"

No one listens, so she shouts, "Quiet!"

Cassie buries her head in the crook of my neck and Conrad sits down hard in a chair, angry. Franklin still stands with his arms crossed, just taking everything in.

Poor little Edwin looks admonished and embarrassed and starts to cry again, albeit silently. She wasn't even shouting at him because she can't see or hear him, but he stays quiet just the same. Simon keeps giving me the "we have to leave" look, wholly uncomfortable at this family argument and confusion.

Mrs. Hannon chides me, "Nickie, what are you doing here at this time of night? These children need their sleep, and so do I. Can't this wait until morning?"

Simon takes the opportunity to inject, "I'm so sorry, Ma'am. We'll be going now." Mrs. Hannon gives him a very distrustful glance, and I just ignore him and answer her question.

"I'm afraid not, Mrs. Hannon. I'm so sorry to intrude like this. Horrible things afoot, and they affect you and Conrad and everyone here rather directly, I'm afraid. Please, just let me speak to Cassie for a few minutes and everything will become clearer."

"Very well," she says. "You've come through for us before, Nickie, so I'm sure you have your reasons." She covers herself up with a housecoat and sits in the chair next to Conrad. Franklin still stands at the kitchen door and, finally, Rufus stumbles out rubbing his eyes and moves close to Franklin, who puts his arm around Rufus's sleepy, slumped shoulders.

"Hello, Nickie," Rufus says. "Is all this fuss about Edwin? I heard a bit. Thought it was a dream at first."

"It is about Edwin, and more."

"Cassie's been seeing him. I haven't, but I'm the only one who believes she does see him. Do you believe her?"

"I do believe her, Rufus. I see him, too. Let me talk to Cassie, all right? We'll sort this all out."

"All right." He settles down at Franklin's feet and leans against his legs. Rufus's eyes try to close again, but he struggles to keep them open and pay attention.

I sit down on the floor with Cassie in my lap, and I say to her, "Please no more screaming, all right? This is very important. Only you and your dolly can help us. This is all very scary, I know. But I'm here, and I'll protect you. All right?"

"You didn't protect Edwin," she says. That cuts deep because she's right. I didn't.

"That's true, and I'm so so sorry about that, Cassie. I was very sick then, but I'm much better now. It's no excuse, I know, and I live with that failure every day. I miss Edwin so much, and I know had I been more alert that night, I might've saved him. I can't forgive myself, but can you forgive me for that, Cassie? Can you forgive me for not protecting Edwin properly and believe that

I will do everything in my power to protect you? That I will never be distracted again."

She nods, tears form in the corners of her eyes.

"Thank you, Cassie. I shan't betray that trust. I shall protect you and everyone here with my very life. Tell me what your dolly said about Edwin. Has she mentioned a priest at all?"

"Yes!! A very bad man! He's a very, very bad man!"

"Yes, he is, Cassie. Very bad. Where is he? Does she know? How can we stop him?"

Cassie whispers to her dolly and then holds the broken thing up to her own ear, nodding here and there and saying "uh-huh" and "oh, my!" periodically. Simon crosses his arms, no doubt thinking this isn't the time for games and childish stories, but he doesn't say anything. Not even another word about leaving. Just listens, rather intently.

Finally, Cassie speaks to me. "He's in a dungeon. With the dead. He's at a big, big desk. Like a table with barrels and wires and stuff, but it's ten times the size of him!" Slight exaggeration, no doubt, but she is a child after all. Things must look very big to her, indeed, since we're all ten times her size. "Bessie, dolly says. He's with Bessie. Oh! He's hurting people, Nickie! He's hurting people and herding vampires and ghosts, dolly says. Like Edwin and so many others. Stop him! He's a bad, bad man! Can you stop him?"

"I can and I will, Cassie. Where is this dungeon? What do you see?"

"Scary bones, Nickie. I don't want to look! Scary, scary bones. Lots of them. Stacks and stacks of them. Crosses, too. A round room. A secret door. Hidden," she says each new word and phrase after listening to her dolly tell her more. "The head of the highest bones. It turns, it does. It opens a secret door. That's where the bad, bad man is. That's where the giant desk is, too. Bessie! That's where Bessie is!"

"By the rectory," I say to Conrad and Simon. "He's down in the rectory, or, at least, near the rectory. It's among some catacombs. It's where the main machine is, I believe. Perhaps that's where Bessie is, too. We can get to both of them at once. Perhaps she's trapped there against her will."

"Who's Bessie," Conrad asks.

"Big, big desk," Cassie says. "Bad, bad man."

"We're not sure," I answer Conrad's question. "I'm assuming she's his lady friend, perhaps forced. Perhaps his partner. We'll find out."

"Big, big desk," Cassie repeats. "Bad, bad man."

"But he's a priest, isn't he supposed to, you know, not have lady friends?" Conrad's disgust shows on his curled lip, likely remembering his confession with Benedict.

"Yes, but he's not supposed to be doing a lot of the things he's doing. That's why we have to stop him!"

"Understood," Conrad said, then shuddered.

"HE's a bad, bad man, too," Cassie says pointing to Simon. "Go away, bad man!"

The pain on Simon's face cut deep into my heart. He turns his face away to hide his covered scar. "No, Cassie," I say gently, "That's Simon. He's our friend. He's here to help."

"No! Bad man in a mask! Bad, bad man! The wrong mask. It's the wrong one!"

Tears form in Simon's eyes. He clenches his jaw, but his cheeks and nose turn the color of his hair.

"Ready?" I say to him, hoping he can see I don't doubt him.

"Let's do this," he says blinking back the tears.

"I'm coming, too," Conrad says and stands up to follow. "Besides, you still haven't told me the other part. You said Edwin was one part. What's the rest? You can tell me on the way."

I look at him, then his mother, then back to him.

Cassie repeats, "Bad, bad man!"

Simon says, "Nickie, let's go!"

It's essential I tell them now. "Sorry, Simon. Just another moment."—then to Conrad— "Did you have your father's service at St. Saviour's? You know, his funeral."

"Yes," Mrs. Hannon says, "Why?"

"I—" I stammer, then look from Conrad to Mrs. Hannon, back to Conrad again. I try to read them, but the only thing on their brow is concern, curiosity. After a deep breath, I just spit it out. "I—I saw him."

Immediately Mrs. Hannon looks betrayed, and Conrad's fists are balled up again in anger.

"That's not funny, Nicole," Mrs. Hannon starts. The expression on her face holds the pain of an old wound, one that I just ripped open. How could I be so callous as to burst it out like that? To even tell them at all? They've been through so much. I should've just left with Simon.

"I'm so sorry, Mrs. Hannon. I'm not joking. I—I shouldn't have said anything. I'm so sorry."

"You saw my father?" Conrad asks. "Among these ghosts in Southwark?"

"Well, not exactly. I saw him on the north bank. Rather, he saw me. I was with Fanny and I consulted the compass while hunting. Then he was there. In a blink. He recognized the compass and demanded to know where I got it, but before I could get much information out of him, he was gone. Fanny couldn't see him at all. Then I saw him again near St. Saviour's."

"It's your imagination, girl," Mrs. Hannon scoffs and sits down hard. She dismisses me with a wave of her hand, but her eyes haven't dismissed it as nonsense. Hope and fear and agony struggle behind those tired eyes.

Simon takes the opportunity to tug me toward the door, but I stand fast and try to recover. "Quite possibly. Look, I'm so sorry I said anything. Just—just forget it. Your mum's probably right, Conrad. It's my imagination. We have to go," I say, looking over to Simon who looks back with sympathy at my faux pas.

All of a sudden, a feeling rises in the pit of my stomach, as if something is happening or something will happen and it will be horrible if I don't get there on time. Perhaps the urgency to get back on the hunt tugs at my gut now, too. Just like Simon said before. Whatever it is, I can no longer ignore it and remain standing. The discomfort is quickly turning to stabbing pain. I cradle my belly with one arm, as if it will make a difference.

"No! You can't just drop something like that and leave, Nickie!" Conrad's face twists in anger or pain or both. His fists and his entire body tenses, ready for a fight.

"I'm so sorry, Conrad, but there are a lot of people in pain, including Edwin and—" but I can't bring myself to say his father again.

Edwin looks up at me and says, "You have to come now, Nickie! Now! He's doing it again. He's doing it again. You have to stop him from hurting us. From making us watch such horrible things."

"We're going. Can you take us there, Edwin?"

Edwin nods and floats out the door. Good thing we have Cassie's description, so at least we'll get close. If she's right. I look back to Conrad, hoping for some semblance of understanding or support, but he just looks at me with his mouth hanging open, shaking his head.

"You really are a nutter," Conrad says, crossing his arms, "And you're not going without me."

"Nor without me," Mrs. Hannon says. "If William is really there as you say, then I want to see him. I want to…say goodbye. I never got a chance to do that before. It's mad, of course, and Conrad might be right about your delusions, Nicole, but I know what it feels like to be called mad when you're really not. You saved me, and I'll never forget that. I owe you at least the benefit of the doubt. Besides, I so want you to be right. I want to see my William one more time." Tears sparkle in her eyes, but she smiles up at me.

"Thank you for your confidence in me, Mrs. Hannon, but it's too dangerous," I say. "I can't put you in harm's way. You either, Conrad. You are my family! Please. Let us do this alone. This Benedict chap is playing with dark forces, and we just don't know enough yet."

"Tough," Franklin says, "We're coming. We're all coming." Rufus stands and takes Cassie's hand. They both nod. Mrs. Hannon and Conrad join the others, and they all look at me with determination.

Pain slices open my stomach, at least that's how it feels. I cringe, but surprisingly don't double over. It would only delay us further. I sigh, defeated. Must get out of here now. Say whatever to make that happen.

"Fine. Stick together and go to St. Saviour's. Simon and I must move faster. Get a handle on things before you arrive, I hope. We've already wasted too much time. Bundle up. It's freezing out there." Ignoring the betrayed look coming from Conrad and the bloody dagger screaming in my gut, I stride across the flat and leave.

CHAPTER NINETEEN

IN WHICH NICKIE NICK BREAKS INTO A CATHEDRAL

Still mentally and emotionally reeling from the visit to Conrad's, Simon and I arrive back at St. Saviour's. Once I started moving, the pain subsides to a dull ache. Too, something's off with Simon. He seems eager to move forward and hesitant at the same time. Perhaps all this reminds him too much of his past.

In a moment of hesitation, the fourth since we left Conrad's, he asks, "How can you just take that little girl's word for it, Nickie? We're expecting a lot from the fantasies of a child."

"No, Simon." I've already said this at least a dozen times in the past five minutes, but I take a deep breath and say it again. "This is a very special little girl. She's a seer. She thinks her dolly is talking to her, but she actually has the gift of second sight."

This time he actually responds instead of getting all quiet and picking up speed. "You mean that broken china doll? I'm quite sure I've never seen anything so disturbing," Simon says.

"Yes, rather unsettling to look at the gaping hole in her face, but Cassie loves that doll. She's never without it. More importantly, a few months ago, she and her dolly helped saved a lot of people's lives. I only wish Fanny were here. We could use her expertise, not to mention her powers. I'd like to make a quick dash over to mine to collect her, but I'm not willing to leave Conrad and the others here alone even for a moment."

"Understood."

"I suppose you could go," I suggest. Perhaps it would give him the out he's vacillating back and forth about. "Especially with the use of your levitation machine on top of your speed. You could make the trip right quick! I'd say twenty minutes there and back. An hour all told."

"And leave you here alone? Never. Not for a minute, let alone an hour!" Simon stops and pulls me in front of him. My knees threaten to swoon, but I lock them and hold my breath. "Nickie, I won't leave your side. We'll do this together, like you said. Let's figure out what we can about this priest, then we can enlist more help if need be. That's if he's even here."

"Agreed," I say and step back from him. No time for romance now, no matter how sweet his lips look or how mesmerizing his eyes are. Not now. Edwin. Cassie. I promised Cassie. No more distractions. "Right. Gather information. Then plan on how to stop him."

"Exactly."

That decision strengthens his determination to face whatever's inside that church. Mine, too. No more dithering about. No more wishing witches were here to help or lamenting my friends will be in danger. Time to act. We cross the courtyard to the impressive building. Its flint sides appear black in the night, like gaping chasms to another realm. Perhaps doorways directly to hell. Quite a disturbing thought, that.

Everything is quiet. The streets, of course, in the wee hours of the morning. It must be nearing two or even three. Nothing is about, not even the ghosts. No sign of Edwin either.

I tug the wrought iron ring, but the tall wooden doors are locked. "Of course," I say. "What did I expect, really? This is where Fanny would come in handy." I'm still wishing my favorite witch was here with us, and for good reason, too. "She can unlock doors with the wave of her hand."

"Seriously?"

"Yes. She's quite a powerful witch," I whisper. "I could break it open, of course, or you could, for that matter, but I'd rather not make too much racket. So far we have the element of surprise, if nothing else."

"I miss Roger even more during times like these, too. He could pick a lock in ten seconds flat. Genius, he was." The sadness on Simon's face touches me.

"Don't worry. We'll avenge his death yet. Tonight, maybe. If I'm right, and my Protector intuition tells me I am, there's a connection between this priest and the Ashen Clan. You said as much yourself. We'll stop them both."

"So," Simon says, looking around the edge of the door then up the tall stone facing, "we have to find another way inside." A window above opens then slams shuts, but I can't see anyone there. We back away from the door for a better look, but there's still nothing. To our left, a door squeals on its hinges and clicks closed. The sound of a lock turning follows.

"That's unsettling," I say. "Do you think he knows we're here?"

"I think his spies do."

"They're the ones who've asked me for help. Certainly they wouldn't betray us now, would they?" Simon shrugs, and mumbles something like those who you least expect it are usually the ones who do. I suddenly feel cold and very confused. The fiery windows on both levels look down on us. Faint candle, or perhaps even gas, light glows from the inside, illuminating those watching eyes. Then, all at once, they go dark.

"We've got to get in there," Simon says, "Ghosts or no."

"Right. You go that way," I say, pointing around to the left. "And I'll go this way. Look for any open or unlocked window or door. Even small ones. There has to be a way inside somewhere. Meet back here in ten minutes."

"Perfect." We part in our respective directions. Every window I come across is locked, or solid, like stained glass. No way in without breaking it, and that would make far too much noise as well. Perhaps it would be best to just break the handle lock on the front doors. Even if it announces our presence, we can face him together. Although, we don't know what he can make these specters do, not to mention the vampires.

The sheer size of this place is awe-inspiring and it takes forever to get around to the back side. The grey clouds illuminated by the moon make the church's central tower a beautiful black silhouette above me. Then a thought occurs. "The basement," I say into the night, then quickly cover my mouth. Although it's the wee hours of the morning, no need to draw attention to myself. Likely no one's about but possibly the ghosts. One never knows. I start looking near the ground for a small window, much like the one I use to sneak in and out of my own house. Too small for most to get through, certainly any adult, but not too small for me.

Thankfully, I'm still thin enough to squeeze through, although I won't be for long if I keep up with those apple tarts. I might come to regret the four I had this morning.

My thoughts wander back to Conrad and the others. They will be here soon, and I'm certain it's altogether a rotten idea for them to come.

"This way," a voice behind me says. I turn to look, and none other than Conrad's father stands before me.

"Mr. Hannon," I say. "What are you doing here?"

"He's at it again. He's hurting her, absolving her. Please, if you can make it stop, please do."

"Do the others like you know we're here? We know that he uses the specters as spies or something."

"They're out getting information, most of them. The others stay hidden far away when he's absolving her. Far, far away. They're here, but hiding. I'm only here to talk to you. You can help." His eyes glaze over and a blank expression covers his face for a moment. Then, confusion. "I know you, don't I? Nicole Hawthorn, my son's friend. Do you know where my son is? I've been looking for him. Yes, him and my wife. Have you seen them?"

"Your son and your wife, Laura, are coming to say goodbye, but I don't think they'll be able to see you."

"Why not? Say goodbye? Why? Are they going on holiday?"

Why do I have to open my big mouth? First with Conrad and now with his father. Neither one nor the other believes the reality I see, besides he's so in and out of lucidity I feel like I'm just wasting time here. I should learn to stay quiet. I try anyway. "You died many years ago."

"Don't be absurd, child! I'm standing before you. Do you want to get in here or not?"

Back to lucid.

I leave it at that. Now is not the time to convince him about his state of being or anything. He leads me to a back door on the lower level and walks straight through it. I stop, dumbfounded.

How am I supposed to follow like that?

"Mr. Hannon," I whisper.

No answer.

I chance a little louder, "Mr. Hannon!"

He materializes back through the door. "Aren't you coming?"

"You just walked right through the door!"

"What are you playing at, girl? I opened it and then held it open for you! This is a tiresome game, child. Horrible things are happening below!"

"You walked through the door. You're a ghost, sir. Please believe me. This is no game. I can't come in this way. You must think I'm being cheeky with you, but I'm not, sir. This is a very serious matter, you're correct, and I'm so sorry you're wrapped up in this."

His face distorts, like it's been stretched from side to side. "No! No! He's pulling me in! Nicole! Help!" I reach out for him, but all that I grab are invisible icicles that slash at my skin.

"What can I do? Mr. Hannon!"

"Help!" With that, he was gone. Dematerialized.

Enough of this. I'm breaking the lock. Bollocks to the noise. I dash back to the front of the church where Simon is already waiting for me. Edwin is with him.

"When did Edwin get here?"

"Just a moment ago," Simon says. "The others will be here in a few minutes, he says."

"Nickie, are you going to stop the bad man?"

Propping my hands on my knees, I lean down to Edwin's height and say, "I'm going to do my very best. Is that bad man trying to pull you in now?"

"No. He can't do that to me, not like he does the others."

"You said he makes you do things you don't want to do."

"He does. He tells me if I don't do what he says, that he will hurt the lady more. I have to do it or he'll hurt her more, Nickie! Then he'll hurt me, too. I see what he does to her, and he said he'll absolve me, too. I don't want to be absolved, Nickie! Please don't make me go back there, but if I don't go back, he'll find me and absolve me!"

"You never have to go back there again, Edwin. We'll stop him." I turn to Simon. "I couldn't find a way in, so break the handle?"

"I did. A small window. I won't fit, but I bet you will. You can come round and open the front door for me. All right?"

"Perfect. Let's do this." Sure enough, he shows me a window that I will barely fit through, but I manage. Rather fortunately, the front door keys hang on a nail next to it. Careful not to let the keys clatter together, I unlock the door and pray the hinges aren't too rusty.

After minimal squealing, considering the age of the place, Simon joins me inside the great hall. That sense of reverence I felt the first time I stood in the grandeur of St. Saviour's has left me, knowing what evil goes on here. How can one appear so pious and pure in public, to his congregation and the world, and be so wicked in private, destroying countless lives with his treachery and vile ways?

First Ashe's betrayal and now this. I don't feel safe anywhere. I can't trust anyone. Fanny and Conrad, perhaps Simon, but no one else.

I suppose that's more than most people have.

The words of Shakespeare return to me as I look at the sweet swan reclining for all of eternity in his cubbyhole. "One may smile and smile and be a villain."

No truer words were ever written.

After I convince Edwin to stay in the main nave and wait for Cassie and the others, Simon and I descend the dark, narrow stairway. Without light this time, I take each step one after another, feeling the edge of the following step before putting my weight on it. About halfway down, if memory serves, I hear the moans and screams. Father Benedict's voice, indeed, but it's also a woman's voice. Could that be Bessie? Is it she who he's absolving? Whatever that meant. Not what everyone else thinks it means, anyway. Hers are screams of pain, agony, and his are sounds of pleasure. My skin creeps up to the nape of my neck, and I pick up the pace.

"She said the head of the highest one, right?" I whisper to Simon as I reach the bottom, even more dimly lit than before with only one sconce burning. The door to Benedict's chamber stands open. Only darkness within. The screams and moans are coming from somewhere inside the wall, just as Cassie saw. A secret room.

Each of the stacks of skeletons ends at the same height.

I remove the sconce from the wall and I hold the candlelight up along the floor to see if I can find scrapes along the floor or any indication what wall might move. No clue found.

"They're all the same height," I say. "There's not one taller than any other and I can't find any indication of one of these walls moving. Now what? Try each skeleton? Each skull?"

"This one, I think," Simon says. He takes the skull in his hand and twists it clean off. "Ooops."

Nothing.

"Blimey," he says, dropping the skull. It cracks on the floor, much more loudly than one would expect.

"SHHHHH," I say to Simon and wait.

The priest stops moaning, and the woman's cries of agony diminish to a whimper, much like the sound of a beaten down dog. I'm going to stop this man and ensure he knows the meaning of pain when I do.

"Who's there?" Father Benedict shouts from the other side of the wall.

Frozen in fear, I don't know what to do next. We've been discovered. Conrad is likely waiting outside with the others, and I've led them right into the den of a madman. Nice work, Protector. Do I run for it or stand and fight this monster? With Simon by my side, I feel confident to fight, plus I promised Cassie I'd protect her.

After transferring the sconce to my left hand, I pull a stake out of my corset with my right. Not a vampire, true, but I feel more comfortable with some sort of weapon. I'm guessing it would do the trick if it comes to that, although it would be quite messier than a vampire's remains. I chide myself for not bringing Franklin's crossbow contraption, as I don't fancy getting close enough to this creep to use a stake. Must do what one can.

The round chamber fills with a host of ghosts. Wall to wall these specters stare at us, moaning themselves. Their moans aren't that of pleasure, however. They are of utter agony.

"Help us. Help us. Help us. Help us. Help us," they chant over and over and over again until the din fills every crack and crevice, not only in the room, but also in my mind. I crouch down, covering my ears, but their words attack me from the inside out.

"Stop it," I shout! "Please! Stop!" The onslaught of projected pain from the ghosts threatens to drive me mad on the spot. I'll be in a room next to Pilkington before the night's out if this keeps up. Simon's arms slide around me, and I start to feel safe again. At least I'm not alone down here. Together we can work this out. Together we'll get out of here alive.

"Silence," I hear, and every ghost moan and rattle and shriek evaporates like the last fading note of a Bach Cello Suite. I look up to see the walls swallow each specter, leaving a near-naked Father Benedict behind.

Frightening sight. A burlap nappy covers his privates, thank goodness, but the rest of his stringy form consists of welts and cuts and fresh blood, save his drawn face curtained by stringy black hair. Not a cut or even scratch on it, but every inch of his skin from the neck down is covered in scars or fresh wounds. His thighs are a mishmash of bloody crisscross marks. A large cross has been burned into his chest over his heart; the skin a thick scar tissue. His beady black sunken eyes look at me amused.

Then. Hands around my throat and a foot kicks the stake from my hand. From behind.

Simon rips Fanny's amulet from my neck and pushes me away.

Benedict chants something in Latin that I don't understand. His words force my eyes closed no matter how much I try to keep them open. The last thing I see is Simon standing behind Benedict, head hung in shame.

The world fades into black.

CHAPTER TWENTY

IN WHICH NICKIE NICK
MEETS BESSIE

I wake up strapped to a table situated on its end, much like a painting set on an easel. Iron bands shackle my wrists, arms, waist, and ankles. Although I struggle against the restraints, they hold fast. The metal just bruises my skin as I try to get free. Since they come directly out of the table, they don't even give an inch to work with. I look around, but I don't see Simon. Did he really just betray me? How do I find these men?

"You have been a very naughty girl," Benedict says. "A very, very naughty girl. Now, you are *my* naughty girl." He smiles and twirls around the room in a psychotic waltz with himself. It would be comical, in that sackcloth nappy, if I wasn't so terrified. "As God's chosen one, I will save your soul from eternal damnation. We will purge together, and you will be clean going into the afterlife. I will absolve you. Yes, yes, yes. Such a sweet one to absolve. I will absolve you again and again until you are clean, child. Until I have taken every ounce of your lust from you."

He runs his hands up and down his scarred torso, slithering and gyrating across the floor towards me.

Despite my bruised flesh, I can't stop myself from trying to get free. Surely my strength will save me from what this horrid man has planned for me. I try not to think about it. My limbs tremble and my flesh crawls.

"Perhaps, if God will it, you, too, can work as one of my Angels! Yes! You, too, may be blessed. Oh, yes! I will be exalted in heaven for my sacrifice, especially for absolving The Protector. Yes, my holy Father in heaven will be very proud of me. Very much. Yes, indeed! I have saved so many souls, sweet girl. So many of my flock are in heaven now because of my continued martyrdom. Yes, I am chosen! I am His representative on earth. Through my sacrifice, my martyrdom, my absolution, they get to rest forever in the presence of God." When he says the word "absolution," he thrusts his hips forward, making the hopsack jiggle in the most revolting way.

My mouth is gagged, so I can't speak or say anything. I look around the secret room again, searching for any way out or even the screaming woman I heard before, but there is no one but me and him. A large desk, ten times the size of a normal desk, dominates the room.

Cassie wasn't exaggerating. It is, indeed, ten times the size of a man. Tubes and wires sprout from along the sides and enter back into other parts of the wooden desk. Some tubes disappear into the wine barrels that encircle it, one about every five feet. In addition to this machine, a wooden table full of surgical and torture devices sits between me and a cot in the far corner that displays fresh streaks of blood on the sheets and other wet spots.

I do not wish to guess their origin.

"You like my collection?" Benedict says when he sees me eyeing the table of devices. He picks up a particularly frightening tool and waltzes over to me. It has six or seven metal prongs at one end, nearly as long as the space between my elbow and forearm, and a pin at the other end. He turns the pin, making the prongs spread wider apart with every crank. "I got this from an old doctor friend. It's called a cervical dilator. Usually a birthing device, but I like to use it to go deeper in rather than let something out. Yes, indeed!" He tosses it back onto the table, and it clanks against the other metal instruments.

Something deep inside my belly cringes, and I try to pull out of my restraints with renewed fervor. The blood from my wrists is starting to lubricate the iron clamps, so perhaps I can slip through. I will rip my own hands off before he gets near me with that thing.

"So many sins have I taken on, child. So many. Gluttony. Stuffing myself sick and letting the obese wither away, salivating as they watch me sacrifice myself to save them. Taking on their sins, then purging. Purging!"

As he continues his monologue, he turns away from me and dances across the room again. More thick, ugly scars cover his back, mostly in a V pattern from each shoulder. Some are dark red, obviously old wounds. Others, raised scar tissue. In between them all, fresh welts still drip blood which trickles down into his burlap cloth. The same crosshatching marks encrust his legs. His entire body has been beaten and bloodied time and time again. From the looks of it, by his own hand.

"I haven't had a live girl for quite some time." He says, salivating and rubbing his hands together. His tongue goes around and around and around his lips. "No. Not for some time. What a treat to have someone here warm and soft and alive. You can be witness to my sacrifice. *And he gave his only son...*and then He gave me. Not in death, of course. Oh, no. Death is relief, isn't it? That final journey. Life is suffering, my dear. Life! I stay alive and stay alive, absolving sinners so that they may rest and sit with God in heaven. Yes! I sacrifice all for my flock, so that they might know the glory of God the way I do."

As he speaks, his arms are thrown out wide, like he, himself, is nailed to the cross, but in ecstasy rather than agony. The two sides of passion. He spins around and around, a gleeful smile on his face and a sparkle in his eyes. Much like the way Ashe looked at me with love, but it's not love. It's obsession. It's deranged passion. He talks of God as one would talk about a lover.

"Every day, He fills me and brings me such pleasure, such pain. He is my life, my love, my everything. All is for Him. All is for Him. All pain, all pleasure. He is mine and I am His. We are one. He chose me! His very special love. I am chosen. I am chosen to take all the lust upon myself and purge. Oh, sweet purge! And absolution." Hip thrust.

The vile vicar takes a long whip off the table and flings it across his back. The loud crack fills the room and echoes off the dirt walls, followed by a cry of ecstasy from Benedict. Tears gleam in his eyes, but there is no sign of pain on his face. He whips himself again and again, laughing loudly with each new snap of the leather. I want to close my eyes, protect my mind from such horrors, but I'm unable to turn away from such a grotesque display.

"Yes! Oh, yes!" he cries. "Exalt me, Lord. Purify me, my sweet Lord!" After a few minutes of this, his breath comes faster and faster until he screams out in ecstasy. Fresh blood and other fluids dribble down his body. "You see, child? You see how I honor God? How I honor you and all you sinners. My vows keep me from pleasures of the flesh, from even having such desires for another human, but the Song of Songs—the Song of Sweet Solomon taught me that God is my lover. Through Him, through the pain of original sin and the agony of humanity, I am exalted. I am chosen!" He flings the whip again and it snaps against his back, drawing fresh blood. His stringy hair falls over his eyes, which roll back into his head while his entire body spasms. A moan escapes his mouth, and he lets his head drop back, exposing a long, skinny neck close enough to slit.

My left hand slides an inch but not enough to wiggle free. Benedict recovers from his moment of climax and trains his eyes back on me. His bony hand pulls that greasy hair away from his eyes, and he continues with his sick story.

"One day, long, long ago, I thought I would damn myself to eternal hell. I thought I must, you see, but God—He saved my life and my soul. He showed me a new way. In a beam of heavenly light, He spoke to me in my dark quarters. Noose around my neck, ready to do the unthinkable and deliver myself into the realm of Satan. You see, I felt I was so unworthy of His love. Fleshly desires consumed every moment, every thought. The young altar boy. The nubile mother. Even her husband. It mattered not, as long as it was a warm body.

Like yours. Yes. Warm! After some time, I couldn't bear it anymore, child. Do you see? I foolishly thought I was a disappointment to God, but it was all a test. All of it! Because I was chosen by Him. Chosen, girl! Chosen as His love. As His special one! He invited me into His metaphorical bed in that ray of light, and I obliged Him, His ever faithful servant. A sacred union with God was beyond transcendent."

With one hand he rubs up and down, up and down over his nappy, then whips himself again across his back and howls anew. "I remain his faithful servant today. He sends me whores and the lustful to purify. He's shown me how to call on a host of angels to do His bidding through me." Once again, he dances around the room in a solitary waltz, cracking his whip in the air and then across his back, crying out in ecstasy. He makes a deep dip in front of a wine barrel and kisses it. "He gave me BESSIE. Through a dream, He taught me of Mr. Tilly the madman. My Heavenly Father told me where to find him and bade me visit this Mr. Tilly in Bedlam, which I did. Poor, poor soul, Mr. Tilly. It was through Tilly's sketches of what he called The Air Loom and through the grace of God that I was able to build BESSIE here." He caresses the wine barrel as one would a beloved's cheek. Then, encircling his hand around the tube extending from it to the main desk, he strokes it back and forth. Back and forth. Once again, his eyes roll up and his body shudders.

I have never been so disgusted in my life.

"MMMMMM--MMMMMM," I manage through the gag, jutting my chin out at him.

"Do you want to speak, child? You want to thank me for my sacrifice, don't you?" he says, clapping his hands together and twirling around. I nod my head eagerly, eyes wide. Anything to get out of this gag. That's the first step.

Benedict waltzes over to me, dipping here and there as he makes his way across the room. Once he stands before me the smell of blood and other fluids fill my nostrils. I want to vomit, but I must suppress it until at least the gag is off. "Promise you won't scream, child? You must promise on all that is holy and good. Swear to God Almighty that you will not scream or cry out for help, not that anyone will hear you. You must pay for your sins, child. I will absolve you here and now and you will know true love, true ecstasy through Him. Do you promise?"

I nod again, making my eyes as sincere as I possibly can through my revulsion. When his hands touch my cheek and stroke it for a moment before removing the gag, I must suppress another retch. I shall never forget the feeling of this vile man's hand on my cheek. It will haunt me the rest of my days. Let's hope I don't have to endure it elsewhere. My mind ferociously works out a plan, any means of escape.

Simon betrayed me, it seems quite clear now, but where did he get off to? Is he hurting the others? Will they be here soon? Perhaps they're already here and they will be this evil man's next victims.

As soon as the gag is free I take a deep breath through my mouth, hoping it will refresh my thoughts and block out the horrid smell of this man's blood and sweat and—other emissions.

"Smile, sweetheart," he says. "I bet you have a beautiful smile. Ever since that first day I saw you, I knew you were special." His foul breath clouds my judgment, lips just inches from mine, and he strokes, strokes, strokes my cheek. His other hand is somewhere below stroking as well. Thankfully, not on me.

"Might I have some water?" I ask. "I'm so thirsty. Once my thirst is quenched, I shall smile. All right? I am ever so grateful that you have chosen me to absolve, Father. I am, indeed, a fortunate girl. But water first, please."

"All right," he says. "Moistening your mouth will be beneficial anyway. Yes, indeed! I'll purge your sins, dear one. I'll take on all your naughtiness and lust, you naughty, naughty girl. Absolve it right out of you! Any girl out so late and dressed like that must be naughty indeed." He suddenly stands straight up with a finger in the air, and with a voice slightly deeper than his own, he quotes, "*A woman shall not wear an article proper to a man...for anyone who does is an abomination to the Lord, thy God.*' Yes, indeed! Shameful, dressed like a boy in those trousers and spats. That's all right, sweetheart. I can treat you like one of my boys as well. So many different ways to absolve a girl. Yes, I'll punish you rightly here on earth so that your soul may be cleansed for your eternal life in heaven. Yes, indeed!"

Stall. Nickie, just stall. Anything just to stall a few more minutes. Something will come to me. I am The Protector. The only one, after all. If I can't protect myself, what good am I to anyone else? Think, Nickie. Think!

"Thank you," I say and let him feed me water. He pours it a little too fast and it flows out of the sides of the glass down my chin. This delights him, so he continues more forcefully. Water drenches my face and blouse and I force myself to keep it down by looking away from his tongue going around and around and around his lips. "That's so much better," I say while he puts the empty glass on the table. "I'm so impressed by all of this Father. Your sacrifice, of course, but Bessie, too! Would you tell me more about Bessie? You said she helps you control the hosts of—"

"Angels! Yes!"

My years of grooming to be the wife of some great fop in the ton comes in handy here. Mother always taught me that men just want to be heard. They want to be admired and loved. We all do, she said, but the way women get that need met is by being completely attentive to their men. Balderdash, I say, but it seems to be working with this lunatic. "Did you build her yourself? She's so very beautiful! Why ever did you name her Bessie? Did God give you that name for her?"

"Oh, no!" he said with great pride and thrusts his chest out, running his knuckles up and down his sternum, like over phantom lapels. He moves over to Bessie, giving me some much appreciated breathing space as I continue trying to work my hands out of the braces. My wrists are already quite bloody at the attempt, but the blood isn't enough of a lubricant. "Naming her BESSIE was my idea. All mine!" He turns his eyes upward, then his face takes on the countenance of a scolded dog. "By your inspiration, of course, my love. Sweet Father in Heaven! All for You!"—back to me with a brightness in his eyes I've only seen in excited children upon discovering something new—"BESSIE. It's stands for Benedict's Electric and Steam Specter Influencing Engine, you see? Isn't that rather clever? So clever and splendid of me. Yes, indeed! Of course it was inspired by God, so, indeed clever. Everything is at the grace of God!"

"Influencing Engine? This is how you control the ghosts?"

In an instant, he was back in my face, furious. His foul breath fogs my face. "I told you!" he screams "There is no such thing as ghosts!"

Before I can even apologize for my slip of the tongue, he is waltzing around the room again, singing himself a jaunty tune. As he passes by the table, he picks up a large pair of scissors, although they are much more the thing one would see in a surgeon's hand than a seamstress. He twirls around the room to some music inside his head, spouting off snippets of discordant sounds here and there. After each spin he snips the scissors twice into the air, then spins again.

"I heard another woman in here before. She sounded like she was in pain," I say. "Were you graciously absolving her as well, Father?"

"Ah! That was Helen. She was one of the Winchester Geese in my younger days. Someone with whom I would indulge before I was recruited by God, before I understood that what I was doing wasn't indulging in lust but rather taking on others' sins and absolving them. Thanks be to God! Thanks be to God! She fornicated with men, and God says,"—that deep voice again—"'Slay, therefore, every male child and every woman who has had intercourse with a man.' Yay! He has spoken! Thanks be to God! Thanks be to God!"

"The Winchester Geese? The ones buried in Cross Bones Graveyard, right? But that was closed over thirty years ago, wasn't it? You don't look old enough for that, Father." I actually even bat an eyelash at him. Flattery. It might just buy me some more time.

"Oh yes, this was long, long ago. Before The Almighty granted me immortality for my sacrifice. I must continue to suffer life and others' sins so that they might be spared the fires of purgatory or even hell! Through my living martyrdom, they know the bliss of heaven, and I know the bliss of God. I deliver them straight into His arms after absolving them."

"How exactly do you absolve them, Father?"

Just keep him talking, Nick. Keep him talking.

"I act out their sins with them, through them at times. Yes, indeed! Gluttony. Avarice. Hubris. Lust. The most of which is Lust." He growls the word and sneers when he says it. Half in disgust, half in hunger. "That alone would damn all of humanity. But not my flock. No, not mine. No! I purge them. I absolve every wife, every wicked woman, and some of the boys, too."—deep voice, finger straight in the air—"'*I will take your wives while you live to see it, and will give them to your neighbor. He shall lie with your wives in broad daylight.*' Yes! So says the Lord, thy God! Helen was the lustiest wench of all the Geese, so she continues to be absolved now, aiding me in my sacred task. She earns her place in heaven through my sacrifice! Through my absolution! BESSIE makes her corporeal enough to be absolved again and again and again. For seventy years now, I have absolved her daily, sometimes several times, so great is her lust, even after she left this plane. She no longer needs absolution for herself, as she's an angel of heaven, thanks to me, but I absolve others through the use of her form, her energy. She pays for her sins by playing proxy to that of others. Yes, indeed! She will sit at the right hand of the Father."

Seventy years? But Benedict can't be more than fifty at the most. What he means by absolve is quite clear now, and that's what he intends to do to me. I shudder and work my hands against the restraints harder, further ripping the skin.

"Enough talk," he says and waltzes over to me. Taking the scissors, he starts at the bottom of my pantelettes and starts cutting along the inside seam. Snip. Snip. Snip.

Just then, Simon comes in, thankfully. He doesn't make eye contact with me, but he distracts Benedict long enough that I finally pull my left hand free, skinning myself from the wrist to the lowest joint on my thumb. With all my Protector might, I knock Benedict's jaw hard just as he turns back to me. The force of my blow coupled with the momentum of his turning head knocks him to the floor, unconscious.

Simon stands stunned, and I shout at him, pleading, "Simon! Get me out of this. I know this isn't you. He's controlling you somehow, isn't he? He's the one who hurt you, who marked you as his."

"I'm his beautiful boy. He blessed me with this scar, marking me as his special one. His very special boy." There's a tremor in his chin, and he speaks as if he's in a daze, much like those mesmerized zombies did.

"But Roger took you from him, didn't he? He saved you?" My right hand is nearly free.

"He did, and I believed him for a while, but when Roger died, Father Benedict took me back in and forgave me for straying. Told me I was chosen to assist him on his sacred duty. My savior. It's my duty to help him. He absolves me of all my sins and bad thoughts."

"So you're not a Protector like me, after all?"

"Roger believed it and convinced me for a time, but my mother was a whore and my father, some nameless, faceless pervert who paid for it. They both need a good, righteous absolution. Roger, too," he says with a sneer. "He took the word of a filthy whore. Blinded by love, he was. I, of course, have strength and speed, as you have witnessed, but Father showed me that it is by the grace of God, not the work of blasted witches. I told you that story, and all the rest, to gain your trust, Nickie. To help you, so that you too can be absolved and sit at the right hand of the Lord. It's a divine power, to fight demons and evil."

Exactly, but when he says it now, those words take on a whole different meaning.

"Your friends are here, by the way. I've detained them above. They will be absolved as well. Each one in their turn. Father Benedict says I can watch so that I might learn the proper way. I'm to take over when he finally gets to rest at the right hand of God after so many years of service. Going on a century for Father Benedict now, so I must learn. Your absolution, I gather, will be quite violent. Necessary to pay for your sins—for Father to take them all on himself to save your immortal soul."

Frantically trying to get my other hand free, I try to keep him talking. Although, I'm not sure what I can do with my hands free, as I'm still strapped by the waist and the feet, but it's something. I can at least defend myself within arm's reach. Almost there. "Did he kill Helen and the others, Simon? Did he kill Roger?"

"Yes," a deep voice answered. "He did kill me, Simon."

"Roger?" Simon says, turning to the voice behind him. A translucent man emerges from the stone wall. It's one of the ghosts I've seen before. The one who tried to warn me. Handsome and strong, as he undoubtedly was in life. Dark hair and kind eyes. "Is that really you?"

"It is, Simon. I've saved you from this monster once, but I didn't know how deep his evil ran until after he had me killed. He controls the Clan of Ashen as well, son. He had them kill me so he could get you back again."

"No!" Simon grabs handfuls of his hair and his face twists in pain. He's so confused and after this life of torment, likely quite insane. "That's not true. Father told me to kill them. To hunt them and destroy them. He told me they betrayed him like the demons they were. That he couldn't control demons enough to do God's work. That the rituals were meant to bind them so they can be destroyed and sent back to hell where they belong. You're lying!" Simon barks the last words to the specter, grasping for any true thing on which to stand. He's been told so very many lies. I can only imagine what he must be going through after a lifetime of deception and horror, as just a few weeks of it had me down for over a month. This poor, poor man.

Roger's voice remains calm and full of love. "He believes he works under the will of God, but God would never wish for the things he has done to you and so many others. Look how he uses us, the dead. Not letting us rest. How could he be absolving us for heaven and then bind us here? We have not felt the warmth of heaven, son. Most of these poor souls don't even know they're dead, but you can release us, Simon. You can release all of us and let us rest in peace. Please."

The room fills with dozens of ghosts. They all echo Roger's words. "Please. Please. Please," they beg in a chorus of desperation. The woman I had seen before, the rather broken red-haired specter, stands next to me and whispers, "I'm so sorry."

"Helen?" I ask, and she nods. "Oh, Helen. I'm so sorry. We'll stop this now. We'll find a way to stop this, and you will be free at last. I just have to get out of here. Can you help me do that?" Even with the help of my bloodied left hand, I can't get my right hand free, no matter how much I rip the flesh.

"We all will try to help you," Mr. Hannon says. "You were right, Nickie. I am dead, and I've been dead for a long time. I saw my son and my wife above, and they've aged, just as you have. Besides, they couldn't see me and I can't touch them, just like you said. I can't do a thing to release their bonds. This fraud tied them up, and they're all so scared. Help us help all of you. What can we do?"

"I'll help you, my dove. Worry not." Fanny says as she steps into the secret room.

CHAPTER TWENTY-ONE

IN WHICH THE GHOSTS OF SOUTHWARK SAY GOODBYE

"Fanny! What are you doing here?" Which is what I opened my mouth to say, but another voice in the room said it first. The familiar voice came somewhere from inside the crowd of ghosts, but Fanny can't hear him.

"Oh, Nickie! You are all right! I'm not too late." She rushes over to me and strokes my face, then upon seeing my bloodied wrist, cries out. "What has he done to you?"

"Nothing yet. Get me out of these shackles, will you? We have to destroy that machine, then free Conrad and the others above."

"Did that on my way down, my lamb. Let's get you free so you can fight properly." With a simple wave of her hand, all five shackles pop open. Powerful witch, indeed, but I get the feeling she's not wielding her power alone. I caress my bloodied wrists and thank God for Fanny's timing. Anger rises. Fury at the betrayal, at what Benedict did to Simon and these poor specters, at what he was going to do to me. Mercy is quickly falling away from my vocabulary.

Simon steps forward to grab me again, and I take a fighting stance, ready to protect myself and Fanny at all costs. But Fanny whips her head around and throws up a flat palm towards him. The force of her power throws him against the dirt wall. His head hits with a dull thud and a grunt. The next moment, he's crumpled on the floor, arms wrapped around himself.

"Some Protector," she sneers. "Stay back, you." She wags a finger in reprimand, and Simon cowers against the stone wall, whimpering and sniveling and crying. Hugging his legs tightly. Broken, he is. Utterly.

"Easy on him, Fanny. He's known horror neither you nor I can begin to comprehend. He's brainwashed, and, I gather, controlled by that machine as well. Fanny, meet BESSIE: Benedict's Electric and Steam Specter Influencing Engine."

"Oh, my," she says. "How perfectly awful."

"Fanny! Fanny!" the voice from the host of ghosts says. "Fanny, it's me, Peter. Don't you remember me?" The dark-haired man makes his way to the front, and with downcast eyes says, "I wouldn't blame you if you chose to forget. I was horrid to you, Fanny. Simply awful."

"She can't hear you," I snap at him.

"Who are you talking to, pet? Are there ghosts in here now?"

"There are. Dozens of them. One of them knows you, Fanny, and is trying to talk to you." I can't bring myself to tell her who I think he is, with the name and his pleas for his bonny lass. My stomach turns, and I can't look at him for what he did to her. Must focus. "First, we have to destroy that machine. How did you find me? I'm just baffled, Fanny. Why are you here? How did you know?"

Fanny speaks as if we're at home enjoying a hot cup of tea. "I've been in contact with my coven, as you know I had planned, and they explained all they knew over the aether. I did as well, plus some catching up amongst old friends, you know. So nice to reconnect, even under such awful circumstances."

"Fanny!" My tone is frantic, urging her to hurry up. We haven't much time before Benedict regains consciousness, but Fanny doesn't seem to be the least bit concerned.

"Well, after sharing what I learned from the book as well, we knew how serious it was. We couldn't take any chances to wait, so we've been doing a circle around all of England for hours. Through that trance, we tracked you to ensure your safety. I saw what was happening here before you even arrived. Disgusting, this man is. Utterly." Fanny grimaces and shoots a hateful glance at the near-naked vicar lying in a heap, but when she looks back at me, she smiles, bright as a school girl who has just been given a new toy. "Powerful to connect with them again, my dove. I'm surging not only with my own powers, but with all of theirs, too. All through me! It is quite the experience."

"Witches," Simon spits. "You will all burn in hell where you belong!" There, curled up against the wall, his body trembles all over. I've never seen anyone so scared. Sweat streams from his brow, drenching his black mask. His eyes plead with me to help, but a moment later, they hold nothing but pain, then confusion, then anger. Emotion after emotion rotates through his features in mere seconds.

"Quite," Fanny snaps, but she's interrupted before she can say anything else.

Conrad and the others come into the room behind her. "Blimey," he says when he sees the torture implements and the giant machine and the unconscious, revolting priest. Rufus, Cassie, and Mrs. Hannon form a chain, all holding hands. Cassie's dolly dangling between Cassie and Rufus, its little hand caught up in theirs. Mrs. Hannon gasps and covers her mouth when she sees the state of me and the room, or perhaps just the sight of the virulent vicar is enough. Edwin stands on the other side of Rufus and reaches out for his free hand. Rufus jerks it away as if stung, then looks around to see what caused it. Little Cassie cries silently between Rufus and Mrs. Hannon, too scared to say anything. Franklin moves in front of the four and stands tall, crossbow raised, ready to attack when needed.

"They shouldn't be here, Conrad," I say. "Get them out of here. It isn't safe."

Conrad ignores my pleas and says to Fanny, "Thanks for releasing us up there, Miss McTavish. Cheers."

"Think nothing of it, dear boy. Back to the business at hand. Nickie's been hurt."

"Are you all right, Nickie?" Conrad rushes to my side and takes my bloody wrists into his hands with such a gentle touch. "I'll kill him for doing this to you," he says, but it's not anger I see in his eyes, not at first. Such tenderness in that moment, but then the anger comes. A fury rises up inside him, and just as Conrad rears back to kick Benedict, Simon gathers the fallen priest up in his arms.

"No," Simon says, "Don't hurt him anymore. He's dedicated his life to helping sinners like you, and this is how you repay him?"

Conrad looks at me with a quizzical expression. "He's mental."

"Long story," I say. "I'll fill you in later. Now, we have to destroy that machine and let all these souls free."

Mrs. Hannon now holds Cassie and Rufus, one under each arm, close to her skirts. "Is he here?" she asks. "Is my William here?" Her eyes scan the room without focus, trying to see what she cannot.

"Mum," Conrad begins in a regretful tone, but I put a hand on his arm to interrupt.

"He is, Mrs. Hannon." Conrad's face changes from anger to sadness back to anger again. Confusion. So much confusion. "Here. These will help." I take the goggles off of the unconscious priest's head while Simon kicks at my feet to get me away from his beloved abuser. I offer them to Mrs. Hannon. She takes them, with tears and gratitude. "Put those on. You'll be able to see them all through those," I explain.

She smoothes back her hair with trembling hands before putting them on, gasping as soon as she does. "There are so many of them! Oh, my goodness! So, so many of them," she cries while looking around through the goggles. "William! Oh, my William!"

"Laura!" he exclaims. They run to each other to embrace, but he passes right through her. She shudders, and I remember what it was like when Edwin moved through me. Icicles. Quite unsettling. "I'm so sorry," he says, facing each other again. "I forget, as I only just realized...I—I'm so confused, Laura. I miss you."

"Oh, William! I miss you, too! I thought I'd never see you again! Just this moment is worth everything I've endured. Just to see your sweet face again, my love." She reaches out to touch his cheek, but then snatches it back to avoid another freeze burn. "Oh! How I want to touch you!" Tears squeeze out from the bottom of the goggles.

My heart is in my throat watching them unable to touch, longing for something that can never be. Just like Ashe. Dead. Fanny and Conrad both stand close to me, and I'm so glad to have the people who mean most to me all here together in this place where such horrors have been committed and endured. In this hall of hell, all of us together fill it with love, and I can see by the faces of all the damned that they feel it, too. They remember joy and love and loss, and they're grateful. Ever since I first saw them, in this moment, they look more alive and serene than I've ever seen them. Confusion, gone. Pain, gone. Their nightmare is over and eternal peace, only a few moments away.

Conrad's eyes, glassy with grief, never leave his mother. I take his hand in support and hold it with all my might.

"I'm so sorry I left you. I was careless that day. Working long hours trying to make more for you, for both of you," he says, looking up at Conrad. "Yes. He can't see me either. Would you give those spectacles to Conrad for a moment so that I might talk with him? Please, Laura?"

"Of course," she said. Through her hesitation—as her hands move toward the goggles, then stop, then move again—I knew it took every bit of will and courage she had to remove the device that allowed her to see her husband again, not wanting to waste a moment, but she did so out of love for them both. She holds them out for him and says, "Conrad, your father wants to talk to you."

A tear spills over his lid and slides down his cheek, breaking his stoic facade. Always under so much pressure to be the man of the house, even before his mother had returned, and now more than ever. He doesn't allow himself to feel much more than anger, except with me. He can be himself with me, can't he? And I can by myself with him, fears and all. He takes the goggles from his mother and puts them on. "Blimey," he says and rears back, likely at the sight of just how many ghosts there are in this room.

"See why we have to destroy the machine, Conrad? All these poor souls are trapped. Your father and Edwin, too."

"Hello Conrad," Edwin says. The young specter waves frantically to his big brother, nearly jumping out of his little ghostly skin in his excitement at being seen. "I miss you so much. You and the others."

"We miss you, too," little Cassie says. She hugs her dolly close and moves into Rufus who protectively puts his arm around them both. Cassie turns into him and hides her face in his chest. Franklin moves behind them both, one arm on Rufus's shoulder, the other still holding the crossbow. Just in case. Big brother to all.

"We sure do, Edwin," he says. "I can't see you, little brother, but I can feel you here, and we miss you so much."

"Conrad. Son," Mr. Hannon says, and Conrad looks up to the voice.

"Father," he says and his face lights up like it's Christmas morning and he's just seen that new bicycle. "You look exactly the same. Like not a day has passed."

"You don't. My brave son. You have grown into a fine man, Conrad. I couldn't be more proud of you."

"Thank you, Father." Conrad bows his head. "I miss you so much. I've tried to be the man you would've wanted me to be. The man you were. I'm taking care of mum the best I can." Tears flow freely now, a little boy once again. "I—I love you."

"I love you, too, son. I see you gave my compass to this fine young woman, and I couldn't approve more. She is strong and kind and brave, all the qualities I see when I look into your face, son. Never let the other out of your sight," Mr. Hannon says to us both. "Love and be happy together."

Conrad doesn't have the heart to tell him we're just friends, and neither do I. He just nods and mumbles, "Goodbye, Father. May you find some peace until we meet again. I love you. Goodbye."

As soon as Mr. Hannon says, "Goodbye," Conrad rips the goggles off and hands them back to his mother to do the same. Stoic again, so I take his hand and squeeze it.

Benedict squirms in Simon's arms, so I urge, "Hurry, Mrs. Hannon. We have to destroy this machine before that evil man wakes up. I'm so sorry we don't have more time."

"I understand," she says. "I'm eternally grateful for these few moments." After the goggles are in place, she reaches out to where Mr. Hannon stands, and she doesn't pull back this time. Her hand touches his phantom cheek. It must be like grasping an icicle, burning her hand in its iciness, but she doesn't move away. "I will never forget you, my dear William. It's you. It's always been you, my love. My life stopped the day you left us, but seeing you again today has given me new hope. I will see you again after this painful life, and I will love you even more. Then, we'll spend eternity together."

"And I, you, my love. Your sweet face will keep me going until you can be in my arms in heaven. Until then, my sweet love. Until then."

"Until then," Mrs. Hannon says. They kiss. Ever so briefly, although one couldn't feel the other at all, they kiss. An expression of pure love.

"Please let me talk to Fanny," that dark-haired man begs. "Please. Just for a moment."

CHAPTER TWENTY-ONE

"No," I say to him. Fury rises. "Haven't you done enough?"

"Please, Miss. Please. I know I don't deserve it. I know I ruined her, and I don't deserve forgiveness. I know I don't deserve any of it, but please, let me tell her I at least know that now. Let me put any part of her mind that still blames herself at rest. Let me give her the peace I took from her. Let me at least ask for her forgiveness, although I do not deserve it. Please, Miss. Let me try to make it a little bit right."

My trembling lips form a scowl, and I glare at him through tear-filled eyes. She deserves peace, after all he's taken from her. I only hope it's the right decision. "Mrs. Hannon, would you let Fanny use those goggles for a moment, please?"

"Of course," she says and wipes her tears off of them before handing them to Fanny. Conrad goes immediately to his mother, pulling away from my hand to comfort her. They hold each other and cry, but contentment and a sense of peace emanates from them.

"Who is it?" Fanny asks before putting them on.

"You'll see. Put them on," I say. Benedict stirs again and groans. Simon squeezes him protectively. "Hurry," I beg, indicating the priest.

"Don't worry about him," Fanny says, and with a wave of her hand, he's unconscious again. Goggles on, she looks around the room in shock at the number of ghosts. "Oh, my. You weren't kidding, Nickie." Then, settling on the man so determined to talk to her, breathes one word: "Peter."

"Hello, Fanny. You're looking well." He steps out from the crowd of ghosts, head bowed in contrition. Phantom hat in phantom hand.

"You're dead," she says, stiffening. "Good."

"I deserve that and so much more. I'm just so grateful you're saying anything to me, Fanny. I was selfish and cruel to you. Horrible, I was. I have no excuse for how I treated you or the way I betrayed you."

"My life was ruined, Peter. Over. I didn't deserve that, not just for loving you. For trusting you."

"No, you didn't. You deserved someone who loved you for the amazing woman you are, Fanny. I didn't know how to love you and I did feel something real with you. Something deep, and it scared me so much that I had to destroy it, push you away. Cut you off. I was a fool. Selfish and cruel. Violent." He says the last with such shame.

I concur with Fanny. Good.

"I hope you believe me when I say that I'm sorry. I have suffered greatly at the hands of that priest, in ways that I cannot bring myself to speak. I've endured myself what I had done to you, and I had to watch countless others as he exacted his treachery, his absolution. But-but I'm not complaining, Fanny." He face brightens a moment. "Oh, no. I deserved every second of it for what I did to you. I have paid for my own treachery time and again. Once that young girl destroys that blasted machine, I suppose I will be released, but I cannot rest in peace without your forgiveness, Fanny. Even if the Almighty takes mercy on my wretched soul, I cannot rest in peace without your forgiveness. Can you, after all this time, forgive a stupid, selfish man? A frightened man. A coward. Not that it excuses what I did," he adds quickly. "No, nothing can do that, but can you find it in your heart to forgive me, even if I don't deserve it?"

"I've never loved, you know. Never loved since you, Peter. I couldn't risk such devastation again. Because of you, I've isolated myself to avoid further harm. You forced your cowardice into me that day. Yes, violently violated me and transferred a piece of your cowardly soul into me. I have lived alone for over twenty years because of you."

"Oh, my." The ghostly white specter turned even whiter at her words. "Then, indeed, I haven't suffered enough to pay for what I've done. Don't forgive me, sweet bonny lass, for I destroyed pure beauty with my selfish, horrid act. I took someone young and free, full of life and light, and squelched it, all for a few moments of pleasure, of power. No. Don't ever forgive me. I shall continue my well-deserved torment for doing such damage as to rob you of a life of love. Don't forgive me.

Ever." Peter shamefully hangs his head and covers his face in utter remorse. Through his ghostly hands, his muffled voice says, "Even after all the absolution at the hands of that evil monster, I shall still rightfully burn in hell. I'm so sorry, Fanny." He turns to move back into the crowd, to hide in his shame, avoiding the eyes of everyone in the room, even the ghosts.

"I forgive you," she says, reaching out to him in his pain. With pity, she retracts her hand once again, knowing she can't touch him. He turns back to her and she looks upon him with such compassion, not a shred of hate or anger or anything else. Compassion and even love. "How can I not forgive you, Peter? I loved you then and I love you still. Once in a woman's heart, you are always there, even when you treat it thus. All I even needed was for you to admit it, to take responsibility and acknowledge the damage you caused. To apologize, offer a sacrifice, and made amends. I see you've done that now. I release you, Peter, and I forgive you. Rest in peace now, and free me to finally love."

"I don't deserve such mercy, Fanny, but I accept your gracious forgiveness. Humbly. Go and love, my dear. Love a good man. A true man with integrity. An honest man. A man who would never do to you what I did— what far too many do," he said with a grimace toward the vile vicar. "May they pay as I have. Go and love, Fanny. Goodbye, my bonny lass. No one ever loved me the way you did, and I tossed it aside, destroyed it out of fear and selfish entitlement. I had everything with you, and I ruined it. I don't deserve this forgiveness and grace, no. Your goodness is proven once again on this day. Goodbye, my dear."

Fanny takes off the goggles and tosses them to me. "It's done," she says and turns from the group to face the wall for a moment alone with her nostalgia, her grief and elation, her long-awaited resolution. Everyone in the room is quiet with her, taking in this reverent moment.

I think of Ashe, frightened and alone. Perhaps he suffers like this, too. Perhaps his fear shattered our love as well, but it matters not. That love lies in ruin; no reviving it. Now, there is only remorse and woe.

Simon cowers and mewls, like a whimpering abused animal. His soul and mind so splintered by the vicar's "love" that his capacity to love has been forever intertwined with betrayal, deception, and horrific abuse. So much pain.

Then, Conrad. He stands with his mother in their grief.

It's Fanny who breaks the silence. She repeats my words, "Destroy it. Now. Let these poor souls rest now. Let them finally rest at peace."

Chapter Twenty-Two

In Which the Clan of Ashen Returns

"NO!" Simon shouts. "You can't destroy BESSIE. It'll destroy him, too." He pulls the grotesque priest off the ground with him as Simon clambers to his feet and holds the vile vicar's emaciated, scarred form in a protective embrace. "You can't. He's my father. He's my protector."

"He's your abuser, Simon," Roger says, moving closer to Simon and reaching out to him. The sadness and regret in his voice are palpable. "Remember, son? Remember?"

Simon's face contorts in his agony, confusion. Face wet with tears and cheeks the color of his hair, Simon shrieks, "You left me! You left! I had no one else. No one but Benedict and Buck. Where else can I turn?" Squeezing the priest against him, Simon kisses his bare shoulder and arms. "He loves me." Benedict shakes his head and begins to wake up.

"Conrad," I implore, squeezing his hand, "Get your mother and the children out of here. Get them to safety. Please."

He clutches my hand desperately and pulls me close to him and his family. "No, I'm not leaving you alone down here with these madmen. We're not leaving you here alone." Then, whispers against my cheek, "I'm never leaving your side again, Nickie."

Forehead to forehead, surrounded by lunacy and death and regret, I appeal to his sense of goodness and love, hoping to show him that the only way we will all make it is if he lets me do my work without having to worry about all of them. "Please. Let me and Fanny finish this. We must focus here, and this is no place for children, Conrad. I'm counting on you to keep them safe. It's all our best chance to get out of here alive.

"All right," he says, releasing his mother's hand to cradle my face and look into my eyes. "Come out of here safely, yourself, Nick. Come back safe to me."

Gently, I lower his hands from such an intimate embrace, for such shows of intimacy terrify me about as much as that horrid priest, after being betrayed by love twice already. Then, I assuage his fears. "I will. I promise. Now, go."

"Goodbye, Edwin," Conrad says into the air. The other three children repeat their own goodbyes in the wrong direction, except for Cassie, who looks directly at him. The other's can't see Edwin, but they all know he's there now.

"No! Don't leave me," Edwin begs and cries, clawing at them desperately. His little hands go right through them. "I want to come, too! I want to come, too!"

But they can't hear him and all they feel is the chill of his phantom fingers passing through their flesh. They huddle closer together and eagerly crowd in the doorway, ready to leave.

"Stay here with me, Edwin. All right? I need your help. Will you stay and help me?" His little bottom lip is pushed out in the most adorable pout, and he nods his agreement. He's but a child, yet he knows he's dead and cannot remain with the living. "Thank you, my sweet." I reach out to take his hand and brace myself for the icy sensation, but I do not pull away from him. Instead, I invite him to come closer. Then, as Edwin cuddles against my side, I mouth the word "GO" to Conrad, and thankfully he does because Benedict regains full consciousness a moment later and tries to escape Simon's embrace. Benedict's face is twisted in anger and he struggles to get free, but Simon, taller and by far stronger than the vile vicar, holds on tighter.

"I can put him out again," Fanny says matter-of-factly. "Just say the word, Nick." She's enjoying this power, even if she's as horrified as I am about the situation. No doubt, she feels a sense of purpose helping like this, and connection with her sisters in magic as well. On top of all that, she's finally found peace from an old demon that has been haunting her these many, many years.

"It's all right, Fanny. I want him to see this, the destruction of his treachery. Then, the police can have him. Keep him contained, if Simon lets go, but conscious."

"Consider it done, my dove." She takes a fighting stance, just as she's taught me, and she focuses her eyes on Benedict, ready to act at a moment's notice.

"What's—what's going on? What are you going to do, girlie? You think you can stop me?" Benedict spits as he speaks. Long dribbles of saliva spill out of his mouth and onto his stubbly chin.

Tears gush down Simon's face. His knuckles and wrists are white from embracing the priest with all his might. Benedict bears his teeth and digs his fingernails into Simon's flesh, but Simon will not let go. Tiny half moon cuts release blood that trickles down Simon's arms. Still, Simon won't let go. "Don't do anything to hurt him," he says. "Please. Just go. Everyone go and leave us alone."

"You're stronger than this, Simon," Roger says gently, still standing near his son. "You're The Protector, remember? You were born to fight against evil like this man. It is your sacred duty."

"No! My powers are from God's grace, not witches, and he's not evil, neither," Simon snaps. "*He* showed me what love was. *He* loved me like no one ever has, and he loves me again now. He forgives me for forsaking him. He loves me with God's special love."

Benedict's definition of love and absolution fills my head with rage, and I see red. That vile vicar hurt Simon over and over through the years, damaged him beyond repair. Yet, Simon holds onto the priest for dear life—his or the priest's, I'm not sure.

Roger stands in front of Simon and the priest now, but without the goggles, Benedict cannot see him. Simon can, because he is, indeed, The Protector, just like me. He snivels at Roger's kind words, unable to let go of the reality that has been forced on him for too long. Even a moment is too long, but after years of such treatment, he would have to believe it was love in order to survive. He can't bear to see it for what it is. Roger knows this and tries to reason with him, but there is no one there with whom to reason. Just a shell of a broken man. Roger's love for Simon, however, refuses to admit defeat. "You're bonded to him in pain, son. You can break that bond. You can see clearly again, just remember what I taught you. Remember what real love feels like. It's not exploitation and violation; it's not what this madman calls absolution. It's pure. It's without expectation, without judgment or pain, without remorse. Remember? Just let go, son. Just let him go."

Simon's grasp relaxes, but Fanny's extended hand keeps Benedict from escaping Simon's hold. Simon's eyes dart back and forth from me to Roger to Benedict. His expression is one of confusion, so desperate to understand, but there is no understanding this. Not for any of us. Simon keeps his arms locked around the priest and pecks tiny kisses over the back of the vile vicar's head and cheek and neck and shoulder. He's past saving.

The host of ghosts take up chanting, "Release us. Please release us. Please let us be at peace. Finally. Please release us."

With so much sorrow and feelings of utter hopelessness, I whisper, "Now, Fanny. Do it now."

"Goodbye, Simon," Roger says with such sadness. The words come not from his throat or mouth but from his very soul. "I love you, son. May you find peace."

"I love you, too, Roger. I love you, too." Simon bawls, but he never lets go of Benedict.

"Do it now, Fanny!"

She releases the hold on the priest and whips her arms around in a wide circle, conjuring up her power and the power of her coven's circle all at once. Benedict shouts, "NO!" and breaks free from Simon's embrace, stopping long enough to slap Simon across the face before lunging toward the table of torture instruments.

Simon holds his injured cheek, and with fresh tears cries, "NO! NO! I can't let you." He dives in front of BESSIE just as Fanny blasts the infernal engine with her combined powers. Simon squeals in pain. His soul flies up and his body falls down.

"Simon!" I shout, rushing to his fallen form, but it's too late.

"I'm so sorry! He jumped in front of the spell. Oh! What have I done? What have I done?" Fanny's hands press into her rosy cheeks and her eyes search mine for forgiveness.

Roger rushes to Simon's soul, now able to touch him since they're on the same plane, and holds him close, telling him it's all right. Everything will be all right. Simon's shade curls up into Roger's arms. Roger hushes Simon's tears over and over, stroking Simon's hair. I tear my eyes away from them and force myself to not look at Simon's lifeless body, telling myself that now he might find some safety and peace. The tragic loss of Simon's life quickly fades into the gulf of calamity around us. BESSIE remains intact. The Ghosts of Southwark are still here. Still trapped. Still suffering. Still wailing to be released. I shout over their clamor, "Again, Fanny. Blast it again. We must let these poor souls know some peace." Then I turn to her when no blast comes, and freeze.

Benedict has a crossbow pointed right at Fanny. "You will not stop me, woman. A tramp like you will never stop a Man of God!"

"Man of God," a gravelly voice says in mockery. Six inhuman, horrific faces scowl at Benedict from the doorway. The symbol burned in their foreheads betrays their identity. "You are even more evil than we are," the one in front says. "And just as damned."

Benedict turns his aim to the vampire and pulls the trigger. The Clan of Ashen vampire snatches the arrow out of midair, just before it pierces its chest, then rushes Benedict. The rest charge in after him.

I push Fanny against the wall and stand in front of her. Our exit is blocked, and now we're not only in danger from this blasted vicar but also surrounded by vampires. I sent Conrad and the others upstairs. Did they fall prey to these monsters? I hope beyond hope they got away in time, but worrying about that now won't do me or Fanny any good.

Fingers blackened with age encircle Benedict's throat and holds his struggling frame off the ground. The crossbow lies splintered below his feet. Benedict gasps and spittle dribbles down his chin. His eyes protrude even more than usual, but despite all this, he laughs. "You think you can destroy me, Christoph?" he croaks. "I'm a soldier of God, you fools. I own you, control you. You work for me, remember?"

"Work for you?" Simon's shade asks, peering out from Roger's arms. "You ordered me to destroy them. You told me they killed Roger."

"Shut your mouth, boy," Benedict hisses. "Do as you're told."

"Did he now?" Christoph says. Its mouth pulls back tight against its pointed teeth into what appears to be an attempt to smile, but it's about as warm as a skull's deathly grin in the catacombs. "How very interesting, Benedict. Playing one against the other, are we? You had us kill Roger in order to get your special boy back. Disgusting as I find your behavior with boys, you offered us something more. Absolution. True absolution, not what you do to these souls. You promised us that when we left this existence, our severed souls would find their way to heaven, so you sent your little doggy out to speed up that process, did you?"

"This is all just a big misunderstanding, Christoph. Let me down, and I'll explain everything." Benedict's tongue darts out and licks his cracked lips. From this angle, it looks forked. "You can't kill me without destroying yourself. Don't you see? You are forever connected to me, to my power. I die. You die." Benedict thumps the vampire on its forehead, right over the branded symbol, then spits on its face.

"You lied to me?" Simon sobbed from Roger's arms. "You killed Roger? Everything he said was true? You had him killed to get me back again?"

"Shhhhh." Roger tries to soothe Simon's agony. "It's over now, son. We're free of him now. Peace is before us now. We'll find that peace together. Just a few moments more."

"I warned you once, boy. Shut your mouth!" Benedict's eyes turn completely black. He cackles and croaks from beneath Christoph's grasp. "Do your worst, Christoph. You and your demonic minions."

Christoph's men spread around the room. Two guard the door. Two flank Christoph, ready to help with Benedict, and the last vampire stands between the exit and Fanny and me. We are greatly outnumbered, and although I'd love for them to take care of Benedict for us, I'd rather we leave alive, too.

Please, let Conrad and my friends be all right upstairs. Please.

I push back against Fanny, moving us both closer to BESSIE and taking a step away from the guarding vampire each time he looks back at Christoph and Benedict.

"What are we to do, Christoph?" one of the other vampires says. "Does he speak the truth? Will we also die if we destroy him? Will we burn in hell forever? Or cease to exist altogether?" Their inhuman features show fear, a feeling shared by all life forms, apparently.

"This is unexpected. He's probably lying, but I'm not willing to take that chance. Of course, we don't have to kill him." Christoph smiles that deadly grin again. "We just can make him wish he were dead. Yes, we will have lots of fun with him, and with them." His eyes dart over to me and Fanny for a moment. They all laugh, including Benedict. Little do these vampires know that pain is Benedict's ultimate pleasure.

"Again, Fanny." I whispered. "It's our only chance. Blast it again! Now, Fanny."

The vampire guarding us takes a step forward, and I spin into a back kick, impaling the fiend on the stake from my boot. "NOW!" I shout. Just as the two flanking Christoph come at me, she winds her arms up again and sends a second blast to BESSIE, this time hitting her in a massive explosion. The force of it blows us all back, including the vampires, who writhe on the floor as if in great pain. Then, in another moment, they melt into piles of dust.

The host of ghosts exclaim, "Thank you! Thank you! Thank you!" all at once, then are gone.

The shrillest scream I've ever heard comes from Benedict's throat, his forked tongue flailing about and face distorted in his horror. Before my eyes, he grows old. Really old. Like over a hundred years in an instant. Wrinkles appear. His skin stretches over the bones, and his black, greasy hair turns silver, then white. It cascades out of his scalp, growing three feet from every direction. His eyelids retract and his bulgy eyes pop out of his head. They fall onto his emaciated cheeks before dropping completely out of the empty sockets and splash on the floor with a plop. His leathery, shrunken skin falls away until nothing but a skeleton is left. In horror, we watch his bones turn to dust.

It's over.

Ashes to ashes. Dust to dust.

Chapter Twenty-Three

In Which Nickie Nick
Gets to Sleep

Fanny collapses into a heap on the stone floor, so I rush over to her. "Fanny! Fanny!" I shout. "Fanny, are you all right?" I can't lose her. I just can't lose her after all this. I look around the room to see if her spirit is here, for she's not breathing at all. "Fanny! Please don't leave me! Please!"

Nothing remains. Not her ghost. Not anyone's ghost. They're all gone. Now, just silence except for the sound of my frantic breath and racing thoughts. "They've all left me alone, Fanny. You can't leave me, too. Please," I whisper into her temple, cradling her in my arms.

"I'm still here," a small voice says.

"Edwin! Oh, my sweet boy, Edwin! Why are you still here?"

"I wasn't with the rest of them. That bad man wasn't making me do stuff like he was the others. I stayed to help you, Nickie. I wanted to help you stop the bad man."

"Oh, sweet Edwin. You did help! You did! But I want you to be at peace, my love. I don't want you to be gone at all, but if you must be, then be at peace."

"I want to be here with you. With you and Conrad and Cassie and Rufus and Franklin and even Conrad's mum, Mimi. I want to be with all of you. You're my family. I want to be with you."

"We all miss you so much, Edwin, but they can't see you. You know that. You will feel so alone here. Go and find peace, my dove, and we will join you soon enough. We will see you again, Edwin. I promise."

Edwin sniffs and looks down at his phantom feet. "I don't know how. This is all I see. Please don't cast me aside, Nickie. Please. I'll be all alone here."

Poor little thing. Perhaps he's trapped here, unable to cross over. "Did you see Fanny pass over? Is she with you now?" The tears cascade down my cheeks now, fearing the answer.

"No. She's with you. She's still with you on that side. See?"

Fanny gasps in my arms: a sharp intake of breath, fighting for air. I pull her onto my lap and rock her back and forth, holding her soft body as close to me as my strength will allow. "Please don't die, Fanny," I say, kissing her brow. "Please. Please don't leave me. Not after all this, you can't leave me, too."

"It's all right, child," she manages. "You can't get rid

of me that easily. Let loose a bit. You're crushing me."

"Oh! Fanny! You're all right! You're all right! Thank goodness," I ramble, and then just let everything spill out to my governess, my friend, my very own protector. "This has been such a horrible time. Is this what it will always be like as The Protector? So much loss? So much pain? So much betrayal? Is this my life? In just a few short months, everything has changed. I fell in love and it was ripped away. Betrayed by him, then Simon, too. Then these horrid people like Pilkington and Benedict. Worse than vampires and demons, they are. Monsters have no choice but to be monsters. Benedict had a choice. Pilkington had a choice. They had free will, and they chose to destroy. They justified their abominations as the will of God or in the name of science. Is this what my life will be? Loss and pain and betrayal?"

"Oh, Nicole," she says in a soft voice. Her rosy cheeks and kind eyes look at me with the same love Roger had when he looked at Simon. "I'm afraid that's what everyone's life is like, my dove. You're an adult now, so you're seeing the world for what it is. This ugly, cruel world. Yet, there is love in it. Never enough, that's for certain. Never enough to push out the evil, but there is, indeed, love, and you have so much love in your life, Nicole. I am here with you, and I will never leave you, never betray you. Together we will make it through. You also have Conrad and the others. Good friends who shan't betray you. They are few and far between, my dove. Cherish them."

"I won't betray you either, Nickie. I promise," Edwin says.

"See, Edwin is here to stay, too."

"You can see him?"

"I can. Something happened, I suppose, when I was unconscious. As the magic passed through me, it left something behind. A residual sense of power or perception or something. Hello, Edwin. I'm so sorry you died."

"Me, too. That wasn't at all fun. I miss running in the sunshine with Cassie and playing patty cake and hide-and-go-seek. I miss the warm hugs of Mimi and Conrad. I even miss being teased and tweaked by Rufus, but I'm so glad you can see me now."

"I am, too."

"It makes me feel less alone. Maybe you can use your magic so the others can see me, too!"

"I can certainly try, dear boy. Let me see what I can learn once I'm back with my books."

"Yay!" Edwin says and then zips up to the ceiling, around the room a few times, and back down by us. "I sure couldn't do that when I was alive! That was fun!"

"That looks like fun," Fanny says. She sits up and smooths out her dress. "What are we to do with Simon's body? He jumped in the way, Nickie," she explains again. "I didn't mean to…"

"I know you didn't. He sacrificed himself to save Father Benedict. After so much damage caused by that horrible man, I think Simon must be better off with Roger in heaven now, or wherever they are. He might find some peace there. As for his body, I don't know. I suppose someone will find it down here or we can bury him ourselves."

"I think that would be best. We can't just leave him here."

"We can bury him in Cross Bones with the other forgotten people, but they'll all be remembered by us. Winchester's Geese, the poor of St. Saviour's, and now Simon, too."

"I want to go home," Edwin says. "Can I go home now?"

"Yes, and I'll see you there tomorrow, all right? Will you watch over all of them for me until I get there? Keep them safe?"

"Yes! Oh, yes! I can do that, Nickie! I like to help you."

"No scaring anyone though. Be a good boy."

"Yes ma'am. I will."

"Remember, they can't see you, at least not yet."

"Cassie can."

"That's true," I say, laughing a little. "She sure can. You go and be with Cassie. Be with your family."

"Bye-bye, Nickie! I love you!" Edwin zipped out of

the secret door and up the stairs, off to be with his family.

"I love you, too, sweet boy," I whisper after him.

Fanny kneels over Simon's fallen form, weeping. "I'm not strong enough to lift him," she cries. "Just a feeble old woman." This has been hard on her, too. On all of us.

"I'll collect him, Fanny. Then let's leave this place forever." Simon's body lay in front of BESSIE's remains, mere kindling now. No one will ever be able to put her back together. I pick up his limp form and carry him up the long, dark staircase. He's still warm, and it looks like he's just sleeping. I hope he has pleasant dreams.

Fanny does a quick spell once we're at Cross Bones to open the earth for Simon, and I say a few words. I remove his mask so that he might go into the afterlife free from shame. Such a beautiful boy, after all. My tears wet his face, and I think how I could've loved him. However, after the life he had known, he could never receive true love. He only knew pain and abuse under the guise of love.

"Rest in peace, sweet Simon."

I lay him in his open grave and watch as all those buried around him embrace him in death. None of them will ever be alone again. The pain in their lives binds them together in death.

Fortunately, Fanny had Wilfred drive her to the east

end. He borrowed the carriage, and we must get it back before anyone notices it's missing. I'm quite pleased I don't have to walk all the way home. It's been a long day.

I admit, I already miss Simon, and I feel very confused about his betrayal. He was quite obviously brainwashed, but he still deceived me. I trusted him, but he didn't deserve that trust.

First Ashe. Now Simon. Throw in Doctor Pilkington and Father Benedict. Leaders of the community. Men we're supposed to trust. A healer and a man of God. How can I trust anyone? So much has happened in the past three months. I ponder on how drastically one's life can change in such a short time, how everything certain can become uncertain. My mind reels from all I've seen tonight, from the agony experienced by the Ghosts of Southwark and by Simon, himself. I wonder what the point to any of it is. Then, Fanny takes Wilfred's hand and pecks him on the cheek when we get home.

Love. She's right about that, too. We do have love.

That's what it's about.

Fanny is still here. She has always been here. She will always be there for me until the day she dies, or I die.

Conrad, too. My best friend. My confidant. Always here.

I sink into my soft bed, vowing not to decide anything tonight, and I drift into a deep, dreamless sleep.

CHAPTER TWENTY-FOUR

IN WHICH NICKIE NICK
SHOWS MERCY

February 20, 1881

After a full day where I do nothing but sleep and eat my fill of apple tarts, I make my way back to the east side, taking my time. So much to think about. I wind up and down the cobblestone streets, my day skirt flapping in the wind, always emerging from the tall buildings again on the south bank overlooking my beloved Thames. Those lovely grey skies reflect in its dark waters. As I get ever closer to Blackfriars, I wonder what I'll say. After everything that's happened, after what Mr. Hannon said about us, I just don't know what to do.

I find that I'm scared. Not of demons or of vampires or even of creepy, vile vicars. I'm scared of love.

My thoughts turn to Fanny and what Peter said to her. She had lived her entire life afraid of love. That can't be me. That won't be me. I must be cautious, is all, but not shut myself off completely.

I wind my way up another dark alleyway and trip over someone hidden in the shadows.

"Pardon me," I say. "I didn't see you there."

"Nickie," a weak voice says.

"Do I know you?"

"I thought you did," he says, and I recognize the voice now. It's one I do not wish to hear. The one I hoped to never have to hear again.

Ashe moves into the relative light, just to the edge of daylight. He looks awful, as if he hasn't eaten in weeks. Hasn't slept or bathed or anything. His black eyes are hollow. His cheeks sunken and grey. His hair, a matted mess.

He reaches out to me, and I, all at once, want to comfort him and recoil in disgust.

"What's happened to you, Ashe?"

"I'm purifying myself for you."

That sounds a little too close to what Father Benedict said, so I back up from him, gaining a safe distance, more afraid of him than ever.

"I'm sick without you, Nickie. Please. Forgive me for my stupidity. Please. Come back to me. I love you. I *need* you."

My heart melts. Something Fanny said rings true. Once in a woman's heart, always in a woman's heart. Despite all he's done. Despite the betrayal. Despite him casting me aside like rubbish. Despite his abandonment. I love him still.

Then, those weeks of agony return and my gut clenches in protest. I love him, so true. Always will. My first love. My Ashe. But I remember Simon, trapped in an abusive bond with a man who used that word "love" as well. It destroyed poor Simon, was his undoing in the end. I will not let that kind of "love" destroy me, for that is not love at all.

"Please give me another chance, Nick," Ashe says, his words and his eyes plead with me.

"Why?" I'm being difficult, and I don't care. Not after what I've endured. "You left. If that's the way you handle problems in a relationship, then how can I ever count on you? I don't want that for my life, Ashe. I want someone who will be there, who I can depend on, who will turn toward love, not run away in fear."

"I won't leave again, Nicole. I promise. I was scared, and I didn't know what to do. This is just all so confusing and so wrong. I'm a vampire, and you're a vampire hunter! How can this..."

"Work? It can't. This proves it right here. Forget what you are and what I am, that's not the problem. It's *who* you are, Ashe. You're asking to come back all while saying it won't work. You need to figure out, not only what you want, which you clearly don't know, but also what you can offer. What you can honestly and realistically offer another person before involving another's heart. It's unfair and cruel."

He swallows hard, but didn't say anything. His top lip curls slightly in anger at the judgement.

"After you left…" I continue, forcing the tears back.

It is still so raw, especially after the rest of the loss. Especially after Edwin, whose death I still hold Ashe responsible. "I didn't know the meaning of heartbreak until you left. I heard the words and heard stories, but nothing could've prepared me for the soul-crushing pain I endured—that you left me in—because of your vacillations and cowardice. I'm not going through that again for you or for anyone. I believed in you, Ashe. I trusted you. I loved you, and you just left."

"I made a mistake, Nicole. Can you forgive me?" His tone is far from kind this time. It had turned as hard and cold as his stone lips. Behind those words, an accusation hangs in the air.

"I can and have, but that doesn't change anything. A very wise woman once told me that one's entire life can be defined by a single choice. Will that choice be made out of courage and integrity or cowardice and what feels good in the moment. This very fleeting moment."

"I still love you, Nickie." Ashe's voice is now small, almost not even there.

"I still love you, too, Ashe," I reply, matter-of-factly, for it's true. "Once you're in my heart, you're in my heart forever. I truly do love you, Ashe, but love is not enough, not in the end. When I look into your eyes I want to forget everything. I want to forget my duty, my family, my friends. I want to forget myself and just be in your arms. I want to give up everything and become a part of you, for you to become a part of me. To merge in body and soul, nothing else is close enough. To be consumed by you."

"My love! I want that, too!" Ashe reaches toward me, hope in his dark eyes, but I pull away, putting my hand up between us. I stop him, and my heart stops with him.

"But then what happens the next morning? I will not go through that again because you don't know what you want. You're right. This—us—we're doomed from the beginning. All this will be for either of us is pain and more pain. We will destroy each other through love, and I choose to love and create, not love and destroy. That's what I choose for me. I would rather have you in my life, fighting by my side, than give into this destructive force between us. Our lives are not our own, Ashe. We have a higher calling."

"I don't know if I can work so close to you and not touch you. Even now, it's as if my body has a will of it's own. It's taking every fiber of strength not to take you here, not to kiss you, not to touch you, not to make you mine."

Words of possession, ownership. Words that echo what Fanny said to me, and his voice becomes a growl near the end. I step back even further.

"I will never be yours or any man's. I am my own. No one owns me, Ashe. No one controls me, certainly not a man. Never ever any man, least of all you."

"But, Nickie. I can't control myself. Your body, your blood, burns my eyes, my flesh."

He reaches out for me, and I deflect his grasp, taking him down. My boot rests on his throat. "I said no, Ashe. I will stake you right here if you persist. You have shown again and again both in action and in words that you care nothing for what I want. It's what you want. Always what you want. It's what you want for me, to do with me, to own me. Never."

"It's torture being with you. It's torture being away from you," Ashe speaks into the snow. His voice squeaks from beneath my boot, and he doesn't even try to escape.

"Passion," I say. "You feel as passionately for me as I do for you. Do you know where that word comes from? It's Greek. Pathos. It means 'to suffer,' and that's what this is between us, Ashe. It's not love, not a healthy love. It's toxic. It's a drug, an insatiable need. We won't stop until we are both destroyed along with everyone we love. Edwin already paid that price for my weakness, for my passion, for your betrayal. No more. Not another will die because of this nonsense."

Ashe weeps blood tears, staining the snow beneath his face.

"Look around, Ashe," I continue. "We're surrounded by predators, by supernatural monsters and even just people out to hurt other people. Out to control, to destroy. There's so much pain, most caused by selfish people, and I'm not going to contribute to that over love, not this kind of love. We have the opportunity to stop it, Ashe! You and me. We have the power to help other people, to save them from pain, from the nefarious desires of bad people. You and me, but we can't do that if we're distracted by this toxic love. No more, Ashe. No more. This is our sacrifice. We must give up each other, despite the all-consuming desire, so that we can save the world. Our love burns too bright, and it will annihilate us."

"How can I let you go?" he says, puling.

"Find a way. You did it once before, so you can do it again. If you can't bear to work by my side, then you can work on my side. For me, for the good of us all, but I will not take a chance in love with you again. You left. That singular decision defined our relationship, defined you. Your actions today have reinforced that. I want someone who will be there, who has always been there. A sustainable love. A trusting love. A fearless love."

I catch my breath and stumble back from Ashe, releasing him from my hold. Realization smothers me like a heavy blanket, warm and safe against the cold February wind. "Conrad," I breathe into the night. The word hangs in the air, trapped in a cloud of frozen breath.

In an instant, I'm under Ashe. In the space of a blink or a sigh. Hard flesh pins me into the snow-covered cobblestones. His eyes angry and teeth bared. "Not that child!" he hisses. "I'm not losing you to that little boy!" He's kicking my legs apart, one hand at my throat, the other pulling up my skirt. I freeze in that moment, trapped beneath the weight and strength of this vampire. Down a dark alley in London where no one will come, no matter how loudly I scream. I'm alone.

Fanny comes to mind. Peter. The word bully.

All maids find out the hard way.

Not this maid. Not today. Not like this.

I don't scream. No need. In my mind, Ashe is already ash, but the stake I ripped from my corset without even thinking just misses his heart. Perhaps it was mine that shifted my aim, perhaps it was bad luck.

Ashe cries beneath me, sobbing apologies in the night, but I have no more tolerance for his sniveling or empty apologies. "The next time I see you, I won't miss. You will never touch another woman. Do you understand? You will stay away from humans. You will feed on rats and other vermin. You will stay underground, coming out only to hunt other monsters like you. But you had better stay away from me. Stay away from those I love. Stay away for good this time, Ashe. That means stop following me, too. If I see you again, I won't even ask. I'll just stake. Is that understood?"

He nods. Blood tears stain his chalky cheeks and the snow beneath his pathetic face.

Head held high, I walk away. Free.

I can trust again because I can trust myself. I can take care of myself, just as I told Conrad again and again. I have been tested, and I have proven victorious.

I can trust myself, so I can love anew.

CHAPTER TWENTY-FIVE

IN WHICH NICKIE NICK
FLIES THROUGH LONDON

I almost run the rest of the way to Conrad's. The heels of my boots fall harder against the cobblestones with each new step. Faster and faster I make my way to my beloved's. How did I not see it before?

It's Conrad. It's always been Conrad.

Throwing myself up against the stone wall overlooking The Thames, I look out over the water. Fear, suddenly, returns. What will I say? I've always thought he felt that way about me, but what if he doesn't? What if I make a fool of myself? What if he laughs at me?

"No," I say to the passing barge on those lovely grey waters. "Fear will not keep me from love. I know what I want. I know who I love. Now it's time to lay my heart out before him to either accept or deny, but I will not be afraid of the unknown."

Running at full speed now, not caring who sees, I turn onto Barge House Street and sprint up their inner staircase. I knock and knock and knock. I knock like

I've never knocked before. Out of breath, hair mussed from the scuffle and nose numb from running in the cold, it occurs to me that I don't look my best. I smooth back my hair just as Mrs. Hannon answers the door.

"Why, hello, Nickie. Come in, dear," she says.

"Is Conrad in, ma'am?"

"Of course. Everyone is here." She blocks me from stepping past her, putting her hands on my shoulders. With deep gratitude and the sparkle of a hidden tear, she says, "Thank you, again, for last night. I can never repay you for giving me the chance to say goodbye. Thank you, Nickie."

Before I can respond, Conrad comes into view. I've seen him a thousand times on a thousand different days, but today my voice got stuck in my throat. "Um," I say. Then I blink a few times, and I say, "Um." Again.

You've got real charm, Nickie.

"Hello, Nick. All right?" Conrad is as casual and friendly as ever. His smile lights up all of London. He pats his mother on the back as they pass each other in the foyer.

"A—all right," I manage.

"Come with me," he says, then takes me by the hand. My heart flutters at his touch and a warm, tingly feeling moves up my arms. "Mum. I'll be back in a bit. Nickie and I are going out," he shouts into the flat.

"All right," she responds from the other room.

"Come home safe."

"I will." He leads me out the door and into the street.

"Where are we going?" I ask.

"You'll see," he says and takes both my hands in his.

"I—I want to tell you something," I stammer, not trusting myself to have the courage later. I must tell him now.

"Wait," he whispers into my ear, so close I must catch my breath. "Close your eyes."

I smile and then bite my lip, wondering what he will do. His arms encircle my waist and he says, "Hold on tight," so I throw my arms around his neck, hoping I never have to let go.

The next thing I know, the wind whips around and up my skirts, blowing my hair into a mess Fanny won't ever let me forget, I'm sure. "Open your eyes," he breathes into my cheek, "but don't let go and don't look down."

We're flying! High above London, and I hug him tighter than ever. "Conrad! How are we doing this? Is this really happening?"

"What? Did you think you'd be able to show Franklin that levitating device without him making (and improving) one of his own?"

The Thames snakes beneath our feet like a long, dark serpent, even more beautiful from this vantage. The cold February wind chaps my cheeks, making me want to snuggle in closer to Conrad, so I do. My best friend. My confidant. My love. He knows me so well, and I him.

He takes me to my favorite place in all of London. People on the streets below point up to us, mouths open wide in shock. We arrive just at the stroke of noon, and those beautiful bells ring out as Conrad and I hover in front of the great clock face. As the jingle of the Westminster Chimes stops and the twelve loud dongs begin, Conrad's smile fades. I have never in all the time I've known him to look so serious, so grown up. The boy I knew was forever gone and a man holds me now.

I hold my breath, wanting to say the words I feel with ever fiber of my being. My whole heart sings out to him, but I'm rendered speechless.

"I love you, Nickie," he says. His eyes search mine for understanding, for hope, for any sign that I'm there with him. "I've loved you as long as I've known you."

"I love you, too, Conrad. I'm sorry it took me this long to figure that out."

"Don't worry," he says, smiling once again. "We're together now."

Then, right there in front of Big Ben, for all of London to see, he kisses me.

It is the greatest kiss in the history of all kisses. Tender and sweet. A lifetime of friendship—a history of trust and a future of passion and children and all the beauty and pain and joy that life and love brings. Everything is in this one, solitary kiss. All of life captured in this perfect moment in time.

Between two friends.

Between two lovers.

~

THANK YOU SO MUCH FOR READING.

I HOPE YOU ENJOYED
THE ADVENTURES OF NICKIE NICK.

PLEASE CONSIDER WRITING A
REVIEW ON AMAZON.COM AND
GOODREADS. JUST A FEW SENTENCES
IS SO VERY APPRECIATED.

PLEASE SHARE IT ON YOUR
NETWORKS & RECOMMEND IT TO
YOUR FRIENDS!

PEACE.

OTHER BLUE MOOSE PRESS TITLES

Rowan of the Wood
Winner of the 2009 Indie Excellence Award
978-0-9819949-2-5 $12.95 trade paperback
After a millennium of imprisonment in his magic wand, an ancient wizard possesses the young boy who released him. When danger is nigh, he emerges from the frightened child to set things right. Both he and the boy try to grasp what has happened to them only to discover a deeper problem. Somehow the wizard's bride from the ancient past has survived and become something evil.
http://www.rowanofthewood.com

Witch on the Water
Rowan of the Wood: Book Two
978-0-9819949-2-5 $12.95 trade paperback
Cullen thought he had enough trouble surviving school, dealing with his miserable home life, and being possessed by Rowan, a 1400-year-old wizard. But when Rowan's wife, the sadistic vampire Fiana, comes back seeking revenge, Cullen and his band of misfits must do what they can to stop her. This time Cullen's favorite teacher is Fiana's first target.

Fire of the Fey
Rowan of the Wood: Book Three
978-0-9819949-6-3 $12,95 trade paperback
Adventures continue for Cullen Knight and his band of misfits in this third installment of the Rowan of the Wood fantasy series. Still possessed by the wizard Rowan, Cullen settles into his new home with his fire elemental sister, Aidan, and their fey uncle, Moody Marlin. But all is not well. A series of fires raging through the redwoods puts Aidan in the hot seat, as the group looks to her for an explanation.

Power of the Zephyr
Rowan of the Wood: Book Four
978-1-936960-94-1 $12.95 trade paperback
Power of the Zephyr continues the Rowan of the Wood fantasy series with further adventure and magical mayhem. The Freak Squad, as Trudy takes to calling them, confront Fiana in the desert of Northern Nevada. She has developed a cult of mesmerized zombies in an intricate plot to capture Rowan and his wand for herself, once and for all.

Other Titles by O. M. Grey

Avalon Revisited
978-0-9819949-5-6 $12.95 trade paperback
Arthur Tudor has made his existence as a vampire bearable for over three hundred years by immersing himself in blood and debauchery. Aboard an airship gala, he meets Avalon, an aspiring vampire slayer who sparks fire into Arthur's shriveled heart. Together they try to solve the mystery of several horrendous murders on the dark streets of London. Cultures clash and pressures rise in this sexy Steampunk Romance.
http://omgrey.wordpress.com

Avalon Revamped
978-1-936960-98-9 $12.95 trade paperback
Arthur Tudor, a vampire for nearly four-hundred years, finds himself bored with life and love, yet again. His tolerance for his newly-turned girlfriend Avalon wanes, and he's on the prowl for fresh blood to drink and succulent flesh to pierce. While investigating a series of mysterious disappearances, the couple comes face to face with Constance, a succubus committed to exacting justice for violated women. The supernatural trio joins forces to stop a serial rapist and murderer. Set in Victorian London, this Steampunk horror novel is about justice, retribution, and redemption. Let true justice prevail...

The Zombies of Mesmer
978-1-936960-92-7 $12.95 trade paperback
Gothic YA paranormal romance novel
Follow Nicole Knickerbocker Hawthorn (Nickie Nick) as she discovers her destiny as The Protector, a powerful vampire hunter. Ashe, a dark and mysterious stranger, helps Nickie and her friends solve the mystery behind several bizarre disappearances. Suitable for teens, enjoyed by adults.

Caught in the Cogs: An Eclectic Collection
978-1-936960-90-3 $12.95 trade paperback
In the midst of war, a beautiful young officer finds love aboard an airship...A woman steals away to fulfill her desire with a phantom lover...A group of thieves seek out a town of women to satisfy their lustful urges, but these ladies have an agenda of their own...

PLUS nine more short stories, angsty love poetry, and twenty-six relationship essays considering topics such as alternative lifestyles, deepening intimacy, opening communication, abusive relationships, and how to end a relationship with respect.

MORE BLUE MOOSE PRESS AUTHORS

Prelude to a Change of Mind
Hidden Lands of Nod: Book One
978-0-9827426-0-0 $9.95 trade paperback
Meg Christmas is found sick unto death in a remote mountain camp. Beings out of legend arrive to save her, emerging from an alternate realm where they live in exile. A quiet, intimate adventure, *Prelude to a Change of Mind* boasts dire peril and brave feats, but also lots of tea with Ekaterina Rigidstick, poems by Jack Plenty, and talks with both about the nature of reality and conditions of being.

Entranscing
Hidden Lands of Nod: Book Two
978-0-9827426-2-4 $9.95 trade paperback
The second book in *The Hidden Lands of Nod* revisits Meg and her friends from the exile realms of the Dvarsh—the metamathemage, Ekaterina Rigidstick, and her cousin, the part-human poet, Jackanapes Plenty—in a vastly different reality twenty years on. This fast-moving follow-on to *Prelude to a Change of Mind* picks up and enlarges the tale of Meg, the Dvarsh, the Thrm, and their collective struggle to save both love and the planet.
http://www.robertstikmanz.com

Fiends: Volume One
978-1-936960-00-2 $35.00 Limited Edition Hardback
978-1-936960-01-9 $12.95 trade paperback
Including Canvas, Tattoo, and Closet Treats, Fiends: Vol 1 is a collection of horror stories by Paul E. Cooley. As a special treat, the author gives his reader a glimpse into the FiendMaster's Scrapbook.

All Blue Moose Press titles are also available in Kindle and other eReader versions. For more information on our current titles, as well as other exciting titles on the horizon, visit **http://thebluemoosepress.com**

GET AUTHOR SIGNED BOOKS DIRECT FROM THE PUBLISHER and SUPPORT INDIE AUTHORS!current titles, as well as other exciting titles on the horizon, visit **http://thebluemoosepress.com**

GET AUTHOR SIGNED BOOKS DIRECT FROM THE PUBLISHER and SUPPORT INDIE AUTHORS!

ACKNOWLEDGEMENTS

Special thanks to:

Erin McLarty for her fabulous ideas
and cherished friendship.

Kevin Keele for proofreading the book
and offering feedback.

My amazing husband Ethan.
You are the very definition of love.

ABOUT THE AUTHOR

Nestled in the mountains of Northern California, Olivia M. Grey lives in the cobwebbed corners of her mind writing Gothic stories and controversial nonfiction. Olivia focuses both her poetry and prose on alternative relationship lifestyles and deliciously dark matters of the heart and soul. Her work has won various awards, been on Amazon's Gothic Romance bestseller list, and has been published in various anthologies and magazines like *Stories in the Ether, Steampunk Adventures, SNM Horror Magazine* and *How The West Was Wicked*. Visit her blog for a list of her complete published works: http://omgrey.wordpress.com

Under the name Christine Rose, Ms. Grey also writes the award-winning YA fantasy series *Rowan of the Wood* with her husband, Ethan. Find articles on publishing, writing, marketing, and meet emerging authors on Christine's blog: http://christinerose.wordpress.com

Connect with her on Twitter: @omgrey
On Facebook: http://facebook.com/OMGREY